Wild, Crazy

HEARTS

The Bradens & Montgomerys
(Pleasant Hill – Oak Falls)

Love in Bloom Series

Melissa Foster

ISBN-10: 194886830X
ISBN-13: 978-1948868303

WILD, CRAZY HEARTS

Cover Design: Elizabeth Mackey Designs

WORLD LITERARY PRESS
PRINTED IN THE UNITED STATES OF AMERICA

A Note from Melissa

I have been looking forward to writing Trace and Brindle's love story for a long time. I laughed and I cried while bringing together these two high-spirited, stubborn lovers, rooting for them the whole time. Trace and Brindle have a love that is unlike any other, and I hope you enjoy their emotional journey to coupledom as much as I enjoyed writing it. If this is your first Love in Bloom book, all of my love stories are written to stand alone, so dive right in and enjoy the fun, sexy adventure!

The best way to keep up to date with new releases, sales, and exclusive content is to sign up for my newsletter. www.MelissaFoster.com/news

About the Love in Bloom Big-Family Romance Collection

The Bradens & Montgomerys is just one of the series in the Love in Bloom big-family romance collection. Characters from each series make appearances in future books, so you never miss an engagement, wedding, or birth. A complete list of all series titles is included at the end of this book, along with previews of upcoming publications.

You can download **free** first-in-series ebooks and see my current sales here:
www.MelissaFoster.com/LIBFree

Visit the Love in Bloom Reader Goodies page for downloadable checklists, family trees, and more!
www.MelissaFoster.com/RG

Chapter One

THERE WERE CERTAIN benefits to being the youngest girl in a family with seven children, such as the fact that by the time Brindle Montgomery could walk, her older siblings had already done so much crazy, stupid shit, nothing surprised their parents. When Brindle hit her teens, Sable—the third oldest, and until Brindle had come along, the most rebellious—had left no troublesome stone unturned. Brindle had always done as she pleased, and she believed in living life to the fullest. That was why, when she scheduled a six-week trip to Paris, no one had given it a second thought. Finding out she was pregnant a week after arriving had complicated things, and she'd extended her stay to try to figure out her life. Though she hadn't told her family why she was staying, they weren't surprised by her change of plans. Now here she was, three and a half months later, counting on those skewed expectations. She didn't think her pregnancy would come as *too* big of a shock to anyone. Well, anyone other than her on-again off-again boyfriend of a dozen years, Trace Jericho.

As she stepped from her car after the longest travel day *ever*, she began questioning her decision to come straight from the airport to the barn bash the Jerichos threw every year for

Halloween. But it was rare to get all of her siblings in the same place at the same time. They were all there for the event, as was Trace, which meant she could deliver her news in one fell swoop. She'd convinced herself they'd rally around her, supporting her decision and taking it all in stride.

Now she called bullshit on all of that.

But her situation wasn't going to change, and she needed to face her future head-on. She straightened her spine, shoved her keys in her coat pocket, and headed across the field toward the barn.

Children darted around adults, who were busy mingling. Just beyond, strings of black and orange lights illuminated the massive barn, which was decorated with scarecrows, ghosts, ghouls, and gauzy fake spiderwebs. It was a typical Oak Falls affair, one that Brindle usually looked forward to. But as she weaved through the crowd, her thoughts turned to Trace and the reason she'd gone away in the first place. She'd loved him for so long, she couldn't think clearly when she was around him, and she was at a point where her feelings had grown so big, she needed to know if they were real. But their relationship was complicated, with as much turmoil as pleasure. And *oh*, what pleasure Trace Jericho could bring! But *relationship* wasn't the best definition of what they had, since neither one had ever wanted a long-term commitment.

Or at least that's what she'd always thought.

"Hi, Miss Montgomery!" a group of girls dressed as princesses, witches, and cheerleaders called out as they ran past.

Brindle waved.

Everyone was dressed in costume, making them hard to identify, which was just fine with Brindle. She only wished *she* had a costume. She taught English at the high school and drama at the elementary school, which meant she knew almost everyone in their small town. Normally, she loved everything about their close-knit community, from events like the barn bash right down to the gossip that many people rued. But she was so nervous about sharing her news, she didn't want to deal with any of that before seeing her family.

And Trace.

Her heart raced with the thought of telling him she was pregnant.

Her stomach knotted as people started noticing her, waving and calling out. She ducked her head and pulled her coat across her stomach, wishing she hadn't always kept herself in prime bikini shape. Most women puked through their early months of pregnancy, but Brindle had been ravenous. She had eaten so much, she already had a little belly. Sable would probably say she was drinking too much red wine and eating too many bonbons.

"Brindle?" Beckett Wheeler's voice startled her from her thoughts. He threw his arms around her. He was dressed in jeans, a white T-shirt, and a leather jacket. His short dark hair was slicked back from his face in a fifties style.

Beckett was a bigwig investor and one of Trace's best friends. He was a nice guy, but Brindle was on a mission and she didn't need him thwarting it.

"I heard you were coming tonight," Beckett said. "I can't believe you've been gone since July. How was your trip? Trace is here somewhere. That man nearly drove everyone crazy while you were gone."

She stumbled momentarily over his comment about Trace, but who knew what that really meant. For all she knew, he was driving them nuts chasing women.

Trying to push that hurtful thought aside, she said, "The trip was amazing and it's good to see you, but it's been a really long day and I need to see my family before I fall over with exhaustion. I'll catch up with you soon."

"Cool. Your family's in the barn. If I see Trace, I'll tell him you're here."

She waved absently and hurried away. *Trace. Oh God, Trace.* Being home made her situation even more *real.* It was one thing to *think* about telling everyone she loved that she was pregnant, but now that she was there, staring at the ground to keep from meeting the eyes of friends, she wasn't sure she could go through with it. What would her family think of her? What would Trace think of her?

I can do this, she told herself as she entered the barn. She'd been telling herself that for so many weeks, she almost believed it.

Music blared from the stage, where a group of people played banjos, drums, guitars, flutes, and saxophones. She was surprised neither Sable nor Axsel was onstage. In addition to owning an auto shop and being a kick-ass mechanic, Sable played guitar in a local band called Surge, and their only brother, Axsel, was the lead guitarist for Inferno, one of the hottest bands around. He was a legitimate rock star.

She scanned the crowd, spotting her family surrounded by Axsel's entourage. Even though they were in costume, she could identify every family member. Her parents were dressed as Sonny and Cher. Her mother looked younger with the long black wig, and her father actually pulled off the fake mustache pretty well. Her chest constricted at the thought of telling them about the baby. They'd always supported her decisions, but would they support the biggest one of all? Or would they be too disappointed to see straight?

She stopped cold at that thought as she watched her tight-knit family laughing and talking animatedly. Youngest or not, she needed to face the truth. Skipping school, partying too much, and sneaking out was nothing like an unplanned pregnancy at twenty-five. This was uncharted territory for their family. Her gaze moved to her oldest sister, Grace, and her new husband, Reed, handcuffed together and dressed as a prisoner and a policeman. If anyone should be announcing a pregnancy, it was them.

Sable's laughter hit Brindle's ears, pulling her from her thoughts. Her family was now focused on Morgyn and her new boyfriend, Graham Braden, whom they'd all met at Grace and Reed's wedding before Brindle left for Paris. Morgyn and Graham had just returned from ten weeks in Belize, where they were building a community of tiny houses for one of Graham's business ventures. Although Brindle was close to all of her siblings, she had a special bond with Morgyn, followed closely by Sable. She had talked to Morgyn often while they'd been away, though Brindle hadn't told her, or anyone else, about the pregnancy. Morgyn had gushed about Graham's adventurous personality, the way he understood her like no man ever had, and just about everything else Graham-related. Her sister had been so happy, she hadn't noticed a difference in Brindle. *Or maybe I'm just that good at hiding things.* Morgyn and Graham were dressed as bride and groom, which was hilarious considering Morgyn, like Brindle, had no interest in marriage. *Single sisters forever!*

Time to pull up my big-girl panties and get this over with.

As she weaved through the crowd, she smiled inwardly at the fact that pulling *off* her big-girl panties was what had gotten her into this quandary in the first place.

Every step made her even more nervous, and when she was a few steps away, she felt like she couldn't breathe.

I can do this. I can do this.

"I'd argue that point," Morgyn said as she slipped her arm around Graham.

Brindle pushed through the crowd, smiling despite her nerves, and said, "What are we arguing about?"

"You're home!" Morgyn squealed, throwing her arms around Brindle. They were the only blondes in the family, taking after their father, while their other siblings were darker, like their mother.

They didn't have time to say more, as their mother, Marilynn, pulled Brindle into a tighter hug than she ever had. Her mother was warm and funny, but having raised seven strong-willed children, she knew how to turn on the drill-sergeant facade when she had to.

"Oh, my sweet baby girl! I have missed seeing your beautiful face."

"I missed you, too, Mom," Brindle said as her siblings all spoke at once.

"Hi, sweetheart," her father said as he gathered her in his arms. "I sure have missed you, pumpkin."

"I missed you, too, Daddy."

Grace grabbed Brindle next, and since she and Reed were handcuffed together, he joined in. Amber weaseled her way in, her golden retriever, Reno, sticking to her like glue as she embraced Brindle, her seizure-alert necklace familiar and present between them. Amber had epilepsy, and Reno was her service dog.

"I'm so glad you're home, Brin," Amber said, absently

touching her seizure-alert necklace. The necklace featured a button that Reno could push with his nose if Amber had a seizure, and it included an internal GPS system to alert family members and emergency services to Amber's location. Thankfully, the alert system had been needed only once, since Amber's seizures were controlled well with medications.

"Wow, you look *hot*," Brindle said, admiring Amber's fairy outfit, complete with bright blue and silver wings and cowgirl boots.

Amber lifted one shoulder in a sheepish shrug. "Thank you."

Their sister Pepper moved in for a hug. She carried a stuffed monkey and wore tan shorts and a matching shirt, hiking boots, and a safari hat. "I'm glad you made it back safely."

"Thanks. Nice legs, Pep," Brindle said.

"I'm Jane Goodall," Pepper explained.

Pepper was Sable's older twin, and she was as proper as Sable was unfiltered. Pepper was a research scientist in Charlottesville, Virginia. She'd developed Amber's seizure-alert necklace when she was in graduate school and had since patented it and sold it all over the country.

"Let me in for a squeeze." Sable, dressed as Catwoman, pulled Brindle into her arms and said, "About damn time. I need someone to party with."

"Whoa, girls," their father said. "We're having a welcome-home breakfast tomorrow, so don't stay out partying too late tonight. I want to hear all about Brindle's trip."

"We won't." Brindle wouldn't be partying anytime soon. Her stomach knotted again. She'd missed them all even more than she'd realized, and now that she was in the thick of them, her courage to reveal her pregnancy was slipping away.

"Well, *I* didn't miss you one bit," Axsel said with a smirk. He embraced her and said, "But I did miss the way you attract hot guys."

Brindle laughed. Axsel was gay, and they'd been checking out guys together forever. "I missed you, too, Ax."

"How was your flight?" Pepper asked. "You must be exhausted."

Brindle groaned. "My flight was awful. I haven't even been home yet. I didn't want to miss seeing everyone, so I came straight from the airport. You guys look great in your costumes."

Reed lifted their handcuffed wrists and said, "Forget the ball and chain. This works much better." He pointed to Graham's and Morgyn's costumes and said, "Bride and groom? Guess you guys are next?"

Sable scoffed. "You'd have to drag Morgyn kicking and screaming to the altar. Didn't you know that about her?"

"No. Really?" Reed asked.

"Well, actually…" Morgyn thrust her left hand out, showing everyone the gold band with cardinal directions carved into a little round disk on her ring finger, and said, "We eloped!"

Amber squealed and hugged her. "Oh, Morgyn!"

"*What?*" Sable snapped. "No way!"

Brindle was dumbfounded.

"Holy cow. You're really *married?*" Grace asked as everyone else congratulated Morgyn and Graham at once.

Ignoring the mayhem, Brindle caught Morgyn's eyes and said, "*Married?* You're *married?*"

Morgyn nodded, teary eyed and grinning like she'd never been happier. "I'm married."

"And you're so *happy.*" Brindle couldn't keep the astonishment from her voice.

"Happier than I ever imagined," Morgyn said.

Not in a million years would Brindle have believed Morgyn would get married. Then again, she never would have imagined herself pregnant. But her pregnancy hadn't been planned, while Morgyn's marriage obviously was.

"What changed?" Brindle asked.

Morgyn looked lovingly at Graham and said, "*Everything*. I've been *his* from the day we met, and I wanted the world to know it." She looked thoughtfully at Brindle and said, "Are you happy, Brin? Did Paris help you figure things out?"

"Yes." Although it had taken Brindle some time to wrap her head around the reality that she was pregnant, she was happy about the baby, and she finally knew exactly what she wanted. But she decided not to steal Morgyn and Graham's thunder. She could tell her family tomorrow at breakfast. Instead, she said, "I guess this summer was good for both of us."

"*Married*," Sable said. "I can't freaking believe it. How on earth did you manage that, Miracle Man?"

Graham looked at Morgyn with so much love in his eyes, even *Brindle* melted a little.

"I didn't," Graham said. "She got me to marry her."

All eyes turned to Morgyn.

"Were you drunk?" Sable asked.

"Yes," Morgyn said, earning a confused look from Graham. "Drunk on *love*."

As Graham pulled Morgyn into a kiss, Brindle shrugged off her coat. "All this hugging and mushy talk is making me hot."

Amber gasped, her eyes drawn to Brindle's belly. "That's a great costume! Where did you find such a tiny baby bump?"

Shit. Why hadn't she worn something looser than leggings

and a tight tunic?

Morgyn spun around, her eyes sweeping over Brindle. She tried to school her expression, but not before Brindle saw shock, and then hurt, in her eyes. She probably should have told Morgyn, but Brindle had wanted to figure out how she felt about the baby without the pressure or input from her family. Now she'd give anything to have told Morgyn so that hurt wouldn't be there—and so she didn't feel like she was standing *alone* and naked on a street corner, with her entire family gawking in disbelief.

"Please tell me that's from eating too many French pastries," Grace said.

"Are you...?" Pepper reached over and touched Brindle's belly.

Brindle turned away. "Stop!" *Ugh.* How could she ever have thought this would be easy?

"Brindle...?" Morgyn looked worried.

"Honey," their mother said, wide-eyed. "Are you...?"

Brindle's eyes teared up as she nodded. Their mother opened her arms and pulled her into them. "It's okay, honey."

"I'm sorry, Mom," Brindle whispered.

"No, baby girl," her mother whispered. "There's no reason to be sorry. We love you, and we're here for you."

Tears slipped down Brindle's cheeks, and she quickly wiped them away, too overcome with emotions to speak.

"Holy crap, Brindle," Axsel said with shock, but not with judgment, and she loved him for that.

Sable crossed her arms, staring at Brindle, and said, "Whose French ass do I need to kick?"

Just as she opened her mouth to try to respond, Trace's handsome face appeared through the crowd, and Brindle's mouth went dry. He casually draped an arm around Sable, flashing his panty-melting smile, his ever-present Stetson firmly in place. In the space of a second, Brindle's gaze drifted to his broad, muscular chest and biceps earned from working on his family's cattle and horse ranch. His tight jeans defined the formidable bulge behind his zipper that she knew intimately. She breathed harder, knowing just how good his hard body felt pressed against her, his thick thighs nestled between her legs. She swallowed a needful sound.

"I'm in for some French ass kicking!" Trace announced, tearing her from her fantasy.

Her strappingly large cowboy was as arrogant as ever. His dark eyes landed on her, and the air around them sizzled and sparked, unleashing the rush of desire that had always consumed them. Her pulse raced. She was sure she was going to pass out.

"Mustang, you're back!" The nickname he'd given her long ago rolled off his tongue like liquid heat. He stepped forward, arms open, and his gaze drifted lower. He stopped cold, the air between them chilling.

Brindle put her hand protectively over her stomach, stumbling backward. She'd thought she could do this, but seeing his desire for her replaced with something dark and traitorous did her in. She struggled to hold back tears as she said, "I can't do this right now." She looked away, trying futilely to regain control. Her heart was shattering inside her chest. With one last glance at her parents, she said, "I'm exhausted. I'm going home. We can talk about this tomorrow."

She pushed past Trace and hurried toward the barn doors.

WHAT THE FUCK just happened? Trace tried to put together the pieces of his fracturing world. He felt like he'd stepped on the prongs of a rake and the handle had smacked him in the face as his Mustang stormed away. Only the pain was lower, burning right in the center of his chest. He took off after her, running out of the barn and into the crowd, and spotted her rushing toward the parking lot. He caught up and grabbed her arm, spinning her into him. Her pain-filled eyes shot up to his like lightning, and the pieces of the last few months started falling into place. *Fuck, Brindle. What have you done?*

"Don't!" she cried, tears flooding her cheeks.

"You were supposed to come back at the end of August," he seethed through gritted teeth.

She clenched her jaw, glaring at him with the same ferocious stare that had first drawn him in. She had the darkest brows and lashes of any natural blonde he'd ever seen, a slim, upturned nose, and lips that made his cock weep. She was just a little thing, but she was as feral, stubborn, and untamable as he was. She could bring him to his knees with a glance or a single sugarcoated sentence, and don't get him started on her touch…

"*That's* why you stayed in Paris for two extra months? You got knocked up by some French asshole?" The accusation hurled from his lungs, anger and hurt slamming into him. "What the fuck, Brindle?"

She tried to pull out of his grasp, but he held tight. He'd been trying to hold on to her forever, but they weren't a hold-on-tight type of couple. They weren't a *couple* at all, and he knew that all too fucking well.

"What don't you get, Trace?" She tore her arm free and hollered, "That I'm *pregnant* and it's *not* yours? Even a big arrogant cowboy like you can understand that."

It's not mine hit him with the force of a freight train. *Holy hell.* He didn't want a kid, and he definitely didn't *need* a kid. But knowing Brindle was carrying another man's child fucking gutted him. He could do little more than stare as she stormed away, her words, *It's not yours*, driving into him like a dagger over and over again.

Chapter Two

TRACE BLEW THROUGH the crowd, his shoulders slamming into everyone he passed. He ignored their angry slurs and the people calling after him. It was all white noise to Brindle's wrathful confession. He couldn't process it, and he didn't even try as he grabbed a bottle of whiskey from the table where his older brother Justus—"JJ"—, the owner of a local pub, was bartending. Trace was the fourth son in a family of five children, preceded by Jeb, Shane, and JJ, and followed by their only sister, Trixie. And right now it would take a hell of a lot more than one of them to calm him down.

"Dude, what the…?" Justus snapped as Trace guzzled the whiskey.

"I heard Brindle's pregnant," he heard a girl in the crowd say. Several gasps and comments followed. The Oak Falls gossip train was already off and running.

He spun around, and Trixie, who was afraid of exactly nothing, glowered at the chick who must have said it and snapped, "Shut your hole. Don't spread shit you don't know anything about." When more people began murmuring about Brindle being pregnant, Trixie laid into them, too. Even dressed in a far-too-short and -sexy costume, his sister was a badass.

Trace stormed away from the lights and the crowd. He tipped the bottle to his lips again, needing to numb the pressure in his chest. As the lights fell away behind him, he took another swig and kept walking. Jeb and Shane caught up a few minutes later, falling into step on either side of him.

"Go away," he seethed, and took another swig.

"Whoa, bro." Jeb reached for the bottle.

Trace smacked his hand away. "Don't fucking touch it."

Jeb and Shane exchanged concerned looks Trace wasn't in the mood for. Trace ran their family's ranch with Shane and Trixie. He could deal with Shane's shit tomorrow. Jeb, an artist who worked with stone, wood, and metals, ran The Barn, a custom furniture shop. Come tomorrow, he'd be on to his next project and not breathing down Trace's neck. All Trace needed was to get off his radar tonight.

Shane grabbed the sleeve of Trace's leather jacket, hauling him into the shadows beside the barn. Trace shoved him away. Jeb's eyes narrowed, and he closed the distance between them, stopping only inches from Trace. The Jericho men were all evenly matched, standing over six feet tall, with dark hair and eyes and strong, athletic builds. Except right now Trace had fire in his veins, and nothing would stand in his way. Not even the well-meaning brothers he'd go to war for.

"I know you're hurting," Shane said angrily, "but if you think I'm going to make up for you dragging ass tomorrow, you're wrong."

"I'm not fucking hurting," he lied, and sucked down another mouthful of whiskey. "And you've never had to cover for me a day in your life."

"Bullshit, you're not hurting," Jeb said. "You've been talking about Brindle coming back since the day she left."

"And she came back with a little more in her pants than you're used to," Shane added with a fucking smirk.

Trace thrust the bottle in Jeb's direction. As Jeb took it, Trace pushed forward, shoving Shane backward. "Shut your damn mouth, asshole."

"Got the bottle away from you, didn't I?" Shane said with an arrogant smirk.

Trace muttered, "Asshole" and strode away.

"Wait, bro." Jeb caught up to him and put a hand on his shoulder. "Talk to me. What'd Brindle say? Is it true she's pregnant?"

"Yeah, it's true." He folded his arms over his chest, grinding his teeth. "And it's not fucking mine."

"She's sure?" Jeb asked.

"This is Mustang we're talking about. When have you ever known her to make shit up?"

Brindle was as honest as she was hardheaded, and Trace loved that about her. They'd been making out since she was thirteen years old, when she'd first dared him to kiss her. At fifteen, he'd had an inkling that she was too young to be kissing, but she'd *pushed* and *challenged*, flaunting her sweet little body and taunting him with her sassy mouth and those sexy lips that made it hard for him to think straight. He'd learned real fast that when Brindle set her mind on something, there was no dissuading her. He'd wanted to kiss her so badly that just the idea had made him hard, but he'd forced himself to hold back. Then she'd pushed him to the brink, questioning his manhood, and his control had snapped. He'd gotten his first taste of the girl who would own him forever. And holy hell, what a taste that had been. That single kiss had opened the floodgates of raging desires for both of them. They'd spent years sneaking out at night, riding the rapids of teenage lust and discovering just what each other's bodies were made for. But the rebel in each of them was too strong to deny, and their on-again off-again relationship had been fraught with as much angst and drama as lust and for him, at least, something much bigger.

Through it all, one thing had never changed: No matter who else's arms they'd fallen into or how many fights they'd had, they always circled back to each other.

Until now.

"Whose is it?" Shane asked.

Trace's hands curled into fists, still grinding his teeth together.

"Didn't you ask?" Shane pushed.

Trace scoffed, telling himself to man up and move on. "Why would I do that? That'd mean I gave a shit." Lying wasn't his strong suit, but the alternative made him a pussy. He snagged the bottle out of Jeb's hand, and when Jeb moved to grab it, Trace shot him a threatening stare. "Don't."

"Come on, Trace. Let's go to the barn and beat on the heavy bag," Jeb suggested. They had a full gym in their supply barn. "Work off some of that anger."

"Fuck that," he said as he strode toward the crowd. "I've got a much better way to work it off."

Ignoring his brother's shouts, he returned to the party, scanning the familiar faces of women he'd gone out with, usually to work off anger from a fight with Brindle and guys with whom he'd played football, ridden horses, and gotten drunk. Their faces all blended together, because the only person he wanted to spend tonight with was pregnant and probably in her apartment with the father of her baby.

"Trace!" Trixie hollered from a few feet away, where she was talking with Morgyn Montgomery and their friend and go-to event planner Lindsay Roberts.

He kept walking.

Trixie caught up to him and took hold of his arm. "Are you okay?"

"Fine," he ground out.

"Well, I wouldn't be if I were you," she said vehemently.

Finally, someone who wasn't trying to calm him down. He glanced at her as he moved through the crowd catching wind of gossipy whispers. His fingers curled tighter, and he stared down a group of girls talking about Brindle until they silenced.

"I'm serious," Trixie said, pulling his attention back to her. "I mean, a baby is serious shit. What will you do? Marry her?"

He stopped cold at the thought of Brindle marrying the father of her baby.

"Morgyn said Brindle didn't tell them whose baby it was, but it's not like we don't know. You two—"

"Well, she told *me*. It's not mine."

Trixie's jaw dropped. "Damn…"

Trace put the bottle to his lips, guzzling more whiskey, his mind reeling back to the night before Brindle left for Paris. There was never any question whether they'd see each other that night. On some levels they were *that* connected, one look was all it took for heat to consume them, and it was all they could do to get to someplace private before tearing off each other's clothes. That night they'd gone out for drinks and ended up tangled between the sheets. They always had great sex, but that night their connection felt different, *magnified*. He'd hated that she was leaving, but he'd learned early on in their relationship that Brindle wasn't into commitments, and if he wanted Brindle, he had to play by her rules. Rule number one was clear:

Don't push a Montgomery girl into a corner or she'll come out fighting. Rule number two he'd learned after making a few mistakes: If he wanted to be with her, she had to believe he didn't want a commitment any more than she did.

He was so damn in love with her, he'd wanted her any way he could have her, even if it included six weeks apart while she went to Paris. Besides, he'd reasoned that if there wasn't a commitment, no one could get hurt, so he'd kept his thoughts about her trip to himself. But the night before she left, he was meeting his brothers to ride horses before sunrise, as they often did, and as he'd gotten ready to leave Brindle's apartment, she'd said she would miss him. He remembered thinking, *Says the girl who planned a solo trip away for weeks on end.* But before he could respond, she'd corrected herself and said she'd miss *this*, meaning the sex, and he'd said, *We both know that once you're overseas I'll be a distant memory.* She'd half-heartedly said it wasn't true, and the sting of the truth had caused his spiteful response. *Don't sweat it, Mustang. There are plenty of warm bodies around to keep me company while you're gone.*

So much for not getting hurt.

He'd been an idiot to pine for her while she was away. She'd obviously been typical Brindle, the untamable wild child, while she was gone.

He spotted Jeb and Shane making a beeline toward him and uttered a curse.

"See ya, Trix," he said, and moved deeper into the crowd. His gaze landed on Heather Ray, a buxom blonde with a reputation for being easy. Just as his brothers caught up to him, he put his arm around Heather and said with more than a hint of innuendo, "What do you say we get out of here?"

She turned, her smile lighting up her green eyes. "I'm in."

She flicked her chin, sending her blond hair over her shoulder as they strode away from his brothers.

"Trace!" Jeb hollered. "Don't do this, man!"

With Heather pressed against his side, Trace raised his other hand, flipped his brothers—and everyone else for that matter—the bird, and kept on walking...

Chapter Three

BRINDLE SAT IN front of her makeup mirror Sunday morning applying concealer to try to hide the puffy dark crescents under her eyes. Her phone had rung off the hook half the night—but not from the one person she wished would call, which was why she'd been awake and upset the other half of the night. She still couldn't believe the first place Trace's mind went when he saw that she was pregnant was that it was someone else's baby. She and Trace had been through more than their fair share of drama, but to say something so cruel after she'd been faithful to him even when they were taking breaks from each other? That had been heartbreaking. She hadn't planned to lie about the father of her child, but Trace's accusation had cut so deep, she hadn't been able to stop herself.

She probably should have expected something like that from him, given the hurtful things he'd said the night before she'd left about there being plenty of warm bodies around to keep him company. She'd made the mistake of telling him she'd miss him when she was in Paris, but the disbelief in his eyes had hurt too much, and she'd quickly reworded her confession for fear of losing him altogether. Saying she'd miss the sex wasn't a lie. It just wasn't the complete truth. She'd been terrified that while she was in Paris figuring out if the overwhelming emotions she felt for him were true, lasting, forever love, or something else, Trace would realize they'd gotten stuck in a holding pattern for years and he was done with her altogether. She knew she wasn't an easy woman to be with. She was stubborn, opinionated, and according to her sisters, she liked sex *way* too much. She also had high expectations of any man she was with. He needed to be strong enough not to get jealous at every little thing. A man who didn't want to tie her down but wanted to run wild *with* her. She loved creek parties, hanging with friends, dancing, and doing the unexpected. There was too much fun to be had to ruin it with visions of white weddings and picket fences. And by *fun* she didn't mean sleeping around. Trace had that area covered. He was just as willing to try new things as she was. Her hot cowboy was the perfect combination of animalistic, domineering, passionate, and loving. Like her, he could change directions on a dime, and he never tired of parties or going out dancing.

But what she'd realized during those first few weeks in Paris when she was painfully lonely for him was that it was being with *Trace*—the man who was just as willing to let her drag him to the dance floor as he was to sneak off into an alcove and make out whenever the urge struck—that made those things so fun. It was laughing together, finishing each other's sentences, and sharing inside jokes. It was the fact that she could rest her head on his shoulder in the middle of a crowded bar and he'd press those magnificent lips of his to her temple and never let anything happen to her. Which was why she had stupidly hoped that absence might make his heart grow fonder and he'd be on the same page as her by now and have decided that he wanted only her.

Her gaze moved to the framed collage of photos on her dresser, with pictures dating all the way back to when they were teenagers. Every year she added more pictures. There were photographs of them laughing, kissing, riding horses, at creek parties, and at community events. Her eyes drifted to the strip of pictures stuck to her mirror with a smiley-face sticker. Those were taken in the photo booth at the last county fair. In the top picture they were giving each other bunny ears. In the next she was sitting on Trace's lap, her arm around his neck, and she was making a face at the camera while he kissed her cheek. He was always touching and kissing her, driving her out of her mind. The third picture was a blur of the back of her head, caught mid-make-out. Trace wasn't just her lover and best friend. She knew now that he was her other half, and in many ways, her better half. She'd probably known it all along, but when she was home, in the thick of it all, she hadn't been able to separate the commitment-phobe Brindle everyone expected—even *her*—and the Brindle who just might want a commitment after all.

Not that that mattered anymore.

Trace had made his feelings clear, and his accusation had forced her rebellious side—the survivor in her—to take over. Her plan to tell him everything and finally confess her true feelings for him were shot to hell. Now she had to put away the truth and figure out what the hell she was going to do.

There was no way she was going to be the girl who got a *pity* proposal or married a man out of his *duty* toward her.

No freaking way.

She wasn't afraid to raise a baby alone.

She looked down at her sweater and leggings. She'd spent a long time looking in the mirror this morning, trying to figure out what Trace had felt when he'd seen her. She didn't look pregnant in the outfit she was wearing today, and her mind started playing tricks on her. If she hadn't worn her tunic yesterday, would she have told everyone about the baby right away? And if she *hadn't* told them, would she have hooked up with Trace like she knew he'd wanted to when he'd first seen her? She didn't want to think about the answers too much. She'd have done anything to spend one more night in his arms, and she wasn't sure if that made her a bad person, or if it just confirmed who she and Trace had always been—a man and a woman whose connection was unstoppable but who were too selfish to think beyond their own needs.

Ugh…

That wasn't right, either.

She streamed music from her phone and turned it up to full volume. It still wasn't enough to silence the voice in her head telling her she should have stayed in Paris. As if that were even an option. She'd had to run her credit cards up to pay for the extra time she'd spent there.

She wouldn't have wanted to stay there anyway. Oak Falls was *home.* She loved the gossip-mongering, so-small-if-you-blink-you'll-miss-it town, home to horse farms and midnight rodeos, where families extended well beyond bloodlines—*and where the man I love hates me.*

She wished she hadn't gone to the party last night.

What on earth made her think she could waltz in and tell her family and Trace she was pregnant as if she were announcing she'd decided to buy a car or change her hair color? The look on Trace's face had made her want to shrivel up and disappear, and if that weren't bad enough, word had traveled so fast, she'd heard people talking about her being pregnant on the way to her car. By now *everyone* probably knew—her boss, her friends, Trace's family…

She'd thought she could handle the gossip, but now her pregnancy felt like a dirty little secret, and it *wasn't*. She didn't want her baby to feel like a dirty secret, but in this town, that's exactly how things would play out. Her baby would be born shadowed in gossip unless she did something about it.

Anger bloomed inside her. *I'm Brindle Fucking Montgomery, and nobody is going to cast shadows over my baby.* She put her hand on her belly and said, "I've got your back, little one. I'll fix this."

FORTY-FIVE MINUTES later, Brindle walked through the kitchen door of her parents' Victorian home. Her mother trained service dogs, and two of her young golden retrievers, Dolly and Reba, bounded over, all wagging tails and slobbery kisses. Reno ambled over, sniffed Brindle, then returned to Amber's side as she set the table.

"Hi, Brin," Amber said, looking beautiful in a fluffy gray sweater and jeans.

"Good morning, sweetheart," their mother said as she flipped pancakes. She wore a sweatshirt from Story Time, the bookstore Amber owned in Meadowside, a neighboring town. "Brace yourself, Brindle. Your sisters have *lots* of questions."

"How many questions can there be? There's only one way to get pregnant. I can't believe anyone even noticed. I'm not that big." Brindle shrugged off her coat and draped it over the back of a chair, then crouched to love up the pups.

"You're showing fast, just like I did," her mother said. "I

swear the minute I got pregnant my belly popped just enough to surpass the ate-too-big-of-a-lunch look."

"Thanks for passing that gene on to me," Brindle said. "I parked behind Axsel's massive tour bus. A few of his bandmates were milling about out front on their phones."

Axsel walked into the kitchen with Pepper and Sable and said, "I was supposed to leave ten minutes ago, but I stuck around to make sure you're okay."

"I'm fine, Axsel," she reassured him.

He looked at her like he didn't believe her and sauntered over. "Mm-hm, and I'm into *chicks*," he said softly.

"*Okay*, fine, you big pain. I *was* doing great, and then last night happened, and it was harder than I thought it was going to be. But I'm better now, really."

He drew her into his arms and whispered, "Bullshit, but you know I love you."

"I love you, too," she said as her father walked through the door, followed by Grace, Reed, Morgyn, and Graham. "Where were you guys?"

As they took off their coats, her father said, "With the horses." He leaned down and kissed her cheek. "Hi, pumpkin. Everything go okay with Trace last night?"

Sable plucked a pancake off the plate by the stove and said, "Obviously not. Trace left the party with Heather Lay."

Their mother scowled. "Heather *Ray*."

Pain sliced through Brindle. She swallowed hard as her father squeezed her shoulder.

Heather Ray's parents owned the feedstore in town. She'd made out with a guy in her parents' barn in middle school, and she'd never lived it down. When she was in high school, guys used to say, *Wanna play? Take Heather Ray out by the hay.*

Heather was a Blake Lively look-alike—curvy, tall, and beautiful. She was a little rough around the edges, but she'd always had to be, given the way people talked about her behind her back. Brindle had never made fun of her, behind her back or otherwise. She'd fought her own fair share of gossip, and she knew how stories multiplied and darkened with each telling.

"Guess it's not Trace's baby…?" Morgyn asked.

Everyone looked at Brindle. They looked hopeful, or maybe they looked fearful; she was too upset thinking about Trace and Heather to think straight.

"Is it Trace's, honey?" her mother asked. "We all just assumed…But last night people said it wasn't."

"He was too angry last night for it to be his," Grace said.

"Too *angry?*" Sable scoffed. "Give the guy a break. If she'd said, 'Hi, I'm having your baby,' it would be a little much for *anyone.*"

Brindle's head was going to explode if they kept talking about Trace.

"It's not his!" came out before Brindle could stop it, digging an even deeper trench of lies, but she couldn't stop herself. She wasn't about to tell them the truth until she figured out how to tell Trace. "It was a guy in Paris, and he wasn't looking for a long-term relationship. It was all supposed to be no-strings attached."

"Remind me," Sable said as she sauntered to the table and sat down. "Does an umbilical cord count as a string?"

"Sable," their father warned.

Brindle paced as they peppered her with questions.

"He doesn't want to help support the baby?" her father asked.

"What's his name?" Sable asked. "All kidding aside, I'm

booking a trip to Paris to kick some French ass."

Brindle rolled her eyes. Leave it to Sable to want to kill the guy when the pregnancy was just as much Brindle's fault.

"Was he married?" Pepper asked, earning a glare from Brindle. "*What?* I didn't say you *knew* he was married. I'm just saying that could be why he doesn't want any attachments."

Brindle threw up her hands and said, "*I* didn't want attachments, either. Do you even *know* me?"

"Yes, we do," her mother said, giving a disapproving look to her sisters. "And we love you no matter what the story is." Her mother turned off the stove and handed the plate of pancakes to Grace, motioning toward the table.

"Plenty of people think they don't want commitments, but they change their minds," Graham said. "Look at my beautiful wife." He smiled at Morgyn, who blew him a kiss. "My brother Beau was like that, and now he's engaged, too. Things can change. Maybe you should keep that door open?"

"If the father isn't interested in a commitment," Grace said as she set the plate of pancakes on the table, "then you should have him relinquish his rights to the baby."

"*Ohmygod,*" Brindle said.

Amber set a pitcher of orange juice on the table and sat down. "She has a point. I mean, what if you want to get married at some point and your husband wants to adopt the baby?"

"Maybe he'll feel differently once the baby is born," Reed suggested as he sat beside Grace and leaned in to kiss her cheek.

"When are you due?" Pepper asked.

Sable leveled a stare on Brindle and said, "What's the asshat's *name,* Brindle?"

"Andre!" came bursting out, and Brindle immediately regretted it. She'd met Andre Shaw in Paris. He was a physician and an artist, and he'd gotten his heart broken two years earlier. He'd shown her around Paris, and they'd commiserated over their complicated love lives and helped each other through many difficult nights. He'd since reconnected with his one true love, and they were happier than ever and traveling overseas. It made Brindle sick to her stomach that after all Andre had done for her, she'd just used him as her scapegoat. "Can we please drop it now?"

Sable's eyes narrowed. "Andre *what?*"

"Why does it matter?" Brindle snapped.

"Wait. Wasn't he the one you told me was in love with someone else?" Morgyn asked.

Shit. She'd forgotten about that. She'd told Morgyn all about Andre when she was in Paris, before Morgyn went to Belize.

"When has that ever stopped a guy from hitting on someone?" Sable said.

"Okay, you know what? Just *stop.*" Brindle sat back, wishing she could tell them the truth, but it was true that the baby's father *didn't* want to be tied down, and telling them the baby was Trace's would only hurt more people.

Axsel's phone rang and he turned away as he answered it. "Yeah. I'm coming out." He ended the call and said, "I gotta go. We have a gig to get to in DC." He pulled his signature knit cap from his back pocket and put it on, and then everyone got up to say goodbye.

"When will we see you again?" their mother asked.

"I'll be home for Christmas." Axsel looked at Brindle and said, "But if you need me, I'll cancel everything and come back."

She stood up to hug him and said, "Like I'd ever ask you to

do that?"

"It made me sound chivalrous, though, didn't it?" He kissed her cheek and then leaned in and said, "When you're ready to talk, hit me up."

"Can I just go with you? I'd make a great groupie," Brindle joked. "And hey, there's no chance of me getting knocked up."

Everyone laughed, and as Axsel said another round of good-byes and then headed out the door, the tension of the morning fell away. Thankfully, as they sat down for breakfast, their mother redirected the conversation, asking Morgyn and Graham about their trip to Belize.

"It was a magical experience, helping all those people," Morgyn said with a light in her eyes Brindle had never seen before. She passed around her phone, showing them the pictures as she described the villagers they'd met and the things they'd done. "I definitely made the right choice closing my full-time shop here and selling my stuff on consignment and out of the railroad car so that Graham and I could travel together."

Morgyn had owned Life Reimagined, an eclectic store in the center of town where she'd created her own fashions and accessories from repurposed, gently used materials. Morgyn had a deep connection with their late grandfather, who had taught her how to repurpose items. They'd spent a lot of time together in the railroad graveyard. Graham had purchased their favorite railroad car and had it refurbished so she could use it as a shop, opening it when they were in town so she wouldn't have the stress of rent and other overhead expenditures. He'd made a deal with Reed for the railroad car to be parked on the property of the Majestic Theater, which Reed owned and was renovating to reopen. It was the perfect solution for Morgyn, enabling her to take off at the drop of a hat.

As Morgyn and Graham shared more details about their trip, Brindle tried to ignore the jealousy prickling up her spine. Morgyn and Graham had known each other only a few months, and they were so in love, so in sync, it radiated off them. Brindle and Trace had known each other forever, and though in private they were fantastically compatible, neither one had ever made the type of time or concessions for the other that Morgyn and Graham had. Not that Brindle wanted gifts or trips, but it would be nice to think past the bedroom sometimes. Sure, they'd confided intimate things, but those midnight confessions came only with their eyes closed. After making love they'd lay and talk, but before revealing anything too private, they'd close their eyes and hold hands or embrace. It would probably seem silly to anyone else, but it was those private moments that Brindle loved so much. She'd even pretended he was with her in Paris, closing her eyes and sending her confessions into her dark hotel room. It was then that she'd realized nobody could replace Trace. She'd heard people say that someone owned their heart, but Trace didn't own hers.

He *was* her heart.

So why hadn't she seen that before? Feeling like she suddenly wanted to cry, she stood up and said, "I'm going to step outside for a minute and get some air."

Reno tipped his nose up, watching her from his perch at Amber's feet.

"Want company?" Morgyn asked.

"No. Finish your story. I'll be back in a minute." She grabbed her coat and went outside.

The brisk morning air stung her cheeks and carried with it the scents of horses from the barn at the far end of the yard. She stood at the railing of the wraparound porch, surrounded by memories of her childhood. She'd spent years sneaking out of her bedroom, hanging from the window ledge and dropping to the porch roof. She could still picture Trace standing in the grass below, smiling up at her as she sat on the edge of the porch roof and then dropped into the safety of his arms. They'd been so *bold*, utterly invincible.

Up until the moment she discovered she was pregnant, she'd thought she *was* invincible. But something had happened when those little pink lines appeared on the pregnancy test—and the next four she'd taken.

The screen door opened, and her parents stepped out. "Mind if we join you?" her father asked as they came to her side.

Her father taught engineering at the local community college. He was patient and thoughtful. Even when Brindle had been in her worst rebellious stages, he'd never judged her or made her feel small for her choices. And now it wasn't judgment she saw in his or her mother's eyes. It was worry.

"Sure," she said as guilt washed through her. "I'm sorry to put you guys in this position."

"What position is that, honey?" her mother asked as she moved a lock of hair over Brindle's shoulder. "You mean making us grandparents?"

Brindle smiled. "That's one way to look at it."

"No, pumpkin. That's the *only* way to look at it," her father said. "You got pregnant." He shrugged. "People have sex, and unplanned pregnancies happen."

"You're not mad?" she asked tentatively.

"You're in your midtwenties. This is *your* life, honey," her mother said. "Why would we be mad because you made a decision you feel is right for you?"

"Because you know what the gossip will be like around here.

Everyone's probably already talking about how 'Brindle Montgomery got knocked up in Paris.'"

"And…?" her mother asked.

"I don't know. Are you embarrassed by it? By me?"

Her parents exchanged a glance, and her father said, "Brindle, you streaked down Main Street when you were playing truth or dare at fifteen. *That* was embarrassing, but mostly because the police hauled your naked ass into the station. Do you think all seven of our kids were planned?"

Brindle shrugged, and her mother laughed.

"Honey, once you have one child, *planning* goes out the window. I think Sable and Pepper were conceived in Daddy's old pickup truck."

"Ew. Don't tell me any more." She covered her face, trying not to imagine her parents having sex.

"Amber came after your mother visited my office wearing nothing but a raincoat—"

Brindle groaned and looked up at the sky. "If you don't stop, I'm leaving!"

They put their arms around her and hugged her.

"Okay, let's talk about the important things," her mother said. "I assume you'll get in to see your doctor? And talk to your job to figure out maternity leave?"

"I go back to work tomorrow, so I'll talk to my boss then, and I'll call Dr. Bryant, too. I saw a doctor in Paris, and I'm taking prenatal vitamins. I'm not going to screw this up, Mom."

"That never even entered our minds," her father said. "But we are worried about you, our daughter, separate from the baby. Are you really okay?"

"You must have been frightened when you first realized you were pregnant," her mother said.

"To be honest, I was in shock more than frightened. Fear came a little later, when I thought about telling you guys." She could time her periods like clockwork, and when she missed one, she was more than a little concerned. A week later, she was fairly certain she was pregnant. But even still, the positive tests had delivered a good dose of shock.

Her mother placed her hand over Brindle's on the railing and said, "How did the father take it when you told him? That must have been awful, hearing he didn't want to be involved."

She shook her head, not wanting to lie, so she told the truth. "We never pretended we'd be anything more than we were." Then she said, more to herself than to them, "I never meant to hurt Trace."

They didn't say anything for a long moment, and she couldn't look at them, because she knew Trace was like a son to them, just like his parents treated her like a daughter. She stared at the gazebo in the distance, where she and Trace had brazenly made love in the moonlight on her eighteenth birthday.

Her father put his arm around her shoulder, pulling her against his side. He kissed her temple and said, "You and Trace have always had a complicated relationship. But your friendship has never wavered. He'll come around, pumpkin."

"And if he doesn't, we'll send Sable over to pull his head out of his ass," her mother said with a smile.

"Why does everyone want to hurt the innocent people in all this?" Brindle asked. "I'm just as much to blame as the father of my child, and for Trace's anger."

"Sweetheart, they're not innocent. Baby making takes two," her father said. "And if you want the truth, Trace was a damn fool not to chase you down and get on that plane or haul your ass off it."

"Oh, Cade," her mother said. "That's such a *man* thing to say. Trace knows our baby girl better than that. If he'd gone after her, Brindle would have pushed him even further away."

Chapter Four

THE LATE-AFTERNOON sun beat down on Trace's back as he tore another board from the old storage shed and hurled it onto the pile of rotted wood. *Fucking Francois, Jean-Pierre, or whatever the fuck his name is.* He grabbed another board, set his boot against the wall beneath, and let his rage fuel his efforts as he stripped it from its tethers and flung it aside. *Goddamn Paris.* He tore through board after board, trying to shake the image of Brindle fucking some other guy, which he'd conjured way too clearly last night. His nightmares were filled with images of Brindle and a faceless, nameless asshole walking around Paris, holding hands, making out in the streets, tangled up in the sheets, her hands all over him.

He threw another board as Shane rode up on a horse. Trace took off his cowboy hat and wiped the sweat from his brow as his brother dismounted.

"You're not answering your phone," Shane said, eyeing the pile of rubble.

Trace gritted his teeth. The last thing he wanted to do was deal with his brother's shit. "So?"

"So, what was that all about last night? Leaving the party with Heather?"

Trace grabbed another board. "What the fuck do you care?" He'd always wondered if Shane had a thing for Heather, which made her an even better choice to leave the party with. Trace tugged at the board, his muscles straining as he tried to wrench the board free.

"Because you're being an idiot."

He released the board and grabbed a hammer. "Fuck off, Shane. I don't need a lecture." He hammered the other side of the board to loosen the nails, then tossed the tool aside and ripped the board from the studs.

"No, you need to tear apart the shed we planned to take down together in the spring, because that'll make things *so* much better," Shane said sarcastically.

"Let it go, Shane."

"That's kind of hard to do, man. You and Brindle have been together forever."

"Correction," he ground out, grabbing the hammer and pounding loose another board. "We've been *fucking* forever."

Each of the Jericho brothers had a different way with the ladies. Jeb was a seriously private dude, mysterious when it came to dating and known around town for his artistic talents and overprotective nature. Shane was a gentleman who liked to have fun, but he kept his mouth shut about his trysts, though he had no problem sticking his nose into his siblings' affairs. Justus was a flirt, but wary of gold diggers, and Trace was the playboy every woman wanted to claim to have been with.

"You're an asshole," Shane said.

Trace dropped the hammer and closed the distance between them. "*I'm* the asshole?" he hollered. He glared at Shane, sending his brother backward as he pushed forward. "She gets knocked up by some guy she just met, and *I'm* the asshole?"

"You had *years* to make her yours, and you dicked around with other women every time you two fought."

Shane tried to force Trace back by puffing out his chest, but Trace planted his feet, refusing to budge, and seethed, "You have no idea what I did or didn't do."

Shane scoffed. "Doesn't every damn person in this town? You aren't exactly discreet."

"People don't know shit."

"Don't they? Or is that you we're talking about?" Shane's eyes narrowed. "What are you afraid of, Trace?"

"Nothing. *Ever,*" he fumed, his hands fisting by his sides.

"Bullshit. Something's held you back from committing to the only woman you've ever really wanted. Afraid you're not man enough for her? Afraid you'll get hurt? Because whatever it is, you screwed up. You weren't man enough to make her yours, and now you're pouting like a child."

Trace's fist connected with Shane's jaw before he had time to blink, knocking his brother flat on his back. Trace's chest heaved as he stumbled backward, grinding out, "Shit. *Fuck.* Goddamn it."

Shane rubbed his jaw as he pushed to his feet. He picked up his cowboy hat and drilled a finger at Trace as he said, "You better get your head out of your ass. That was your one shot. Next time I'll tear you apart."

"Dream on, and while you're at it, how about fucking off?"

"It's time for you to grow up, bro." Shane's lips curved up in an amused smile and he said, "Stop being selfish—"

"Selfish? I give everything I have to this ranch. Dad *never* has to worry about shit getting done."

The ranch had been passed down through two generations. Their father suffered from arthritis and did what he could. But he'd taught Trace and his siblings well. They'd been raised to work hard, herding cattle, calving, and working their fingers to the bone practically since they could walk, getting up before dawn, taking care of chores before and after school, and knowing better than to gripe. In addition to being Oak Falls's go-to cattle ranch, they'd earned a reputation for their horse-training expertise. The joke around town was that the Jericho men could finesse the wildness out of a horse as well as they could charm the panties off women. Though Jeb and Justus had followed their passions elsewhere, there were only two things Trace had ever wanted beyond the ranch—one of them required too much time away from the ranch and the other was pregnant with some other dude's baby.

"You just don't get it." Shane held his gaze as he said, "*Selfish*, as in how do you think Brindle feels right now? The whole town is talking about her."

"This pregnancy was her choice."

"Was it? Her choice, I mean?"

Shane paused, and Trace knew he was giving his words time to sink in. He had no idea if her pregnancy was a choice or not. For all he knew she was in love with the French asshole who got her pregnant.

That thought burrowed deep into his gut, burning like a disease.

"At some point all this anger is going to wear off, and you're going to be left with only the hurt. Trust me, when that happens, no amount of faceless, nameless fucks will take it away." Shane mounted his horse and said, "You should have thought about giving *Brindle* everything you had, and then maybe you wouldn't be in this mess."

That had been all he'd thought about since the moment

Brindle told him she was going to Paris. "If I'd tried to fence her in, she'd have jumped the rail faster than I could tell her not to." She'd nixed any thoughts he'd had about revealing those feelings when she'd made it clear that it was the sex she'd miss while she was gone, not *him*.

Shane scoffed. "You've never met a filly you couldn't tame. Like I said, man, what are you afraid of?"

As his brother rode off, Trace said, "It doesn't matter anymore, does it?"

He picked up the hammer and set to work tearing apart the rest of the shed.

Hours later, as the sun set and the rubbish pile grew, his hands burned, a sheen of sweat soaked his shirt, and he was still chewing on nails. But his brother's words were still pummeling him. *How do you think Brindle feels right now? The whole town is talking about her.*

Where the hell was the father of her child? Why wasn't he with her when she told her family? Why wasn't he there, front and center, shutting down rumors and showing his face to the people who loved her? Trace had been protecting Brindle since he was fifteen years old, and the idea of anyone talking shit about her made his gut roil.

But she was no longer his to protect.

She never was.

"Bullshit." He dropped the hammer and headed for his truck.

BRINDLE PASSED THE mirror on the way into her bedroom, catching sight of her messy bun, cutoffs, fluffy bootie slippers, and the off-the-shoulder sweatshirt with UNTAMABLE written across the front of a wild horse, which Trace had given her for her twenty-third birthday. Except for the fact that she couldn't button her shorts, she looked like her old self, though she sure didn't *feel* like her old self. She felt discombobulated, like she didn't know how to fit into her old life anymore. She wasn't a liar, and yet in the space of one rebellious moment that's what she'd become. And then her sisters had started in on her, driving that guilt even deeper. She'd escaped their scrutiny with the excuse of having to unpack and clean her apartment. She'd changed into comfortable clothes, and she'd had every intention of getting to work, but she'd gotten sidetracked by her guilt.

She shoved a spoonful of strawberry ice cream in her mouth, surveying the open suitcases on her bed and floor. There were clothes strewn over the mattress and dressers and bags all over the floor. She'd been so distracted when she was leaving Paris, she'd accidentally left behind the gifts she'd bought for everyone—including Trace, *the big bastard.* It was all too much to deal with. Shoveling another spoonful of ice cream into her mouth, she turned on her heel and headed back to the living room. She flopped onto the couch beside the stuffed dalmatian Trace had won for her at the last county fair.

She kicked her feet up on the coffee table, knocking off an empty pizza box, and eyed the open bag of chips, the box of cookies, and a bottle of water. If she didn't get control of herself, she'd gain fifty pounds with this pregnancy.

With this *heartbreak.*

Ugh! This sucks.

She set the ice cream container on the table and picked up

the dalmatian, absently touching its ears and remembering how much fun she and Trace had had at the fair. Reed and Grace had just reconnected after a decade apart, and Brindle remembered talking to Grace about the play she was working on with the drama club. Grace had said she'd help, and Reed had immediately offered to build the sets without even being asked. Brindle had made a comment to Trace about how nice it was that some guys made time to help, and Trace had said, *Darlin', I've got a ranch to run. But if you want to spend the time we have together building sets instead of our other extracurricular activities, that can be arranged.* She'd nixed that idea and promptly changed the subject. She liked their extracurricular activities, but that was just one more thing that had gotten her thinking that maybe she wanted more than he wanted to give.

She sighed and debated calling Morgyn. She needed to talk this shit out before she said or did anything else to make matters worse.

A knock at her door sent her heart to her throat. Maybe Trace had gotten his head on straight and was coming over to apologize. *You'd better have an apology on those sexy lips, or you'll be kissing your way back out the door.* She pushed to her feet, hoping they could clear up their misunderstanding and move forward.

She pulled the door open, and there he stood, Stetson firmly in place, looking hot as ever, except for the anger in his eyes as he barreled forward, pushing her backward with his massive chest. *So much for an apology...*

His dark eyes shifted as they passed the bedroom, and his jaw clenched. He smelled rugged and manly as he set those angry eyes on her and fumed, "Where is he?"

"Not here," she lied as her back met the wall.

"Do you love the fucker?" he seethed, his big body hulking over her.

Yes, more than anything, was on the tip of her tongue, but she didn't like the way he was yelling at her. "Why does it matter? Why do you *care?*"

He ground his teeth together, and Lord help her because his muscular thighs pressed against her, and his body heat ignited her traitorous hormones. Despite how angry she was, she wanted to tear off his filthy clothes and get lost in him the way she always had.

"Because I'm your..." His eyes searched hers, and she saw him struggling with his words.

"Because you're my *what*, Trace? What exactly *are* you?"

He put his hands beside her head on the wall, boxing her in as his dark eyes drilled into her. But he didn't have an answer, and that hurt even more than if he'd just said he was her *friend*, and more rebellion poured out.

"He was just looking for a fuck," she said spitefully. "Not a lifelong commitment, and nothing says forever like a bun in the oven."

His eyes dropped to her belly, his hips pressing into it. He shifted back slightly, relieving the pressure but keeping the connection as he lifted his eyes to hers. She swore she saw a flash of hurt in them seconds before they turned nearly black, and his hands landed on her hips, holding on to her like he always had. Like she was *his* to protect. There were so many conflicting emotions rushing through her, she was drowning in them. Her whole body arched forward, reaching for him, and it was all she could do to try to force that desire away.

"What kind of guy leaves a woman to deal with this shit on her own?" he growled, his chest heaving against hers. "I don't want a kid right now, but I'd do right by you no matter what. The guy needs his ass kicked."

He didn't want a child right now.

I was so stupid to think you'd want us.

Hurt swamped her, and she struggled to keep those emotions in check, but the hurt broke free anyway. "That's just what every woman wants. Someone to stand by her out of *duty*, not love."

His eyes narrowed. "Damn it, Brindle. Answer the question. Where is he? I want to see the guy face-to-face."

She lifted her chin, willing herself to say, *Look in a mirror,* but all that came out was, "Let it go, Trace."

His fingers curled tighter over her hips, and he touched his forehead to hers, his hat brushing the top of her head. "I can't," he said in a low voice full of emotion, sending rivers of heat skating beneath her skin.

Neither one of them moved. She wasn't even sure she was still breathing as her hands moved to his sides, and she slipped her fingers into his belt loops. He sighed with relief, and it made her heart squeeze.

"Mustang," he whispered, and pressed his lips to her forehead. "Talk to me, darlin'."

"We don't *talk*," she said, struggling to keep her tears at bay.

He pushed one arm around her waist, holding her tighter, and brushed his scruff along her cheek, the way he always did right before he drove her out of her mind, and said, "That's bullshit." He moved his lips beside her ear and said, "I know all your secrets, Brin."

Her stomach sank. *Not all of them...*

He pressed his lips to her cheek, and she closed her eyes as he said, "Talk to me, wild one."

"Trace…" she said half-heartedly. She should let go of his jeans and move out from within the confines of his strong arms, but there was no place else she'd rather be.

He threaded his fingers into her hair, angling her face up beneath his, and just that small, familiar motion, which usually was the start of them ending up naked, made lust simmer inside her. He stared into her eyes and said, "I'm not letting you do this alone. You know that, don't you?"

"You don't want a baby." She slammed her eyes closed, wishing she hadn't said it but knowing she needed to.

"OPEN YOUR EYES," Trace demanded. When she did, hurt and anger warred in them, shocking his heart into overdrive. He wanted to kill the motherfucker who had abandoned her and made his stubborn, brave girl look fearful.

"*That* has nothing to do with *this*," he said emphatically. "You're my best friend, my lover, and my feral mischief maker. If you think for a single second that I'm not going to stick by you when that assfuck is too weak to do the right thing, you're wrong." Positioning her face so he had her undivided attention, he said, "I've got you, Brindle Montgomery. I've always had you, and I always will."

He didn't think as his mouth descended on hers, taking what he'd needed since the day she'd gotten on that plane and left him behind. She rocked forward, rubbing seductively against him as his hand traveled around her waist, holding her soft curves against him. The world swayed as he deepened the kiss and she moaned into his mouth. *Man*, he'd missed her—

her kisses, her sounds, her sexual *greed*. He lifted her into his arms, and as her legs circled his waist, her hands dove into his hair, knocking off his hat and making him hard as stone. They ate at each other's mouths, urgent and messy, as if they needed each other to survive. And Lord knew he needed her just that much.

He tugged her head back and sealed his mouth over her neck, sucking and licking the way he knew drove her to the brink of madness.

"Trace—" she begged as he tasted his way lower, kissing and biting her shoulder, earning one sensual sound after another. "God, I missed you."

He drew back to weigh the honesty in her eyes. "You *did* miss me," he growled with more than a little surprise. "You fucking destroy me, Mustang."

A wicked grin curved her lips, and she wrinkled her nose, tripping up his heart as only she could, and said, "Shut up and kiss me."

He kissed her hard and deep, until she was whimpering needily. He eased his efforts to torturously slow and intensely deep, greedily taking whatever she was willing to give. He'd missed everything about her—their fights, their kisses, their sexual electricity, which never failed to blow him away. He slid his hand down the side of her breast, along her ribs and waist, and brushed his thumb over the new little curve of her belly. His heart ached, but he didn't want to think about the reasons why.

He stepped toward the bedroom, and she tore her mouth away, worry simmering in her eyes.

"Wait," she said breathlessly.

"Don't worry, darlin'. I've seen your messy room before."

"It's not that. We can't." She pushed out of his arms and tugged her sweatshirt down. "You don't want me, Trace."

He glanced down at his throbbing erection and said, "I think we both know that's not true."

Hurt rose in her eyes. She lifted her chin defiantly and said, "I'm a package deal now. You need to go."

Every muscle in his body corded with that harsh reality. "Brindle—"

"*Don't.* Just go." She crossed her arms over her stomach and looked down at the floor.

Damn it. "You really want me to leave?"

She nodded sullenly.

"I've waited months to see you, to *hold* you, to *laugh* with you, to *kiss* you. Leaving is the *last* thing I want to do."

The apartment door opened and Morgyn peeked in. "Knock, kno—*oh*. Sorry. Am I interrupting? Your door wasn't closed all the way."

"No." Trace looked at Brindle, and she shifted her eyes away. "I'm just on my way out." He gritted his teeth, sure they'd crack he'd done it so often lately.

He picked up his hat, and as he turned to leave, "Sorry" fell from Brindle's lips like a secret.

Not half as sorry as I am.

"OH MY GOD, Brindle. What was *that* all about?" Morgyn asked after Trace left.

Morgyn had braided aqua ribbons into two locks of her hair, which framed her face. She was wearing an aqua-and-tan fringed wool poncho with skinny jeans and cowgirl boots she'd decorated with colorful belts and feathers, and she looked too bright for the dark mood hanging over Brindle.

"I screwed up, Morg," Brindle said as she sank down to the couch.

Morgyn sat beside her. "By the looks of Trace, I'd say you didn't *screw* anything. I swear testosterone was seeping from his pores. He looked ready to explode."

"Yeah, we're always like that. Combustible, and arguing only makes us even hotter for each other." She nibbled on her lower lip, tasting Trace and struggling to keep from falling apart.

"I know you guys are. That's why I'm here." Morgyn's brows knitted. "Brindle, why didn't you tell me about Andre? We talked so many times while you were in Paris, and I even said something about you and that guy hooking up. You swore it wasn't like that. Why did you lie to me?"

Tears slipped down Brindle's cheeks. "I didn't lie to you. I lied to everyone else. The baby isn't Andre's. It's Trace's." The words were out before she could stop them.

Morgyn gasped. "Trace's?"

"Yes. I'm due at the beginning of March. But you can't tell anyone that until I figure out how to tell Trace." Brindle pushed to her feet, her heart slamming against her ribs. "I never intended to lie to Trace or to anyone else. But last night the first thing Trace did was accuse me of spreading my legs for some guy in Paris. Do you know how much that *hurt*?" She paced, swiping at her tears. "And then Sable was all 'What's his name?' and I didn't want her to say or do anything to Trace, because *he* didn't know."

"Oh God, Brin. Did you tell him just now?"

Shaking her head, she slumped onto the couch and covered her eyes as she sobbed.

"When I came home, I thought he'd want us. That it might take some getting used to, but he'd want me and the baby. But he doesn't. He told me he didn't want a kid, and that if he were the guy from Paris, he'd do right by me *anyway*." She looked at Morgyn and said, "I don't want him to be with me just because he feels *obligated*—" Sobs stole her voice.

Morgyn held her as she cried. "It's okay. We'll figure this out. He's just hurt and angry right now. If you think we were shocked that he wasn't the father, how do you think he feels?"

"I don't care anymore. He hurt me so bad. Do you have any idea what it felt like when he asked if I stayed in Paris because some stranger got me pregnant? I mean, come on. I have a little belly already. Do the math! I can't…I just…We're *done!*" Even though she couldn't see Morgyn's face, she said, "And don't roll your eyes. I mean it this time."

Morgyn leaned back and smiled. Her smiles were so honest, they were contagious, and exactly what Brindle needed at the moment. "I rolled them."

"You suck," Brindle said with a choked laugh, brushing her tears away.

"You've been done with him at least once a month for so many years, I could track it like a period."

Brindle fell back with a groan and stared up at the ceiling, protectively putting one hand over her belly. "I *know*. That's why I went to Paris in the first place, because I felt so much for him, but we're always so intense, I wasn't sure if it was real."

"Oh, it's real, and everyone knows it. You're both so full of passion, you can't help it." Morgyn said it so matter-of-factly, it felt true. "I used to think the way you two were either madly in love or at each other's throats was a problem, but after the first four or five *years*, I knew it was just who you two were."

"It took you that long?" Brindle said teasingly, because she needed levity or she was going to cry forever.

Morgyn smiled and said, "I don't remember exactly. But I've also learned a lot from being with Graham. You know how some guys thought I was flighty?"

"That's because they were idiots. You're brilliant and whimsical."

"Thanks, but we both know I'm not everyone's cup of tea. But Graham loves *all* of me. He understands my inability to plan and my love of following the universal energy where it takes me. He knows that's who I am, and without all those pieces of myself I wouldn't be *me*. He says he loves not knowing what I'll come up with next. I think that's how you and Trace are. You're both bullheaded about some things, and you love so hard, it comes out in arguments, but they're not hateful arguments. They've never been hateful arguments. I mean, right now he's hurt, and rightfully so, and you are, too. But usually you're both just too stubborn to admit how you feel about each other, so you get hurt or jealous, and you argue. Let's face it, Brin, if you guys weren't so volatile, you'd probably get bored."

Brindle looked at her sister, wondering when she'd gotten so relationship savvy. "So, basically, you think I'm a freak who can't have a calm, stable relationship?"

"I never said *freak*," Morgyn teased.

"I hate you a little right now, but you might be right. Not about my inability to have a stable relationship, but about the getting bored part. I don't like *easy*, do I?"

"You don't even know the meaning of the word." Morgyn picked up the ice cream container and handed it to Brindle.

"So, you're going to tell him the baby is his, right?"

Brindle stirred the melted ice cream. "Right now I'm going to eat this and anything else I can find." She ate a spoonful of ice cream, remembering the venom in Trace's voice when he'd accused her of being pregnant by someone else. "He really hurt me."

"He's hurt, too. How would you feel if he…?"

"Came home pregnant?" Brindle smiled. "It's not fair that things don't work that way. I don't even know how he could tell I was pregnant. I'm not that big."

"You're not big, but you have a little pooch, and we were all still in shock when he joined us last night. I think he heard us saying, *Pregnant? Brindle's pregnant?* And then he looked at your belly, and it was like a light went off in his eyes. Sable and I wanted to go after you when you took off, but Mom told us not to."

"Were Mom and Dad mad? They said they're not mad or embarrassed, but…"

"No, which surprised all of us. But Mom said that we all probably thought you were full of piss and vinegar, but that you're *human*, like the rest of us, and beneath that tough exterior is a sensitive, loving girl who was probably scared shitless, or something like that."

"I didn't know how scared I was until I saw Trace. I'm glad you didn't follow us, because it would have hurt more if you had heard him accuse me of sleeping with someone else." Brindle stirred the ice cream and said, "I want to tell him the truth, but now I know he'd stick by me even though he doesn't want the baby. I need time to figure out how and when to tell him. You can't say anything."

"Give me that." Morgyn gestured toward the ice cream

container. "Now I'm stressing out." She took the ice cream from Brindle and said, "I'll give you a week."

"What are you? The pregnancy police?"

"No! But I can't keep secrets. You *know* that about me."

"Morgyn!" Brindle grabbed her arm and said, "Oh God, you *can't* tell Graham."

Morgyn's eyes widened. "*What?* I won't lie to Graham. If he outright asks if the baby is Trace's, I'm telling him. But don't worry. He's good at keeping secrets." She shoveled ice cream into her mouth. "I hate secrets."

"Can't you just kiss him every time he brings up the pregnancy? Distract him from asking anything too specific?"

"I can't lie to Mom, either." Morgyn ate more ice cream. "Do you want me to kiss her, too?"

"I forgot that you with a secret is like using the withdrawal method as birth control. It's only a matter of time before you spill your secrets in all the wrong places." Brindle answered the question in her sister's eyes. "*No,* we didn't do that. You know I use the birth control patch. I'm just the lucky one percent it didn't work for."

"Oh, Brindle." Morgyn set down the ice cream container and said, "You know what this is?"

"Do *not* say it," Brindle warned. Her sister believed the universe guided her, while Brindle believed life was what she made of it, and sometimes accidents happened.

Morgyn grinned. "I'm sayin' it."

Brindle covered her ears and closed her eyes. "Nanananana. I can't hear you!"

Laughing, Morgyn pulled Brindle's hands from her ears and said, "It's *fate!* You and Trace have annoyed the universe into taking steps beyond your control."

Brindle rolled her eyes.

They talked and ate soupy ice cream and cookies, and then Morgyn helped Brindle unpack. Brindle told her about the forgotten gifts and how that just added to her guilt. By the time they plopped down in front of the television, Brindle felt a little better. But still a little *off*, and she knew it was because she needed to tell Trace the truth.

"Were you scared when you first found out?" Morgyn asked later that evening.

"I was a lot of things, and scared was definitely one of them. But never once did I consider not having this baby, so I figured that was a sign."

"See? You *do* believe in signs!"

"No, but I believed in me and Trace."

Chapter Five

TUESDAY WAS LADIES' night at JJ's Pub, and as Trace looked over the sea of horny cowboys and scantily dressed women on the dance floor, he couldn't ignore the pinch in his chest. He'd come to JJ's without Brindle while she was in Paris, and he'd hated every minute of it. But it beat the alternative, sitting alone in his cabin thinking about her. He'd spent the last two days trying to keep from going to see her, but all that did was make him an angry bastard.

"Have you seen Shane?" Jeb asked, sliding onto the barstool beside Trace.

Trace hiked a thumb in the direction of the mechanical bull. "Lindsay told him the girls had a bet about how long he could stay on." Lindsay was one of Brindle's best friends, and it had taken everything Trace had not to ask her or Trixie if they'd spoken to her. He took a drink of his beer.

"Hey, JJ," Jeb called over the bar. "Hit me up when you get a sec."

JJ lifted his chin in acknowledgment as he helped a gaggle of women.

Jeb straightened his ever-present baseball cap with the FARM BOY patch on the front. Like Trace, Jeb was proud of his country-boy roots. He locked serious eyes on Trace and said, "Why aren't you out on the dance floor?"

"Not feeling it tonight." Trace thumbed out a text to Brindle. *It's Tuesday night. You coming out?* He met his brother's watchful eyes and said, "But Sable's band is really killin' it, huh?"

"Yeah. Did you hear Tuck's solo? That dude is awesome." Tuck Wilder had gone to school with Trace. He was an incredible guitarist with cocoa skin and what Brindle called *soulful* eyes, but he'd had a hell of a life. His parents were rough as nails, and he'd been in and out of juvie since losing his twin a while back.

"The guy can play." Trace's phone vibrated with a message from Brindle. He read it as Justus set a beer down in front of Jeb. *I'm pretty sure pregnant women aren't supposed to hang out in bars.*

Jeb eyed the phone and said, "She's pregnant with another guy's kid. You've got to move on, man."

Trace thumbed out another text, ignoring his brother. *Are your legs broken?*

"I'm serious, Trace." Jeb took a swig of his beer. "You know I love Brindle. The two of you have had great times together, but you're setting yourself up to be let down, and I'm not about to let that happen."

Trace lifted his eyes to Justus, expecting to either catch more shit or maybe support, but he shrugged and said, "Hey, man, I'm staying out of this one."

The band took a break, which amplified the silence between Trace and Jeb. Trace leveled a warning glare on Jeb and said, "I've had her back for more than a decade. I'm not stopping now."

Jeb nodded. "You're loyal, Trace. I respect that. But she's made a choice, and someone's got to look out for you, because I'm not sure you're thinking straight. Hell, I don't think any one of us would be in a situation like this. I think you need to give her some space, man."

"I've spent years playing by her rules, and I've spent the last two days keeping my distance. I'm done with all the bullshit." Trace's phone vibrated with another text from Brindle—a GIF of a pregnant woman dancing.

Space was exactly what she *didn't* need. Brindle didn't do well with space. She liked people, camaraderie, *attention.* She liked to be taken care of, despite acting like she didn't need it. She needed a man who took control, but she also needed to feel like she was the one holding the reins. Nobody knew her like Trace did, and though he appreciated his brother's efforts, he didn't need his coaching. Not where Brindle was concerned.

"Good. I'm glad to hear it," Jeb said.

"Now, how about you worry about yourself?" Trace finished his beer just as Sable sauntered over.

She took off her cowboy hat and shook out her thick brown hair as she called over the bar to Justus, "Hey, handsome, how about a beer?"

"You got it, darlin'," Justus said with a wink.

She put her hat back on and set her hands on her hips, eyeing Trace. "Morgyn said you were over at Brindle's yesterday." Her jeans were painted on, her leather belt was the same dark color as her hair, her tight, V-neck shirt had SURGE imprinted across the front, and her green eyes held a threat that brought Trace to his feet.

"So...?"

"So, she's my baby sister." Sable crossed her arms, as if the look in her eyes should be enough to shut him up.

"She's hardly a baby." Nothing would shut him up where Brindle was concerned. "If you've got something to say, spit it out, because I've got someplace to be."

"She's pregnant, Trace, and despite her I-can-handle-anything attitude, she's got a lot of shit to deal with. She doesn't need whatever brand of bullshit you're bringing."

"That's where you're wrong." Trace picked up his cowboy hat from the bar and put it on, his gaze never wavering from Sable's. "If anyone knows what Brindle needs, it's me."

He turned to leave, and Jeb pushed to his feet. "Hold up. I'll go with you."

Trace looked over his shoulder and said, "I'll be back. Why don't you and Sable have a drink? Maybe it'll chill you both out."

"AXSEL, YOU SHOULD have heard the rumors going around school," Brindle said into the phone as she paced her apartment. "Yesterday everyone was whispering and giving me sideways looks. Even some of the other teachers gave me the stink eye, as if they've never had sex." Her brother had called to check on her, and he couldn't have called at a better time. She'd had no idea what to do with herself after work. She usually went out with Sable or Morgyn, and if they were busy, she went out with Lindsay and Trixie. But she was pregnant, and they were at JJ's Pub. If she showed up there, she'd spark even more rumors.

"That sucks, Brin. But you survived your first day back. Was today any better?"

She sighed. "Yeah, a little. I know it'll take some time for the rumor mill to calm down. Remember Natalie? The sophomore who helps me with drama club? We got together after school to go over some details for next week's drama club meeting and she told me there were all sorts of crazy rumors going around, like I don't know who the father is because I was with so many guys in Paris and that I married the father and then left him. Where do they get this shit? Can you believe my students are actually discussing this?"

"There isn't much else to do in Oak Falls besides stir up trouble."

"I know you think that. You couldn't wait to escape and make your mark on the world, but I love it here, so hopefully this will die down." She thought about telling Axsel the truth about Trace, but she promised herself she wouldn't tell anyone else until she told Trace.

"It will. You know how these things go. When I came out there were rumors for weeks, remember?"

"Yes. But then Trace told everyone he was bisexual, and he got his brothers to do the same. That shut everyone up." She'd been floored that Trace had put himself in that position for her brother, and she'd been equally grateful and proud of him. "No one knew what to believe."

"Yeah, except he got my hopes up." Axsel laughed.

"Back off, big boy."

"Hey, when he came over the other day—before you sucked face—did you ask him about Heather Ray?"

"Oh shoot! No. I totally forgot." Her heart sank. "I guess it's a good thing I didn't sleep with him."

"Are you trying to convince yourself?"

"I don't know, Ax. I miss him."

"That's why I waited until Tuesday to call. I know you guys hit JJ's Tuesday nights. I wish I were there. I'd go to JJ's with you and we could dance the night away."

"I don't think I'll be going there anytime soon. Knowing me, someone will say something obnoxious and I'll deck them. Then there will be a hair-pulling bitch fight, which I'll win with one knee to the gut, because I can't let anything happen to the tender morsel I'm carrying, *and* it'll fuel even more rumors."

"Wow. You really ran with that one, didn't you, sis? You don't hit people. You give verbal lashings. But just in case those pregnancy hormones are changing that, let it be known that I don't think you should be *decking* anyone. And what about me? I'd stand up for you."

"Oh please. You'll be too busy checking out the guys who are watching us, because everyone knows guys love girl fights—and you love guys. See? Win-win."

There was a knock at her door, and she said, "Someone's here. Care to wager on who it is? Five bucks says it's Sable wanting Andre's address and phone number so she can go knock some sense into him." *Which is exactly why she can't find out this is Trace's baby.*

"I'm surprised she wasn't waiting on your doorstep Saturday night. I've got to go, too. Call me anytime, and let me know what our hot cowboy says about Heather. Love you!"

"Love you, too. Good luck with the tour." She ended the call and answered the door.

Her broody cowboy barreled in. "Get your hot ass dressed, Mustang. We're going dancing."

"Um, no, we're not," she said as she closed the door behind him. She crossed her arms and said, "Maybe you should take Heather Ray dancing."

"What?" His brows slanted in confusion. "Let's go. It's Tuesday."

She pressed her lips together, looking at him expectantly.

"You seriously think I *slept* with Heather?"

"You've hooked up with her before."

He crossed his arms with a freaking smirk on his face. "I've never slept with Heather."

"Don't even try to play semantics with me, country boy. I've got a vocabulary list way longer than that python in your pants."

He stepped closer. Heat rolled off his body, circling her from the ground up, consuming her like a whirlpool. Her mouth went bone dry as he stared into her eyes and said, "I like knowing you're thinking about the python in my pants."

"*Ugh!*" She pushed past him. "You fucked Heather. Go get *her.*"

"I didn't *fuck* Heather," he seethed.

She rolled her eyes. "Okay, let's see, *hooked up* with, *banged,* or the one that makes me sick to my stomach—*made love to.*"

"Brindle," he warned with fire in his eyes.

"Everyone knows you left the barn bash with her, so don't play me for a fool."

He strode across the room until his chest and thighs bumped hers, hulking over her as he said, "You're nobody's fool, Brindle. Come on. Get dressed. We're going to JJ's, and you can ask Heather for yourself."

She scoffed. "That's *just* what I want to do, right after I shoot myself in the foot."

"Fine. Have it your way." He grabbed her hand and dragged her toward the door.

"Trace! What are you doing?"

He stopped, his eye boring into her as he said, "It's Tuesday night and you're sitting in the apartment probably bored out of your mind, stewing over me and Heather. That's not who you are, and one day you'll realize it's not who I am, either." He grabbed her keys from the table by the door and shoved them in his pocket. "We're going dancing, and we'll clear up this Heather shit while we're there."

She wrenched her hand free and huffed out a breath. "Since when do you manhandle me?"

"Darlin', I'm not *manhandling* you. I'm saving you from yourself. You're in no condition to be stressed out over bullshit."

"It's not a *condition*, and everyone is already talking about me. I have no interest in looking like a jealous ex to one of your trollops and feeding that fire."

The corners of his lips tipped up. "Don't you trust me?"

"Trust is a very *broad* subject." A smile tugged at her lips, and she tried to stop it, but his grin was irresistibly devastating, and it reached all the way up to his eyes, creating the crinkles at the corners that only came when he was being playful. That was the look that had done her in at thirteen. Its effect had only grown stronger with every passing year.

"You trust me, darlin', or you never would have let me into your bed. I told you that I've got you, and you know I'm a man of my word." He leaned against the door, crossed his legs at the ankles, and folded his arms over his broad chest. "Now, I've spent sixteen Tuesdays without you and I hated every single one of them. It's our night and I'm not leaving this apartment without you. You can either hurry your pretty little ass up and change your clothes, or not. I think you look hotter than the sun itself in that cute little outfit."

She looked down at her black shirt with the shoulder cut-outs and lace trim, holey jeans, and cowgirl boots. Her shirt covered the rubber band she'd looped through the buttonhole to create a skosh more room for her belly.

Trace pushed from the wall, grinning arrogantly as he took her hand and said, "Nobody pens my Mustang in. Let's go show this town just what they can do with their gossip."

Chapter Six

JJ'S PUB WAS as familiar as the cleft in Trace's chin, but for the first time in her life, Brindle was nervous about going inside. Why had she let him talk her into coming? After all he'd said, she no longer thought he'd slept with Heather. But she was still nervous about what gossip she might cause by being at a bar when she was pregnant.

She stopped before the entrance and said, "Wait one sec, please."

Trace stopped walking, looking curiously at her.

"I need a minute. I don't think this is such a good idea. Everyone's already talking about me, Trace."

"And…?" He stepped closer. "Brin, people have been talking about us since our first kiss. Why do you care?"

"Because they're not talking about *us*. They're talking about my baby, and I don't want my baby to grow up shrouded in gossip."

He arched a brow. "Darlin', this is Oak Falls. It wouldn't matter if you were three-years married; people would find something to gossip about with that pregnancy."

He had a point, but still. "I have to think past myself, Trace." She put her hand beneath her coat, covering her belly.

"I don't want to make things worse."

He pressed his rough hand to her cheek, and she leaned into his comforting touch. "Changing your life because of rumors and avoiding the people you like to be with will make things worse. You're Brindle Montgomery, and there is not one woman in that bar who is sexier, funnier, kinder, or smarter than you."

"How can you say that with everything we're going through?"

The muscles in his jaw bunched, and he seemed to contemplate his answer before finally saying, "Because I know you better than anyone does. I said it before and I'll say it again. You're my best friend, and you have been my lover forever. I'm not going to let anyone think you're any less important to me than you always have been, including *you*. You're a pain in my ass, but you're the only woman I'd let drive me crazy." He patted his chest with both hands and then he splayed his hands with an arrogant grin. "I'm Trace Jericho, darlin'. If you're with me, you're the best there is."

He draped an arm over her shoulder and said, "Let's go have some fun and show people that nothing will stop you from living life on your own terms."

"How do you do that?" she asked as they headed inside.

"What?"

"Always know how to ease my worries?"

"Years of trial and error." He pressed a kiss to her temple and pulled the door open. "After you, beautiful."

Music and the scent of cowboys and lost inhibitions greeted them in the dimly lit bar. Adrenaline coursed through Brindle's veins as the familiar rush of the night enveloped her. Brindle loved music, dancing, and being around people as much as she loved teaching. Both filled her with a sense of irreplaceable happiness. Her mother always said she was born dancing, because even as a toddler she'd preferred dancing to playing with toys. According to her parents, she'd danced when there was no music, as if a beat lived inside her.

Trace helped her off with her coat and tossed it into JJ's office on their way in. As they passed the arched entrance to the room with the mechanical bull, Brindle saw Chet Hudson, a local firefighter, riding the bull, and she spotted Lindsay and Trixie in the crowd cheering him on. She couldn't suppress her smile. She and Trace had been trying to get Chet to ride the bull for months before she'd gone to Paris.

"Chet's riding!" she said over the music.

Trace leaned closer and said, "Sable goaded him into it with a dare." His eyes heated and he pulled her against him. "You Montgomery girls and your dares. *Mm-mm.* I know just how hard they are to resist."

How could things feel so normal between them when they were anything but?

Trace kept her close as they weaved through the crowded bar, and Brindle tried to ignore the sideways glances and whispers behind hands. She didn't have to ignore them for long, because as quickly as she noticed them, Trace shut each one down with a threatening stare.

"Trace!" Sinclair "Sin" Vernon, the athletic director of the No Limitz youth center, waved them over. He stood by a booth where Jeb and Shane sat drinking beer.

Brindle tried not to react to the disapproving look in Jeb's eyes as they approached. Trace must have noticed her bristling, because he lowered his voice and said, "I've got you, Brindle. Don't ever doubt that."

She hadn't ever doubted it, which was why it had hurt so badly when he'd accused her of carrying someone else's baby. But over the last two days she'd had time to realize Morgyn was right, that Trace had probably said what he had out of hurt. Or at least she hoped so.

"Hey, man," Trace said to Sin, and then he looked at Jeb and said, "We're here to have a good time, so if you've got something to say, you say it to *me* or you wipe that look off your face."

"I wasn't going to say anything." Jeb shifted a friendlier gaze to Brindle and said, "Congratulations."

"Thank you," she said, but while she loved the way Trace had shut him down, she didn't want her pregnancy to cause a rift between any of them.

"Trace, I could really use your help with the youth league for a few hours Saturday, if you've got time," Sin said. He was a big man, like Trace, with dark hair and sharp features.

"Sure," Trace said casually, shocking the heck out of Brindle. "I'll see what I can work out."

"*Whoa*," Brindle said. "Was that actually a *yes*?"

Trace had played football in high school, and he'd gotten a full scholarship to play wide receiver for three West Coast colleges. He'd turned them down, telling Brindle he didn't want to be that far away from her. Trace had stayed home to work on his family's ranch. It was a bone of contention between Trace and Brindle, not because he'd never gone to college, but because all she'd ever wanted was for him to be happy. She knew he loved working on the ranch, but she also knew how much he'd enjoyed football and the camaraderie of the team. Brindle had fond memories of watching him and his buddies practice late at night when they were teenagers. Over the years she'd encouraged Trace to do more with football, and when the youth center had opened, she'd pushed harder. It was a topic that had caused several breaks in their relationship over the years.

Trace shrugged. "It's not a big deal, Brin."

"It's a *huge* deal." She was thrilled that he was taking this step.

"Well, it sure helps me out," Sin said. "You're great with the kids. I really wish you'd think more about coaching next year." He glanced at Brindle and said, "Maybe you can persuade him to help out the kids around here."

"I'll see what I can do," she said, already planning to nudge a little harder in that direction.

Trace looked down at her and shook his head. "Don't make a big deal out of this."

She smiled noncommittally.

"I was just about to get drinks," Sin said to Trace. "Help me carry?"

Trace's hand slid to Brindle's lower back, and he said, "Do you want iced tea? Water? Wait, can you have caffeine?"

"I think so, but water's good, thanks." She was still on a high about his helping Sin coach. The fact that he'd thought of her baby's well-being was icing on the cake.

Trace pointed at Jeb and said, "Behave."

After they walked away, Brindle was too antsy to sit down, and she still felt the need to stand up for herself. "Jeb, I know a disapproving look when I see it," she said firmly. "I get that you're protective of Trace, but you *know* me, and I hope you know that hurting your brother is the last thing I want to do."

"I'm sure it is," Jeb said. "Just tread carefully. He's not as tough as he lets on."

"Brindle!" Trixie gushed as she and Lindsay rushed over and

embraced her. "I'm so happy you're here!" She was as dark as Lindsay was blond. Her hair fell in long layers over the shoulders of her plaid button-down shirt, which was tied at the waist in pure Trixie style.

"Hi," Brindle said, glad for their cheerful distraction. "I missed you guys."

"We missed you, too, and, *girl*, we need to talk," Lindsay said as she and Trixie dragged her away from the table. "And not just about the baby shower I am *definitely* throwing for you." Lindsay was an event planner and photographer. She'd handled Grace's wedding and just about every other major event in the area. "I want all the details on this pregnancy, and the father…"

"That's going to have to wait," Trixie announced. "*What* is going on with you and Trace? The other night he was ready to kill someone over your pregnancy, and now you two look like nothing's changed."

She glanced at Trace leaning over the bar, women ogling his broad shoulders and muscular ass. Jealousy clawed at her, but he was focused on JJ, not the other women. And he'd come to get her from her apartment when he could have been with any of those women. That made her feel all kinds of good—and all kinds of guilty for lying to him.

Trace glanced over his shoulder, catching Brindle watching him, and heat rushed to her core.

But he doesn't want a child right now, she reminded herself.

"When have I ever known what Trace and I were doing?" Brindle finally said. "He came to get me, and you know Trace; he wouldn't take *no* for an answer."

"Well, *good*," Trixie said. "You should be here with us."

Lindsay nodded in agreement. "The entire Oak Falls universe was off-kilter when you were gone. Tuesdays are *Trace and Brindle* nights, and he was a total grump when you were gone."

"Really?" she asked, watching him approach, laughing at something Sin said. All the Jericho men were attractive, but Trace had the sexiest mix of edginess and playfulness, which kept her on her toes—*and on my back.* She felt her cheeks flame and looked away so he wouldn't notice as he walked past and set the drinks on the table.

"Yes, really," Trixie said. "The big bastard even tagged along with me to pick up a horse from Nick Braden in Pleasant Hill, Maryland. He *never* does that." Nick, a freestyle horse trainer, was one of Graham's brothers. He and Trixie often helped each other out, and he'd been teaching Trixie freestyle training techniques well before Morgyn had met Graham at a music festival in Romance, Virginia.

"Totally cramped her style," Lindsay added. "You know that's where she goes to party with Nick's sister, Jilly." Jillian was a clothing designer and she owned a high-end boutique in Maryland.

Even though Trixie was in her twenties, her brothers were still as overprotective as Sable was, which made it impossible for Trixie to hook up with guys around Oak Falls. They all feared the wrath of the Jericho brothers.

"Next time you decide to go to Paris, *please* take Trace with you. I don't care if you bring him along as a *babysitter*, just get him away from me," Trixie said.

"Speaking of babysitting, I still can't believe you're pregnant. How are you breaking it to your students?"

"Oh gosh, they *know.* You saw how things went down at the barn bash. Not exactly how I'd planned, but what am I going to do?"

"*Nothing*," Trixie said adamantly. "You don't have to explain yourself to anyone."

"She's right," Lindsay said.

If only that were true. She appreciated their support, but she knew she had to explain things to Trace at some point soon.

"Come on, let's dance." Trixie pulled them onto the dance floor.

They danced to a few country songs, laughing and having a great time. Brindle felt the heat of Trace watching her from beside the booth. His mouth was moving like he was talking, but his dark eyes were trained on her every move. Oh, how she loved that! She danced sexier, shimmying up and down Trixie's and Lindsay's bodies, her arms over her head, swinging her hips seductively, giving him a real show. His appreciative look made her want to dance even sexier. This was just what she'd needed, to be out and about and not stewing over what jealous coworkers or immature high schoolers thought of her.

She watched Trace cutting through the crowd, eyes on her.

"Sorry, ladies," he said as he draped an arm possessively around her shoulder. "I've waited long enough to dance with my girl."

He took her hand and spun her into his arms. "Ready to show them how it's done, darlin'?"

"You know it."

They'd been dancing together for so many years, they fell right into sync to their own version of the triple-step country swing. People gave them a wide berth, and they took full advantage. They dipped and twirled, laughing as they changed up their steps to match the songs. Sable was watching them like a hawk from the stage, but Brindle was having too much fun to care. Shane and Sin came over and danced with Lindsay and

Trixie.

When the band played a line dancing song, Brindle glared at Sable. Sable knew how much she loved dancing with Trace. Sable smirked, obviously pleased with herself.

Damn her.

When that song ended, Trace took Brindle's hand and pulled her in close. "You've still got it, Mustang."

"Thanks! It feels so good to be out with you. Thank you for pushing me to come."

He winked, and then he leaned in close and spoke in a low, gravelly voice. "You know how much I love making you come." Every word was laced with innuendo, accentuated by a pulse of his hips.

"Let's go," Trixie said, waving them toward the booth.

"Whew, you keep that up and I'll need to bathe in the ice water you got me," Brindle said, fanning her face as they followed the others off the dance floor. She took a gulp of water as Trixie and Lindsay climbed into the booth.

"I've said it before and I'll say it again. Brindle, I'd give anything to be able to dance like you," Lindsay said. "I bet when your belly's big and round you'll still be rockin' it on the dance floor."

"I don't think so," Brindle said, glancing at Trace, who was standing beside her with one hand on her lower back.

"How far along are you?" Lindsay asked.

"Just far enough to have to pee *all* the time. I'll be right back." She turned toward the ladies' room, and Trace grabbed her by the waist, walking beside her. "I'm okay," she reassured him. "I can go on my own. I don't feel funny anymore."

"If you think I'll let the most beautiful woman in here walk around like she's available, you're wrong."

"Oh please," she said softly. "It's not like guys are clamoring to hook up with the pregnant girl."

She was relieved to see a few friendly faces on the way to the ladies' room. Maybe Trace was right. She'd never been afraid of gossip or shied away from the people who spread it. Why should she now?

"I made a mistake letting you go to Paris on your own," he said too casually for such a serious statement. "I'm not making another one."

She opened her mouth to respond, though she had no clue what she was going to say, and a group of girls burst out of the ladies' room in fits of giggles. She took advantage of the distraction and said, "I'll be right back."

She ducked into the ladies' room, exhaling loudly as the door closed behind her. She used the facilities and washed her hands, mulling over what he'd said.

The door opened and Heather Ray walked in. They both stood stock-still, staring at each other.

Brindle forced herself to feign a smile and said, "Hi," as she waved her hands under the dryer.

"Brindle, hi." Heather shifted from one foot to the other. She looked cute in skinny jeans and a purple sweater. "I didn't expect to see you here."

"I didn't, either. Trace dragged me out." She focused on the hand dryer to keep from looking at Heather.

"Listen, I just want you to know…I'm sure you've heard that Trace and I left the barn bash together."

So much for avoidance. "Mm-hm."

"Well, nothing happened. We just talked about you all night. He was really hurting, and, well, you're one of the only people around here who doesn't talk smack about me, so I thought you should know."

Brindle had believed Trace, but hearing it from Heather made her feel ridiculously emotional. "Thank you," she said. "Trace told me you didn't fool around, but I didn't know he talked about me. I'm sorry. That must have been uncomfortable for you."

Heather shook her head, her brow wrinkled. "Not really. I've been his sounding board since you went away. And lots of times before that. Just so you know, we've never hooked up or anything. We kissed once when you guys were broken up a long time ago, but he hated himself for it."

Brindle's heart squeezed. "So you never...?"

"No. Never. But you know how people talk. I don't know what's happening with the father of your baby, but I know Trace is a good man, and he loves you."

Brindle's eyes teared up as emotions slammed into her. She knew Trace loved her on some level, and even if it wasn't in the way she needed, to know he'd conveyed it to Heather, purposefully or not, was overwhelming. She looked up at the ceiling, fanning her eyes dry. "Hormones. Sorry!"

Heather headed for a stall as she called, "Good luck with the baby."

Brindle took a moment to pull herself together before she left the bathroom. Trace was waiting by the door, and she threw her arms around his neck, went up on her toes, and kissed him on the lips. "Thank you."

"For waiting outside the bathroom?" he asked with a lift of his brows.

"No. For being you."

"How about I be me on the dance floor? They're playing our song. Let's go." He pulled her toward the dance floor and led her to the front of the crowd.

"Our song?" she asked.

He cocked his head, indicating for her to listen. She recognized "Fucking Perfect" by Pink, and her stomach flip-flopped.

"Our song, darlin'."

He was an amazing dirty dancer. He kept her close as he wedged his thigh between her legs, and their bodies swayed and connected like mating snakes. Her gaze swept over the stage, and she caught Sable glaring down at them again as she played. Trace's hands moved down her hips to her ass, bringing her attention back to him, where it belonged.

He mouthed the lyrics, singing about her being *fucking perfect*, and she felt herself getting lost in him. She'd been so nervous earlier, but as always, Trace had obliterated everything in his wake. Their bodies bumped and brushed as the music moved through her, eating up any remaining worries like an unstoppable lover. When Trace dipped his head, singing the chorus directly into her ear, all of the emotions she'd been holding back came rushing forward. His broad body moved with her, *against* her. He felt so good, so *right*, months of longing surged to the surface. She ached for his touch, and she gave herself over to the beat, bumping and grinding, holding nothing back.

When the song ended, Trace kept her close, eyeing Sable with a victorious look.

My two bodyguards. She loved them both so much. When Sable began rocking out to Halestorm's "Love Bites," leaving the rest of her bandmates to try to catch up, Brindle had to chuckle. But Trace didn't miss a step. He kept her close, slow dancing to the chaotic beat as people jumped and danced wildly around them.

Trace clutched her butt, pressing his hard heat against her as they moved in perfect harmony. His hips thrust, his hands wandered, and she didn't care who saw or who might gossip, because she was right where she wanted to be, and nothing could pry her away. Not the next angry song Sable played or the one after that. She was vaguely aware of her friends greeting her as they came and went from the dance floor, but their words didn't register. At some point she became aware of the song "Bad Things" playing and Trace singing the lyrics in her ear again as they dirty danced, lost in their own private bubble of eroticism. When he pressed his lips beside her ear and his tongue slicked over her skin, her nipples rose to hard, tingling points. He continued kissing, trailing his warm lips over her cheek, down her neck, and when he brushed them over her lips, his penetrating gaze consumed her.

She knew he was seeking her approval, and she pushed her hands into his back pockets, squeezing his ass the way she had so often. A sinful smile appeared, and he slanted his lips hungrily over hers. Their tongues tangled, and their bodies writhed. She was finally in Trace's arms after months of missing him. The last of her inhibitions flitted away, and as she lifted her wings to fly, she remembered...

She wasn't the only one who would fight the gossip caused by her actions.

She had to think of her baby.

She drew back, breathless and dizzy, forcing the words to come. "Trace, we're just adding fuel to the fire."

"When have we ever lived our lives on other people's terms?"

And there it was, their shared love of rebellion, their determination to never allow anyone else the upper hand, the reason they'd always been perfect for each other.

BRINDLE PRESSED HER fingers deeper into his back pockets, the green light she'd been giving him for so many years. He'd missed it when she was a million miles away. The lust in her eyes belied her hesitant plea, but as he lowered his mouth to hers, he couldn't rid himself of the things she'd said earlier. *I don't want my baby to grow up shrouded in gossip.*

He forced himself to pull back and said, "You want to get out of here?"

She nodded vehemently.

He took her hand, and then he tucked her beneath his arm, needing her closer. He led her through the crowd and away from prying eyes. When they reached his brother's office, he walked over to the desk to retrieve her coat and heard the lock click behind him. He turned and found Brindle beckoning him with her finger, hunger brimming in her eyes as she did the nose-wrinkle shoulder-shrug thing that lit him up inside. His control snapped, and he hauled her against him, capturing her mouth with savage intensity as they clung to each other, struggling to kick off their boots and fumbling with the button on each other's pants.

There was something around her button. He tore his mouth away long enough to pant out, "What the...?"

"Rubber band. Needed space." She pulled his mouth back to hers with one hand as she fiddled with her button with the other.

They feasted on each other as they shed their jeans. Three

and a half months felt like forever, and as they kissed and groped, bit and nipped, he wanted to strip her naked, to feast on her sex and tease her nipples until she begged for more, but he needed to be inside her more than he needed his next breath.

"God, I've missed you," he said as he lifted her onto the desk and wedged himself between her legs.

"Show me," she challenged.

He reached behind her, pulling her forward as he buried his cock to the root in one hard thrust. He stilled at the feel of her tight heat surrounding him. "*Fuck*, Mustang. It's been too long."

She moaned loudly, and the sound soared through him, feeding his carnal desires. Their mouths crashed together, and he drove into her. The pulsing beat of the band hammered through the walls, her fingernails cut into the back of his neck and arm as she went wild, rocking and grinding with all her might. There had never been any pretense of holding back with Brindle. They let all their sexy flags fly—using silk ties, secretly having sex in public places, no holds—*or holes*—barred. But he'd never wanted to do any of it with anyone else. Not when he was pissed off or when she'd left him behind to traipse around Paris, but sometimes a woman needed to get a little jealous to realize what she had. And he'd found ways to do that without having to put his hands on anyone else.

Somewhere in the back of his mind he worried about hurting her or her baby, but she was making sinful sounds, clinging to him like she needed him to survive, and he was torn between ecstasy and responsibility. He tried to push thoughts of her baby away, but it was impossible, and he eased his efforts for fear of hurting her. It wasn't lost on him that he was worried about Brindle and her baby, and *not* the fact that it was some other dude's baby.

"Harder," she pleaded.

He recaptured her mouth, kissing her deeper, trying to drown that thread of worry. But it gnawed at his gut like a disease.

She tore her mouth away and said, "Why are you slowing down?"

"The baby—"

"It's fine!" she panted out. "The doctor said it's *fine*! Don't hold back, Trace. I've waited so long for you—"

For me...

Those words brought out the animal in him, and he lifted her into his arms, kissing her as he pushed in deeper. He clutched her ass, unable to get enough of her. He needed her naked, needed hours to devour every inch of her, to reclaim her as *his*. He carried her forward, using the wall for leverage as months of passion roared out. He sealed his mouth over her neck, her sex clenching tighter with every suck. She whimpered and moaned, and her legs flexed around him. He gripped her hips, helping her move faster the way she needed. Her head fell back, and her eyes slammed shut as his name flew from her lips, loud and greedy, and he followed her into oblivion.

They clung to each other as aftershocks rumbled through them.

Brindle went limp in his arms, resting her head on his shoulder, breathing hard. When he stepped back from the wall to put her down, she held on tighter and said, "Can you just hold me for a minute?"

"Of course. I've got you, darlin'." He kissed her shoulder. "I've always got you."

He closed his eyes, soaking in their closeness, knowing that in about a minute everything would get awkward, because as hard as he fought to forget, Brindle was carrying someone else's baby.

"Trace?" she whispered.

"Yeah?"

She didn't say anything more, just tightened her hold, nuzzling against his neck. God, he'd missed this. Her scent, her love of being held, her neediness. She was so right in his arms, he wanted to wrap her up and take her home to his cabin. To the place she'd always belonged.

But she wasn't his any longer, regardless of how much he wanted to pretend she was. The asshole who got her pregnant might realize what an idiot he was and beg her to take him back.

Let him try. I'll fucking kill him for leaving you in the first place.

After a minute of silence, he said, "What is it, Brin?"

"Nothing," she said a little sullenly. "Thank you for taking me out tonight."

Chapter Seven

PATTY ANN STALEY walked out of the Catch Up Diner in Meadowside Thursday evening as Brindle was passing on her way to Amber's bookstore, which was nestled between the diner and Magnificent Gifts. Patty Ann was a boisterous brunette who had a knack for making people see the good in things. She was also a friend of Brindle's parents and had babysat Brindle and her siblings when they were young.

Patty Ann set her hands on her rounded hips, smiling brightly, and said, "Well, look who's back in town. How are you doin', sugar?"

Sucky, sad, and confused. It had been two days since she'd seen Trace. Two days since she'd almost told him the truth before chickening out. As close as they'd felt, he didn't want their baby, and no matter how she framed her apology, she had lied, and lies always stunk. But those weren't Patty Ann's problems, so she said, "I'm well. How are you?"

"Better now that you're back in town. This place was too quiet while you were gone." She stepped closer and lowered her voice as she said, "I hear you've got a bun in the oven."

"*Yes,* the rumors are true."

"Congratulations, honey. And don't you fret. Those rumors

will die down, and then everyone will be talking about how adorable you look with a big ol' baby bump. Your mama must be pleased as punch. She's been achin' for a grandchild."

"Thanks. I think she's pretty happy."

Patty Ann's brow wrinkled. "And how about you? Are you happy about it?"

"I am," she said honestly. "It was a shock, but I'm excited."

"That's my girl." Patty Ann hugged her. "How's Trace handling it? Word around town is that it isn't his. That kind of blew me away, but I'm sure Paris was romantic and wonderful. No one can blame you for following your heart in another direction."

Brindle's chest constricted. She skipped over Patty Ann's question about Trace and said, "Paris isn't as romantic as everyone thinks."

"Oh, well…" An uncomfortable silence hung between them, and then Patty Ann said, "I guess you're on your way to see your sister?"

"Yes." She put her hand on her belly and said, "I want to pick up a few baby books."

"Oh, how fun! I'll let you go. Just do me one favor." She pointed to a sign in the window for the upcoming Oak Falls 5K Turkey Trot, which took place every Thanksgiving and was sponsored by several Oak Falls and Meadowside businesses. "Does that look straight to you?"

"It's a little crooked, I think. Too low on the left." Trace and most of their friends took part in the race, while Brindle usually walked it to set a good example for her students. But this year she wanted to be on the sidelines, cheering on her man.

"That's what Berle said, but it looks straight to me." Patty Ann tapped her finger just below her eye and said, "Guess I'd better get my eyes checked. I saw Grace and Reed the other day. I know your parents are thrilled that she's moved back. That Reed, he's a dear, isn't he? Grace is a lucky lady. Well, sugar, I'd better get inside. Good to see you. Don't be a stranger. You know I've always got a piece of pie with your name on it." She waved as she headed into the diner.

Grace wasn't just lucky; she was smart, stable, and careful, which Brindle used to think made her boring. But now she realized her oldest sister's careful nature was what allowed her and Reed to have a stable relationship without drama or jealousy. Maybe Brindle should start taking notes.

The bell above the bookstore door chimed as Brindle walked into Story Time, greeted by the familiar scents of warm cinnamon and relaxation. Amber, Grace, and their friend Aubrey Stewart stood by a display of bookish gifts. Aubrey and Amber had attended Boyer University together, where they'd bonded with a group of girls who shared a love of writing. They'd started their own sisterhood called the Ladies Who Write and lived in a shared house like a sorority. Aubrey and two other LWW girls owned LWW Enterprises, a multimedia corporation in Port Hudson, New York. Aubrey ran the film and television division.

"Hi, Brin," Amber said as Reno ambled over to greet her. "We missed you at Mom's this morning."

"Sorry. I just need a little space to deal with life right now." Brindle and her sisters often had breakfast with their mother before work, but the last thing Brindle needed was Sable questioning her every move. She petted Reno and said, "Aubrey, it's good to see you. I didn't know you were in town."

"And I didn't know you were knocked up," Aubrey said with a tease in her eyes. She hugged Brindle and said, "You're as gorgeous as ever. I hear Paris was *very* good to you."

"Thanks, but I'm glad to be home. I didn't know you were coming into town."

"She was checking out a bed-and-breakfast about an hour away for Charlotte's movie and stopped by to discuss the script," Grace explained. Charlotte Sterling was another LWW sister, and an erotic romance author. Aubrey was turning one of Charlotte's books into a movie, and she'd hired Grace to write the screenplay.

"Don't you have underlings to check out locations for you?" Brindle asked.

"Do you really think I'd let anyone else decide what locations to use for *Charlotte's* movie? No freaking way," Aubrey said as they headed for the nook of comfortable couches and mismatched armchairs in the back of the bookstore. "Besides, I needed a change in scenery. Sexy times have been a little *sparse* in Port Hudson."

Brindle followed them back. "What? Ms. Single Billionaire can't find a guy to hook up with? I don't believe that for a second."

"Her go-to hookup is in *Belize*," Amber said as she sat on the couch and Reno settled in at her feet.

"*Belize?*" Brindle asked. "As in the place Morgyn and Graham just returned from?" Aubrey's silence told her she'd hit the nail on the head. "Are you talking about Graham's business partner? Knox Bentley? Morgyn told me he'd stayed in Belize to negotiate another deal."

Amber's grin and Aubrey's effort not to meet Brindle's eyes confirmed her deduction.

"Holy crap!" Brindle exclaimed. "I knew you had a guy you hooked up with all the time, but how did I not know it was

Knox Bentley? If I were you, I'd jet my ass over to Belize. That man is *hot.*"

"Yes, he's hot and impossibly good at sex." Aubrey ran her fingers through her blond hair. "But we're not like that. We just like to have fun, so please keep this to yourselves. I'd hate for Graham and Morgyn to get the wrong impression."

"I won't say anything," Brindle promised, but she couldn't keep from making the correlation about how she'd fooled herself into thinking she and Trace were just having fun, too, and that she didn't want more out of their relationship. *Look where that got me. Pregnant, with my heart breaking because I'm stuck in a lie I can't figure out how to undo.*

"'The lady doth protest too much, methinks,'" Amber said with a smile.

Aubrey scowled. "Don't use that literary prose on me, missy."

"I vote for jetting over to Belize." Grace waggled her brows and said, "Becca said you've been bitchy for the last few weeks, and now we know why." Becca was Aubrey's assistant.

"You've all lost your minds. Knox and I are fuck buddies, nothing more." Aubrey crossed her legs and said, "You'll see. I'll go out tonight and find a hot cowboy who's looking to score. Then you can all kiss my perfect ass."

Just stay away from my hot cowboy and we'll be fine.

While the girls talked, Brindle admired her sister's store. Amber put her heart into every aspect of it, adding homey touches and offering events that made people of all ages feel welcome. She held contests and let the winners choose the books that were featured in the front window, and she was always open to local authors running book clubs and giving talks. But Brindle's favorite part of the store was the children's area, where vines and flowers snaked up the sides of a cylindrical bookshelf made out of stacked wooden crates. A multitude of potted plants and ivy sat atop the shelving unit, giving it a treelike appearance. Carpet mats were stacked for children to move around and sit on while they read. Amber had such an easy way about her, and that carried over to everything she did. It struck Brindle that one day her child would use those carpets and lay on the floor reading while her mother and aunt chatted nearby.

Holy cow. She touched her belly, remembering why she'd come to the bookstore in the first place. It hadn't been to visit with Aubrey and her sisters while Aubrey talked about her upcoming movie and Grace gushed about Reed. She needed to prepare for her baby. *But maybe what I really need is a book on how to communicate with Trace…*

Trace had texted her several times since Tuesday night to check on her *and* taunting her with dirty innuendos, just like old times. It had taken all her willpower not to invite him over or take him up on his offer to come to his place. They couldn't be near each other without wanting to touch, and she felt guilty enough for having sex with him before telling him the truth. She didn't want to see him again until she'd figured out how to undo her lie.

Her stomach knotted, and she pushed to her feet, blurting out, "I need baby books."

"Look at my wild sister acting like a grown-up," Grace teased.

"I told you guys I wasn't going to screw this up. Are you going to help me find books, or talk about Reed all evening?"

Amber and Aubrey stood and headed for the parenting aisle.

"I'd much rather talk about Reed," Grace grumbled, which

made Brindle smile because before Reed, Grace had spent a lot of time telling her siblings what they were doing wrong with their lives.

They leafed through baby books and parenting books, talking about the benefits of each and helping Brindle decide which books to purchase. After Grace and Aubrey left, while Amber was busy with customers, Brindle went in search of the self-help section, where she checked out books on committing to and creating positive relationships. She gathered the stack of books she'd chosen and carried them up to the register. Her head was so full of information, she could barely see straight.

"Wow, Brin. Do you really think you need"—Amber counted the books—"five baby and parenting books and *four* relationship...Wait...you probably need those." Compassion rose in Amber's eyes. "Are you okay?"

"I'm not even sure I know what *okay* means anymore. I didn't realize how much there was to learn, and looking through these books made me realize something else. I'm not like you and Grace. I don't know how to live a quiet life and be content reading or relaxing at home."

"Brindle, stop worrying. You're going to be a great mother. Who says you have to live a quiet life? I don't think Mom and Dad have ever lived a quiet life."

"That's because there were seven of us, and we were noisy. But what if I suck at being a mother? What if I screw this baby up? What if I teach it to be rebellious and opinionated like me?"

Amber laughed. "Then Mom and Dad will probably take pleasure in your frustrations." She came around the counter and said, "I think your baby won't be able to help being rebellious and opinionated. It's *your* child, Brin, and that's *not* a bad thing. You've never worried about who you were, so why are you worrying about this?"

"Because I'm not sure I'm a good person anymore." The confession came unbidden, but she realized it was true. "I don't want this baby to be like me in that way. I don't want it to hurt the people it loves most."

"You didn't hurt any of us by getting pregnant. Oh, wait. Are you talking about *Trace*?"

Brindle nodded, tears sliding down her cheeks. Damn hormones.

Amber put her arms around her, holding her without saying a word. It was just what Brindle needed, to cry the tears she hadn't realized she'd been holding back. If she wasn't careful, she'd tell Amber the truth. She'd already told Morgyn, who had texted her first thing Wednesday morning asking if she'd told Trace yet. It felt like a betrayal that Morgyn knew and Trace didn't, but every time she told herself to call, or decided to tell Trace the truth, the pain of knowing he wasn't ready for a child held her back.

When she stopped crying, Amber handed her tissues from a box on the counter and said, "Brin, Sable said you and Trace were looking pretty cozy Tuesday night. Was that just for show? Have you had another falling out? She thought you two had made up."

"No, he's been great. I'm just losing my mind because of hormones or something."

"Do you want to hang out tonight?" Amber offered. "Watch a Hallmark movie?"

Only Amber, her sweetest sister, would suggest she watch a sappy Hallmark movie. She'd tried to watch one once, and she was so frustrated by the characters hardly ever kissing and *never* making out, she couldn't finish it. Real life included kissing, touching, arguing, and incredible makeup sex.

"I love you for asking, but I have a lot of reading to do tonight." She patted the stack of relationship books.

"That's okay. I know you're more of a Cinemax girl, anyway."

"Actually, these days I'm more of a *Cinnabon* girl. In fact, after I pay for these, I think I'll head over to Pastry Palace and *eat* my worries away."

Amber put the books in a bag and pushed them across the counter. "Keep your money, Brin. You'll need it for my new little niece or nephew, and enjoy every second of that delicious treat you're going to get. You deserve it."

"You're the best. Thank you!"

Ten minutes later, Brindle's was salivating over pastries in the bakery when Trace's mother walked in. Brindle froze at the sight of the chestnut-haired woman who had always treated her like a daughter. Nancy Jericho was lovely and sweet, but that sweetness might have turned sour given Brindle's current condition and the lies surrounding it. Brindle was sickened by the thought that her lie had probably hurt his parents, too.

Nancy looked uncomfortable, forcing a troubled half smile as she said, "Hello, Brindle. Welcome back."

"Hi," she said meekly, and they moved in for an awkward embrace.

"I would ask how Paris was, but I hear congratulations are in order, and I assume it was a nice trip."

The hurt in her eyes sent Brindle's emotions into a tizzy again. She wanted to tell her she was sorry and that the baby was Trace's, but all that came out was, "Yes, thank you."

Nancy looked down at the bag in Brindle's hand, her mouth twitching as if she were struggling to keep her own emotions in check. When she looked up, sadness brimmed in her eyes. Trace shared his mother's cleft chin, and when she truly smiled, they shared a look that had no name because it was too bright for words. Brindle would give anything to see that look right now, but she knew she didn't deserve it.

Her throat tightened and her chest ached. She had to get out of there before she broke down like she had with Amber. "I'd better go," she said shakily, motioning toward the door. "It was nice to see you."

When she turned to leave, Nancy touched her arm, stopping her.

Nancy's eyes dampened as she said, "I always thought it would be you and Trace having babies, but life changes, and I wish you nothing but happiness."

Brindle had no idea how she managed to thank her, or if she really had before running out of the bakery and toward her car, determined to tell Trace the truth.

SHE PARKED BESIDE Trace's truck in front of his two-bedroom A-frame cabin. Her heart hammered against her ribs as she raced toward the front door. His house sat on several wooded acres overlooking a creek. They had taken full advantage of his privacy over the years, making love in the grass, on his porch, down by the creek, *in* the creek, and just about everywhere else, including on the hood of his truck.

She banged on the door. "Trace!" When he didn't answer right away, she pulled it open and hollered, "Trace?"

"Upstairs, darlin'. Come on up."

She dropped her keys by the door, shrugged off her coat, and raced upstairs. "We need to talk," she said as she entered his bedroom.

He came out of the bathroom wearing only his jeans and a smile, and *damn*, she lost her train of thought. Not because of his bare, broad chest, muscular arms, or the treasure trail that disappeared beneath his unbuttoned jeans. It was his smile, those crinkles at the corners of his eyes, and the way his eyes simmered with as much desire as happiness as he closed the distance between them.

He tugged at one side of the scarf she'd forgotten she was wearing, and it slipped from around her neck. He tossed it on the bed and said, "Tuesday night was not enough for you either, huh?"

"I...*no*...but that's not why I'm here."

He dipped low, pressing his warm lips to her neck. "I'm just about to get in the shower." He began unbuttoning her shirt. "Perfect timing."

"Trace, we need to talk," she said as his adept fingers reached the bottom button.

He gazed into her eyes as his hands slid beneath the shoulders of her shirt and pushed it off. His lips tipped up as he dragged his finger down the center of her chest, stopping at the clasp of her bra. "My favorite pink bra. Nice touch."

"Trace," came out as a half warning, half plea. She had never been able to deny him a damn thing.

"Come on, Mustang." He brushed his lips over her cheeks and then traced the shell of her ear with his tongue. "We do our best talking naked."

He bit her earlobe, sending a shock of pleasure between her legs. He soothed the tender spot with his tongue and then he gazed into her eyes and gripped the front clasp of her bra. "Want me to stop?"

Somewhere in the back of her mind she knew she should say yes and tell him what she came to say. But what if this was the last time he looked at her this way? The last time she would ever feel his body against her, *inside* her? She had a fleeting thought about being selfish, but if this was all she would ever get, she'd take that chance, because going the rest of her life without him would be punishment enough.

"No," she said. "But I wanted to talk about something important."

"Being together *is* important." He unhooked her bra, and as he slipped it off, his gaze ignited. "God, you're beautiful, Mustang," he said, full of heat and so much more.

It was the more that shredded any remaining doubt about giving herself—giving them—what might be their one last chance to be together.

He ran his fingertips over her breasts, circling her nipples, bringing them to burning peaks. He stepped closer, his chest hair tickling her skin as he lowered his mouth over hers, kissing her so deeply and slowly, so *thoroughly*, she couldn't hold on to a single thought. His arms came around her as he intensified the kiss, taking and giving in equal measure, until she was wet and needy. He pushed down her leggings, and she was so dizzy with desire she couldn't remain upright. At least she had enough sense to cover her little belly. But as he bent to help her step out of her leggings, he pushed her hands aside and pressed his soft, warm lips to her baby bump. That single, thoughtful kiss made her love him even more.

He ran his hands down her thighs and abruptly buried his mouth between her legs.

"Oh *Lord*," she cried out, clutching his shoulders.

He knew just how to lick and suck to make her lose her mind, taking her right up to the brink of release, and then he rose to his feet. She was trembling and panting, and her legs felt like wet noodles. He unzipped his pants, his erection straining against his briefs, the broad head poking out from beneath the waistband. He kept his eyes trained on hers as he stripped bare, his thick arousal bobbing between them.

THE LOOK IN Brindle's eyes as Trace took her hand and led her toward the bathroom was everything he needed. It said he *owned* her, at least for now, and hell, he wanted to live in that fantasy as long as he could. He was sure she wanted to talk about Tuesday night. She probably felt guilty about having sex at the bar, but he wasn't about to let her feel that way, and he sure as hell didn't want to hear it. All he wanted to hear was his name coming off her lips in the throes of passion.

They stepped beneath the water, and he scrubbed clean as fast as he could. Then he drew her into his arms, kissing her so deeply he wanted to disappear into her. As his hands moved over her slick body, he told himself to go slow. But she was rubbing all her softness against his erection and grabbing his ass, nipping at his lips. She knew how to make him crazy with desire. Slow didn't have a chance around naked and needy Brindle. They'd never been good at *slow* or *no*.

"I want all of you," he said against her lips as his hand moved between her legs.

He kissed her again, rougher and more demanding, earning

a greedy sound as he dipped his fingers inside her, expertly stroking over the secret spot that made her buck and quiver.

Her fingers dug into his arms, and her head tipped back. "*God*, what you do to me," she said in a throaty whisper.

He sealed his mouth over hers, taking her up and over the edge until she cried out with pleasure. He lowered his mouth to her breast, sucking hard enough to send her soaring again. Every time she came, every time she cried out his name, it fed a beast deep inside him that wanted to see Brindle happy and complete in every way. He dropped to his knees, needing more than the taste he'd gotten in the bedroom. She leaned against the tile and he took his fill, feasting his way to her next orgasm. She came hard, pulling his hair, begging him not to stop. As if he ever would before she was completely satisfied.

When she came back down to earth, he kissed his way up her belly. Her hands moved to cover her new curves, and he felt a pang of hurt, but his love for her pushed it aside. He moved her hands as he had earlier and kissed the crest of her belly before rising to his feet.

As he lowered his mouth toward hers, she put her arms around him and began kissing his pecs. He tried to pull her mouth back to his, but she fought his efforts.

"Let me," she said. "I've missed touching you."

With those words, she could do anything she wanted. He buried his hands in her hair, soaking in the feel of her glorious mouth. It had been so long since he'd felt her mouth on him, he could come just from her sucking his nipples, her fingers pressing into his muscles, and the sinful, appreciative sounds she made. She kissed a path down his stomach. Her hands traveled hungrily over his flesh as her wicked lips loved their way directly to his cock. He couldn't take his eyes off her, and when her eyes flicked up to his and her pretty mouth curved up as she lowered it over his hard length, his chin fell to his chest with a greedy *hiss.*

Her cheeks hollowed with every suck, but the smile never left her eyes as she worked him just the way he liked it, tight and slow. Fighting the urge to come, he ground out, "It's been too long. I'm not going to last, and I want to be inside you when I come."

There were women a man fucked and women a man made love to, and then there was *Brindle*—the only woman he'd ever wanted to do both to. Only there was no fucking with Brindle, because everything he did with her, *to* her, was wrapped in love.

She released his cock, still working him with her hand. "I want you inside me," she said seductively. She sank lower and licked his balls, smiling devilishly up at him as she did it.

"Aw *fuck*, Mustang."

He hauled her to her feet, turned off the water, and swept her into his arms, making her laugh—a sound he'd never tire of hearing—and carried her into the bedroom. They tumbled to the mattress in a tangle of limbs and fervent kisses. Their bodies took over and the rest of the world faded away.

A LONG WHILE later they made their way to the shower again, this time lovingly bathing each other. It was as natural as their overpowering, animalistic need for one another. Brindle was the only woman Trace had ever showered with or had in his bed in his cabin. His *sanctuary*. As they lay together afterward, Trace sitting in his briefs with his back against the headboard,

Brindle tucked against his chest wearing his softest T-shirt, he noticed she was strangely quiet. Brindle always had something to say. It was one of the things he loved about her. She was so smart, she was always thinking, sharing her ideas and opinions, which pushed him to think differently about many things. And yeah, sometimes she pissed him off with her opinions, but he loved that, too. He'd always been mind-fucked over her, and he wouldn't want it any other way. But the last time Brindle went reticent, she'd told him about the six-week trip she'd booked to Paris.

"Close your eyes," she said, causing a knot in the center of his chest.

They only closed their eyes when they needed to have a serious talk. His mind began taking him places he had no interest in going. Was she thinking about the father of her baby? Had she showered with *that guy* in Paris? Was she going to tell Trace she was in love with that guy and this was a mistake? That *their* relationship was over?

His arms were already around her, but now he put his hands over hers, lacing their fingers together, unwilling to let her go that easily. The trouble was, he knew he would never be ready to let her go.

"They're closed," he lied.

She inhaled deeply and blew it out slowly, and he tightened his hold on her.

She leaned to the side and tipped her face up. *Shit.* In all the years they'd been sharing secrets, she'd never once looked to see if he closed his eyes. He was her protector. How could he protect her if he couldn't see an assailant—especially when sometimes assailants came from within. Brindle was her own worst enemy. He was probably the only person in the world who saw her that way, but he knew how she worried about the things she did, the way she acted. Not that she worried about being judged; she just didn't like to hurt others. And sometimes that caused her to overthink and hurt herself with blame and guilt in the process. She had been building walls around her true emotions for so many years, showing everyone the brave, untouchable woman she'd taught herself to be, that sometimes even *she* didn't see her pain. That was one reason he needed his eyes open, to protect her from those self-deprecating attackers.

The other reason was simpler. He never knew when she'd fly the coop, and he didn't want to miss a second of their time together.

"Your eyes are open," she said with a hint of surprise and a *lot* of annoyance.

He was caught, and he wasn't going to talk his way out of it. He shrugged.

She turned and crossed her arms, accusations flaming in her stormy eyes. "Have you *ever* closed your eyes? This is *our thing*. We close our eyes to talk."

"You close your eyes, darlin'. I never have."

Her jaw dropped, and a sound of disbelief escaped. "*Never?*"

"Not once. I don't want to miss a second with you."

Her mouth twitched, as if she was going to say something, and then her lips pressed into a thin line and her shoulders slumped. Her dark brows knitted over her beautiful, tormented eyes, tightening the knot in his gut.

"Well, I can't talk to you like this," she said. "Not about something this important."

He reached for her, but she leaned out of his reach. "Mustang, you can talk to me about anything."

She shook her head, the torment in her eyes turning to

sadness so ripe he pulled her into his arms despite her struggles.

"What's going on, Brindle?"

She shook her head again, tears welling in her eyes.

He was a proud *man*, raised to work his fingers to the bone and to keep his head held high even if his world was crumbling around him. He thought he'd feel rage at the idea of Brindle telling him she wanted someone else, but as he gazed into her sad eyes, his heart broke into a million pieces. Nobody had ever taught him what to do when Brindle's world—the world of the person he loved most—was crumbling right before his eyes.

So he did the only thing he knew how to do, protect her from the hurt of having to say it herself.

"You're in love with the father of your baby," he said, to save her from having to tell him.

She nodded, tears sliding down her cheeks.

Pain like he'd never known slammed into him, crushing his chest until he could barely breathe. He gritted his teeth to keep his own damn unexpected tears at bay, but all-consuming loss swept through him like an evil villain.

"That's why you didn't call me when you were in Paris," he said through clenched teeth. "I knew I never should have let you go alone. Is that why you went in the first place? Did you know that guy before? When we were together?"

"Yes! But not like you thi—"

"The fuck it's not!" he hollered, anger intertwining with his hurt. He flew to his feet, unable to stop the pain from exploding from his lungs. "Why'd you come back at all? Because he didn't want you? He tossed you and the baby away and—"

"Stop!" She stepped toward him, trembling all over. "Stop accusing me of horrible things!"

"Accusing *you*? I *love* you, and you trampled on that love."

She stood with her mouth agape, sobbing, her chest heaving, but he was in too much pain to stop the words from coming out. "Do you know how it felt when you planned a fucking *six-week* trip without me?"

"I had to figure out if what I felt for you was real!" she cried.

"Well, guess what. If you needed to go halfway around the world to figure that out, then how real can it be? I was fucking miserable without you. Even the thought of you going had me all messed up. And then I get a *text* telling me you're not coming back for even longer? Like I'm enough when you need a warm bed, but—"

"Stop! Please!" She covered her face. "I reached for the phone a thousand times to call you!"

"But you never made it happen. I don't need an explanation, Brindle. I might be just a dumb cowboy, but I get it this time."

"*No*, you *don't!*" She dropped her hands, her entire body shaking as she stalked toward him in a furious rage and poked her finger into his chest as she yelled, "You want to talk about *accusations?* The minute you found out I was pregnant, you accused me of spreading my legs for another man. Who does that to a woman they've spent years with? Who they supposedly *love?* You didn't even give me the benefit of the doubt and *ask* if it was yours."

"Why would I? Every time we fight, you run off and hook up with another guy."

"Oh yeah," she said sarcastically, oceans of tears streaming down her cheeks. "That's *exactly* what I do. Just like you fucked Heather and you're not the father of my baby."

"You know I didn't fuck Heath—" Understanding crashed into him, and he stumbled back with the impact. "Are you saying…?" *It's mine? Your kid is mine? Our kid?*

She crossed her arms, her lower lip trembling. "It's *yours*, but I know you don't want a kid right now, so it's not a big deal. I can handle this on my own."

"Not a big deal? You're pregnant with my *child*. You've lied to me for, what? Weeks? *Months?* This is a *very* big deal. How long have you known?"

"Why does it matter? You don't *want* it, and that's not going to change based on how long I've known." She reached for her leggings and he reached for her, but she yanked her arm free and started getting dressed. "*Don't*, Trace. This is so messed up."

"You're fucking right it's messed up," he hollered. "How can I know *what* I want? You're giving me thirty seconds to commit to wanting a child, when you have had more than a decade to commit to being mine and you couldn't even do that."

"Really? That's what you think?" She closed the distance between them, glowering up at him. "I have been with only one other guy, and that was *years* ago, when I was at college and we were on a break! We fight, we break up, we make each other jealous. That's who we are, and it obviously doesn't work, because I had to get away from us to figure out that what made my life full was having *you* in it. And you know why that was?" she hollered.

He was too stuck on *one other guy* to form a response.

"Because when I'm with you I can't *think*. I love you so damn much everything tangles together in my head—love, jealousy, happiness, hurt—like one big spiderweb. I had to get away to figure out if I was the spider or the prey. But all it took was *one night* in Paris and I knew what I felt was real, and after more time I realized I'm not the spider or the prey. I'm the fucking *web* itself, and I'm *trying* to change that. I know I suck as a girlfriend. I'm not easy, and just in case I ever forget," she said through her tears, "everyone around here reminds me all the damn time. I may not be capable of loving in the same way Morgyn or Grace do with their men, where everything is fluffy and flowery. But I *love* you, Trace Jericho, and I fucked up bigtime by lying to you about it when you accused me of sleeping with someone else. But that doesn't change the fact that my love is *real*, and I know that when I walk out that door I will *never* love anyone like I love you, because you own *all* of me—the good, the bad, and the frustrating."

BRINDLE STORMED TOWARD the bedroom door in a fit of anger, hurt, and relief from finally telling Trace the truth. But she didn't want to leave. She didn't want to be that person anymore. She stopped and spun around—smacking right into Trace's chest.

"You can't just drop that bomb on me and walk out," Trace said as he hauled her back into the bedroom.

"Stop saying what I'm thinking! Why do you think I turned around?"

He sank to the edge of the bed, pulling her down beside him, still holding her wrist. "You lied to me, Brindle, for a longass time. How can I trust anything you say?"

"Want to go one for one? How can I trust that you don't think I'm a whore after you've accused me of sleeping with someone else?"

The sadness that twisted his face cut through her like a knife.

"I never have and never would—*ever*—think of you as a whore. Even if you had been pregnant by someone else, I wouldn't have thought you were a whore. Don't you get that? If I thought you were a whore, do you really think I'd have had sex with you again? Damn it, Brindle! You're the only woman I have ever wanted to be with, and I guess that screws with my head. I've spent so many years playing by your rules, convincing myself I didn't want a commitment because *you* didn't want one, that I don't know what I want beyond spending my life with you."

He was talking so fast, she couldn't get a word in.

"Did I say something shitty?" he said with fire in his eyes. "Hell yes, I did. Do I regret it? More than you can ever imagine. Do I want a kid? Who knows? I've always seen a future with you any way you'd let me have it. I have spent years hoping that one day you'd realize you've got the best man around, and I was ready to tell you as much months ago. Then you dropped the news about having booked your solo trip to Paris. I was going to tell you again the night before you left, but you made it perfectly clear that you'd miss our *sex*—not *me*—and that hurt, Brindle, more than I care to admit."

"I *told* you I'd miss you, and you looked at me like you didn't believe me," she snapped. "How do you think that felt?"

"I *didn't* believe you. Why would I? Nobody forced you to put thousands of miles between us for six weeks. That was *your* doing." He ground his teeth together, rubbing his hands over his thighs, pressing his fingers into his skin, as if he needed to channel his anger.

"I just told you why I needed to go alone," she said, trying to process everything he was saying and feeling more overwhelmed than ever before.

"But you didn't tell me *why* you extended your trip if you realized you loved me after one night. What are you so afraid of?"

"Everything," she said honestly. "I knew I loved you, but then I found out I was pregnant, and that's a lot to take in. I don't want to be with anyone else, but I'm so afraid of things changing. I love to dance and hang out with our friends, go to creek parties. That all makes me happy, but I realized in Paris that it's not those things that make me happy. It's doing them with *you*. And that was another thing that scared me, because I never thought I needed a man."

"No shit," he said sharply.

"I was *wrong*, Trace. I might have a full life with my own career and a great family, but without you my life feels empty. I want you, Trace, and I *need* you. I'm not afraid to admit that anymore. But I can't put myself or my needs ahead of this baby. I can't be with you at the *expense* of a baby you don't want. And I really don't want to end up being one of those sad, boring couples who fall out of love, carry around resentment, and take each other for granted."

"Jesus, Brindle," he said more calmly. "We *do* take each other for granted. It's just who we are. We fight, we walk away, and we come back knowing damn well we'll fall into each other's arms again. We're both too damn stubborn to be sad or boring."

"And *resentment*, Trace? Should we add that to the list? What if you resent me for getting pregnant? You already gave up a shot at playing pro ball, doing the thing you loved most, because of *me*. Do you have any idea how much guilt I have because of that? Do you think I don't live every day knowing that at some point you're going to stop getting all hot and bothered over me and see me as the person who held you back? Add the baby to it, and…That is *not* a role I want to star in, and I'm already freaking there. It's like a ticking time bomb. And then to find out from *Sin* that you are getting involved in coaching? I am thrilled about that, but why did it take me going away for you to finally do it? Why didn't you talk to me about it? I'm no relationship expert, but I think that needs fixing, too."

"Why are you always pushing me to get involved with football? Let it go already. And as far as helping Sin goes, I've helped him out a couple times. That's really not a big deal."

"It's a huge deal, and I push you because you *love* it, and you turned down the scholarships because you didn't want to be far away from *me*."

He raked a hand through his hair and ground out a curse. "That wasn't completely true, but it sounded a hell of a lot better than the rest of the truth."

"You *lied* to me?"

"*No.* I honestly *didn't* want to be away from you. But with my father's arthritis, who would run the ranch? If I went away, Jeb or JJ would have had to give up their dreams of running their own businesses to help him out, at least until he could have hired the right people. I wasn't about to put that on their shoulders. Besides, I like football, but I love my family more than any stupid game."

"That's even worse," she said absently.

"How is that worse?"

"It's loyal, but if you can't negotiate or fight for your *own* happiness within your family, the people who love you most, then not only can you never really *be* happy, but how can you ever fight for your wife or child's happiness?"

"Are you kidding me? All I've done is try to make you happy. Letting you leave instead of fighting things out? Not chasing you to Paris? Living by Brindle's no-commitment rules? *That's* fighting for *your* happiness, darlin'. But none of what you just said explains why you stayed in Paris longer than you originally intended."

She looked down at her lap to keep from tearing up again. "Because I wanted to break the patterns we'd fallen into. I thought I might be pregnant when I left, but I wasn't sure. After a week I took a pregnancy test. Several, actually. I wanted to call you so many times, but I knew our relationship needed help and I didn't know how to fix it. Mostly because I knew *I* was the problem. I'm impulsive, and when I get hurt or jealous I react without thinking, and that caused you to get hurt or jealous."

"We both do it. You're not alone in this."

"But I do it more than you do. I push, I run, and then I come back hoping you're still there. If I'd told you I was pregnant while I was away and you were here, it would have only made things more confusing for both of us. I'm sorry. I should have told you right away, but I had so much in my head, and when we're together I'm not good at putting my thoughts out there in a way that makes sense. I wanted to figure out *how* to fix that before I came back, and I thought I had, but I obviously screwed that up. I guess I didn't realize how badly I get all caught up in us, and some things come out wrong when we're together."

"Really? I could have clued you in," he said with a biting tone.

"It's not like you're a great communicator, either."

"Tell me something I don't know," he said less harshly. "At least I made an effort to show you when I couldn't tell you. But every time I tried to get closer, you pushed back. If I said you were the prettiest woman in Oak Falls, you rolled your eyes. When I asked you to go to your prom with me, you said you'd save me a dance but you were going with your friends. When you went to college, I said we could make a long-distance relationship work and you said—"

"Why label it," she said as new fissures formed in her heart. "You're *right*. I told you I was at fault."

"We both are for different reasons. I pushed you away too, because with your every reaction, I learned to act like I didn't want those things. I know you don't like to feel fenced in. I get that, because I don't either. The difference is, I *do* want to be fenced in with *you*. And I wish I could wrap my head around this baby being ours right now, but you've had months to accept it. I've had thirty chaotic minutes, and as much as it sucks—and trust me, it sucks for me as much as it does for you—I need time to process all this."

She closed her eyes, telling herself not to react, not to speak, to count to five the way Andre had taught her to. The hell with five. She counted to *ten*, because she really wanted to figure this out. As she counted, she realized that as much as it hurt, this was what she'd asked for. The truth.

"I do want to be fenced in with you, Trace. I just didn't know it until a few months ago. Where do we go from here?" she asked. "We can't pretend our relationship can go on like it always has. I don't want to be a bad influence on our baby. Even if you don't want to be involved in our baby's life in a bigger way, I *do*, and I don't want our baby to ever feel like we don't love each other." Tears filled her eyes as she said, "If that means we have to only be together as friends, for the good of our baby, then…" She turned away as a sob stole her voice.

"Brindle…" He put his arm around her and pulled her closer, pressing a kiss to her head. "I *love* you, and I can't imagine a life without you, but how can I commit to raising a child with you when I can't be sure you really want to commit to me?"

"Did you not just *hear* me say how much I love you? How I'm trying to *change* because I want us to last? How much I *want* to communicate better? I'm sorry I had to leave to figure it out. You can hold that against me, but I hope you won't."

"I'm not holding it against you, and I'm glad that you're willing to make changes. I love you, and you know I love our baby regardless of how screwed up my head is right now. We created that baby out of love and lust and all the things that make us *us*. Of course I want to be in our baby's life. But *I* need to change, too, and you might not like that."

"Why not? I'm all for it if it'll make us better. That's the whole reason I stayed away, to figure out how to change. I love you so much, Trace. Can't you see that?"

"Yes, but I can't play by your rules anymore, Brin. I've fought for your happiness, and now it's time I fight for mine."

Her nerves prickled with fear. "I don't know what that means."

"It means that maybe we need to start over. Not as thirteen-year-old Brindle and fifteen-year-old Trace. But as adults." He pushed to his feet and made a clearing motion with his hands. "We wipe the slate clean and figure it out."

"O-*kay*," she said. "But how?"

"We start by trusting each other explicitly. You need to

believe that I will not ever let you down."

"I do—"

"You thought I slept with Heather. That's not explicit trust, Brin."

"You're right. I just know I'm not easy to be with, and other girls are, and that—"

"Doesn't mean *shit*." He stood over her, his dark eyes holding her captive. "If I wanted easy, we never would have gotten past that first kiss. Suck it up, darlin', and accept the fact that this man right here"—he banged his chest with both hands—"is as loyal as the ocean is deep. If you want me, you need to believe that."

"I will," she said softly. "I *do*. But how do we do this without falling right back into our old ways?"

"We start right now." He turned on his heels and walked out of the bedroom.

"By walking out? Trace!" She pushed to her feet to go after him.

He strode back into the room with a coy smile on his face and his cowboy hat on his head.

He tipped his hat and said, "Howdy, darlin'. I'm Trace Jericho. I run a ranch here in town, and I'm wondering if you'd like to go out sometime."

"Well, *hello*, cowboy—"

"Nope. Try again," he said with a serious expression.

"*Trace*," she said, feeling ridiculous.

"I'm not fooling around, Brindle. I want to do this right and so do you. If we go straight back to sexy talk, we'll never make any headway."

"You like my sexy talk," she argued.

He scowled, looking unfairly *hot* in his boxer briefs and hat.

"We're playing by *my* rules, or we're not going to be playing for long."

"Fine!" She looked up at him, remembering the first time she'd challenged him to kiss her. He wore the same strained expression now, like it took all his control not to put his arms around her and take everything he wanted.

Even after all this, you still look at me like that.

She had to be the luckiest woman on earth, and she wanted him to know he was the luckiest man, too. She schooled her expression, prepared to give them her all, and said, "Hi. I'm Brindle Montgomery. I teach at the high school, and I run the drama club at the elementary school. I love to dance, so if you're into that kind of thing, I'd be happy to go out with you. But you should know I'm pregnant, and I'm due the beginning of March."

He swallowed hard, emotions swimming in his eyes. "*March.* I think I can handle that."

"I need my rest, and I can't stay out too late."

"You might be a little *too* good at this," he said as he pulled her into his arms and kissed the top of her head.

She pushed free and said, "And I don't kiss on the first date."

He feigned a cough to cover "Liar…"

"Excuse me, Mr. Jericho," she said primly. "We've only just met. Please don't assume you know me. And really, you should put on pants, because I'm a *lady* and I don't need to see your bulging…*thighs.*"

Chapter Eight

BRINDLE AWOKE FRIDAY morning excited about having cleared the air with Trace and equally worried about what *starting over* really meant. After she'd gone home last night, she'd studied the relationship books she'd bought and realized how far off the mark their communication skills were. They'd learned to communicate as teenagers, and now they needed to learn to communicate as adults. She'd known this, but reading about it really drove the point home. Coming clean to Trace was only the first step in making changes to how she handled herself. As she got ready for work, she gave herself a pep talk about telling her family the truth. She thought she was ready to face them at breakfast. But as she parked behind Sable's truck and Amber's car in her parents' driveway, her nerves prickled again.

She climbed from the car and headed up the driveway, walking past her father's truck. It felt like just yesterday that he'd taught her to drive the old clunker. *If you can handle old Stargazer, you can navigate anything.* Her father wouldn't part with that truck because it was the one he and her mother used to lie in the back of and stargaze. Brindle knew a lot more than stargazing had gone on in the bed of that truck.

She saw her father coming up from the barn and waited for him by the kitchen door. He had pieces of hay on his shirt, and the front of his hair was tousled, hanging over his eyes. He pushed it back as he approached.

"There's my beautiful girl." He kissed her cheek and said, "I thought you wanted some space. We didn't expect to see you for a while." Her parents would never truly be empty nesters, and she knew they liked it that way.

"I wanted to see everyone. Do you know if Morgyn and Grace are coming over?"

"They're not, but I'm glad you're here. Amber and your mom are making omelets."

She wasn't about to repeat this morning's announcement for each sibling. She'd just have to get the others on the phone before she said anything.

"Sounds delicious," she said as they went inside. "I swear I'll gain fifty pounds with this pregnancy. I'm hungry all the time."

Reno, Reba, and Dolly greeted them as they walked in.

"What a nice surprise," her mother said as she set a pitcher of orange juice on the table. "I'll grab another place setting."

"Thanks, Mom." Brindle took off her coat and hung it on the back of a chair.

Amber carried a plate of toast to the table and said, "Good thing we made extras. You have perfect timing. We're ready to eat."

Amber looked cute in a pretty multicolored blouse and a long navy skirt. Her sunny disposition underscored the difference between her and Sable, who was leaning against the counter in dark skinny jeans, a tight black T-shirt with BORN WITH A WRENCH IN MY HAND, A FIRE IN MY SOUL, AND A MOUTH I CAN'T CONTROL across her chest, black cowgirl boots, and her cowgirl hat. Her eyes were trained on Brindle, and there was no smile tugging at her tight lips.

Great.

Brindle and Sable had a complicated relationship, even though they were close. Sable was the toughest of all her siblings, and she had always taken on the role of being everyone else's protector. But she'd also been Brindle's confidante when her confessions had been too racy or off-colored to share with Morgyn.

"Have fun the other night?" Sable asked as she sat down.

"Yes, actually." Brindle sat at the table and poured herself a glass of orange juice. "It was exactly what I needed. I was glad Trace came over and dragged me out of my apartment."

"I'm glad to hear he's man enough not to abandon you like that other guy did," her mother said. "Then again, he's always been there for you."

"He sure has," Sable said with an edge to her voice as she buttered her toast.

Brindle pushed the food around on her plate, too nervous to eat. "That's what I want to talk to you guys about. But I kind of want to tell everyone at once. Would it be okay if we got the others on the phone?"

Her parents shared a concerned glance.

"Honey?" her mother said. "Is something wrong?"

"Actually, I think things are finally going to be *right.*" Brindle grabbed her phone from her coat pocket and sent a group text to Grace, Morgyn, Pepper, and Axsel. A minute later, several phones rang. "Answer them, please, and put them on speakerphone. I'm only doing this once." She answered Axsel's call. "Ax, hold on a sec. I need to put you on speaker." As she pushed the speaker icon, her mother answered Morgyn's call.

"Hi, Gracie," Amber said as she answered her phone.

Sable eyed her as she put her phone on speaker and said, "Hi, Pepper. You're on speakerphone."

"What's going on? Is something wrong?" Grace's voice came through the phone.

"No," Brindle said, trying not to let her nerves get the better of her. "I wanted to tell you all at once that I lied about the father of my baby."

"No shit," Sable said flatly. "I saw this coming."

Brindle glared at her. "Do you mind? When I was in Paris, I met two guys, Andre Shaw and his friend Mathieu. Mathieu is a screenplay writer, and he was only there for a week, but Andre stayed much longer. Nothing happened with either of them. They showed me around Paris and we talked *a lot*. After Mathieu left, Andre and I talked even more, and he helped me understand a lot of things. It wasn't fair of me to use him as a scapegoat when he's the one who showed me that I needed to slow down and listen when Trace talked and to stop being afraid of the truth. That's what I intended to do when I came home from Paris. To tell everyone the truth, that *Trace* is the father of my baby. But as always, Trace and I managed to miscommunicate and screw things up."

"Oh, thank God you admitted it." Morgyn's voice boomed from her mother's phone. "The secret was killing me!"

"About freaking time," Sable said.

"Did you really know?" Brindle couldn't keep the astonishment from her voice.

Sable nodded. "I wasn't sure until I saw you dancing with him the other night. I saw it in your eyes."

"We had a feeling, too," her father admitted, sharing a glance with her mother. "But we didn't want to say something and then be wrong."

"I had a feeling, too," Axsel admitted. "But I thought you'd have told me."

"Me too," Grace said.

"You guys didn't believe my story and you didn't call me on it?" Brindle crossed her arms. "I'm not sure if I should be thankful or hurt over that."

"Wait," Amber said softly. "How did everyone figure that out except me? Brindle told us it was someone else. Why didn't you guys believe her?"

"I didn't know, either, Amber," Pepper said. "I took Brindle's word as gold. She's rebellious, but she's never been a liar."

"Thank you," Brindle said with a dose of guilt. "I'm sorry for breaking your trust."

"I understand. But I *was* concerned that being pregnant by someone other than Trace would destroy you," Pepper said. "I'm glad it's Trace's. But is *he* happy about it?"

"He's in shock, and he's not happy with me for lying about it, but he said he will love our baby, and he loves me."

"We know he does," her mother said, placing a hand on Brindle's arm. "But why did you lie about something so important?"

"I've thought about that a lot since I first lied about it. The easy answer is because Trace said something that hurt me in retaliation to his own pain, and once the words came out, I just kept digging a deeper hole. But I'm trying to change the way I do things, and I don't want to take the easy way out anymore—"

"When did pigs start flying?" Sable asked, earning a chuckle from several of their siblings.

"*Sable*," her mother warned.

"The harder answer," Brindle said softly, because this was

difficult to admit in front of her entire family, but if she could do it here, she could face anything, "is that Trace and I always take the easy way out. We argue, accuse, storm off. We say things we don't mean, and even though we always forgive each other, it's not a good pattern."

"It's good that you two recognize that, honey," her mother said. "We all come to realize things at different points in our lives, and I'm glad you're trying to work through this together."

"Thanks, Mom. I really want to be a good mother, and I want to be a good girlfriend. We've never officially been girlfriend and boyfriend, and I know our relationship has always been up and down, but our love for each other has never wavered."

"You're just *passionate*," Morgyn hollered through the phone.

"We are, but there's more to it. We had a long talk last night about how to fix things. I don't want our baby worrying about if we're going to fight or walk out on each other. Neither one of us is very good at communicating when things get tough, so we're going to work on that, but I need your help."

"This should be interesting," Sable quipped.

"Sable, give her a chance," Grace said. "Brindle, I've seen you with your students. You're an excellent communicator."

"In school, I think that's true. But for whatever reason, I'm not with Trace. I think part of that is because I love him so much, I'm afraid of losing him, and it's easier to walk out than face my faults. But I want to fix that, among other things. I think I need a meeting of the married minds to help me learn how to communicate more effectively. Morgyn? Grace?" Brindle looked at her mother and said, "Mom? Would you be willing to help me?"

Grace said, "Sure," at the same time Morgyn said, "Of course."

"Honey, you know I'm always here for you," her mother said. "Whatever you need, and I'm proud of you for wanting to work on yourself. That's a hard thing to admit."

"Thank you. I would ask the rest of you for help, but I think I need to focus on *relationship* communication for right now, and they're the only ones who have relationships."

Her father cleared his throat.

Brindle smiled at him. "I love you, Daddy, but I think I need to get a female perspective."

"It's fine, pumpkin. My only advice is to lead with honesty and to end everything you do with love."

"In other words," Sable said, "when you tell him he's an asshole for not doing something, tell him you love him anyway on your way out the door."

"*That's* why I'm not asking Sable for advice," Brindle said. "Anyway, I just wanted to let everyone know before you heard it around town. Oh *shoot*. Do you think I need to address the rumors?"

Sable scoffed. "When have you ever addressed gossip?"

"I *haven't*, but now I have to think about my baby and what he or she will grow up dealing with."

"You probably should have thought about all that before you lied." Amber didn't have a judgmental bone in her body. She spoke so matter-of-factly, it drove her point home even stronger. "You know how this town gossips. This is bound to spark even more."

"Thinking ahead isn't my strong point," Brindle said. "What do you think I should do? I don't want our baby paying for my mistakes."

"Your baby will be just fine," Sable said. "We'll all have its back."

"You're right, Sable," their mother said. "But I'm glad to hear you're thinking beyond yourself, Brindle."

"You guys, I have to get off the phone. I have a meeting," Pepper announced. "Brin, you and Trace have lasted about twelve years, which is longer than the average marriage. You're both stubborn, so if you want this to get better, it will. I love you. Call if you need me."

"Wait. There's one more thing I have to say," Brindle said quickly. "Trace didn't sleep with Heather, and I know you think or have heard otherwise, but I've only slept with two men in my life."

Their father covered his face. "Can you please keep this part of your confession between the females in the family?"

"I, on the other hand, have had many men," Axsel said with a laugh, bringing on a round of jokes.

When Brindle told them about accidentally leaving all their gifts behind, it added fuel to their lively banter. Brindle put her hand on her belly, listening to her rowdy siblings, and the upended pieces of her life started falling back into place. She rubbed her belly. *Hear that, baby? That's the sound of love, and you're going to be surrounded by it.*

TRACE CLOSED UP the barn and gazed out over the pasture, trying for the millionth time that day to wrap his head around the fact that he was going to be a father. He'd always wanted more with Brindle, but because she was so anti-commitment, he'd never let himself picture the pieces of their lives together in a way that made any sense. Today he'd begun envisioning a real future with her. A *traditional* future as husband and wife, as *parents*. He knew they had a long way to go before he should think like that, but he'd buried those desires so deep, they were popping up like plants reaching for the sun.

"Hey, you okay?" Shane asked, pulling Trace from his thoughts.

Trace wiped his hands on his jeans and said, "Yeah. I was just heading up to the house."

"I'll walk with you," Shane said, and they headed across the lawn.

They were having dinner with their parents, and Trace was going to break the news about the baby to his family. He'd been trying to figure out how to tell them all day, and finally he'd decided he just needed to put it out there. His father might give him hell for being irresponsible, but he could handle that. He knew his parents would love the baby no matter what. His mother had been bugging them all about giving her grandchildren. A bigger worry was whether he and Brindle would be able to find stable ground. He sure as hell hoped so, but the only thing he was certain of was that he wanted Brindle and he wanted their baby, but this time it had to be on *his* terms, and that meant a real commitment.

"Feel like going out later?" Shane asked.

"No, thanks. I'm going to lie low tonight." There was too much going on in his head to go out partying. He also had to be up early to get the work done on the ranch before he headed over to the field to help Sin coach.

Jeb met them on the way up the front walk and said, "Trix and JJ are already here. JJ said he's got to blow out early, though. Are you coming out with us tonight, Trace?"

"No."

Trace pulled open the door, then followed his brothers into the rambling two-story farmhouse. The house had been passed down through several generations. It boasted an enormous eat-in kitchen, a family room with horrendous orange-and-cream wallpaper his mother refused to let them tear out—*Why spend money fixing something that isn't broken?*—a wood-paneled den, three bathrooms, and six bedrooms. Memories rose to greet him as he passed the living room where he and his brothers had spent many nights wrestling, the dining room where they celebrated everything from birthdays to sports victories, and the staircase that led to the bedrooms he and his brothers had hidden *Playboy* magazines in and snuck out of at night. Trixie had snuck out a few times, but much to his sister's chagrin, one of them had always dragged her ass back home.

He followed the delicious aroma of his mother's cooking toward the kitchen.

JJ stood in the doorway with a strange expression on his face, watching Trace come down the hall. Trace lifted his chin, silently asking what was up. JJ motioned for him to walk past and see for himself.

"Congratulations, bro," JJ said just as Trace saw Brindle sitting at the table with his parents and Trixie leaning against the counter, grinning.

Brindle looked nervously up at him. "Hi. I just came by to—"

"Congratulations, *Daddy*," Trixie blurted out.

"*Daddy?*" Jeb and Shane said in unison.

"You told them? I was going to tell them over dinner." Trace tried to read his parents faces as he circled the table to where Brindle sat. His mother wore a pleasant expression, which gave him hope. But his father, Waylon Jericho, was a serious man. His deep-set dark eyes and tight jaw gave away nothing. Trace felt his brothers watching him, but he'd deal with them after he made sure Brindle was okay.

"I'm sorry." Brindle pushed to her feet. "I texted you to say I was coming over to talk to your mom."

"Don't be upset, honey," his mother said. "I saw Brindle in town yesterday, and she just came by to apologize for not being honest with us from the get-go. She thought you already told us."

"It's okay. I never saw the text." He took Brindle's hand and turned his back to his family as he asked, "Are you okay?"

She nodded, a small smile lifting her lips.

"I would have—"

"I know." She put her hand on his chest and said, "And I didn't mean to beat you to it."

He faced his parents and said, "I should have come by this morning, but I had to fix a fence on the lower pasture, and then I just...I needed to figure out how to tell you. I wasn't trying to avoid it."

"Nobody thinks you were, son," his father said evenly.

"Brindle, why don't you stay for dinner?" his mother asked.

"Thank you, but I have a million things to do tonight." Brindle stood to leave and said, "I appreciate you spending the last hour with me, and I'm sorry for spilling the beans before Trace could."

Trixie pushed from the counter and hugged her. "I'm thrilled! I'm going to be an *aunt*, and I sure hope you have a girl, because—*look*—we need a little *evening out* of things around here." She pointed at Brindle and said, "I know you have a gaggle of sisters, but I'd *better* be a bridesmaid."

Brindle's face blanched. "Oh, we're not talking about marriage yet." She glanced nervously at Trace and said, "We have a lot to figure out before we get that far."

They did, but one day…

"Well, you two love each other, and I'm sure you'll figure things out." His mother stood up and embraced Brindle. "This is a blessing. We're so happy for both of you."

Brindle turned to his father and said, "I just want to say again, I never meant to lie about any of this, and I appreciate your candor with me."

Candor? Trace put a protective arm around Brindle. His father could be harsh, and he hoped to hell he hadn't said anything too strong or hurtful to her. "I'll walk you out."

When they descended the front porch, he said, "I wish you'd waited for me."

"I know. I'm so sorry. Yesterday your mom was devastated when I saw her. When I got your text this morning and you said you were going to talk to them, I figured you would have done it by the time I came over. But when I got here and saw that they had no idea why I was here, I started to tell them that I was sorry for the rumors and for putting you in that position. I wasn't going to come clean until we could do it together. But then your mom looked so sad, I had to tell her. And after I did, I realized I shouldn't have been so impatient. I should have waited to hear back from you no matter how long it took."

"It's okay. We have a lot to learn about how to communicate with each other. I hate that I wasn't there with you. What did my father say to you?"

She lowered her eyes and said, "Nothing that I didn't deserve."

"*Damn it.* This is why I wish you had waited. I should have been there to protect you."

"I don't need *protecting*," she said firmly.

He gritted his teeth. On many levels she was right, but he knew she was even more sensitive than she let herself believe. If his father had said anything harsh, she would overthink it until she felt like she might explode. That usually led to her confronting the offender, which could go any number of ways. Most of which weren't great when her opponent was his father.

"What'd he say, Brindle?"

"He said I was lucky you were such a good man, and he's right. The more I think about how I handled this, the more I realize I should have let you know right away. I shouldn't have let you think, even for a second, that this was someone else's baby, and I'll never be able to erase that from our relationship. But I'm going to try to do the right thing from here on out." She lowered her eyes again and said, "I mean, starting *now*, since I messed up by talking to your family first."

He pulled her into his arms and said, "You couldn't stand to see my mom sad. Your big heart gets you into trouble and my big mouth gets me into trouble. We're quite the pair."

"I think it was different parts of us that got us into this particular trouble," she said with a playful expression. "Now kiss me. I've got a hot *first* date tomorrow night with a pushy cowboy, and I need time to prepare."

After several steamy kisses, he stood on the porch watching her drive away, knowing in his gut they'd get through this. Jeb and Shane joined him on the porch.

"She's got balls," Shane said.

Trace glared at him.

"I meant it as a compliment," Shane said. "Not many girls

are strong enough to face Dad like that."

"So it's definitely yours?" Jeb said.

"It's mine, and I should have known it from the start."

Jeb crossed his arms and said, "I guess we all should have."

"Why'd she lie, man?" Shane asked. "That's the only part I don't get."

Who knows was on the tip of Trace's tongue, and it's how he probably would have responded before last night. But comments like that fueled speculation about their relationship, and he was done making that mistake. "That was my fault," he admitted. "I accused her of sleeping with someone else in Paris."

The door opened, and their father stepped outside. "Jeb, Shane, go help your mother. I'd like a minute alone with Trace."

Trace squared his shoulders as his brothers headed inside, each giving him a silent, *Good luck.* His father was six foot four and stocky, with more salt than pepper in his short, thick hair. Even with his limp from the pain in his joints and his gnarled hands, he had a commanding presence. It wouldn't matter if he was five feet tall. Trace had more respect for his father than he had for any other man on earth.

"You okay, son?" his father asked.

"Yeah. I'm good."

"Then you're better than I was the first time I found out your mother was pregnant. I was scared shitless."

Trace nodded. "I'm right there with you, Dad. But I didn't want you to think I wasn't man enough to handle things."

"Son, we raised four good, strong men, and one good, strong woman who's going to do to a man just what Brindle has spent years doing to you. That's what strong women do; they butt heads with the best of us."

"Brindle's pretty good at that," Trace said.

"Yes, we know. And I'm sure you're just as good at driving her crazy. But part of being a good man is owning up to the things that scare you. Everybody gets scared. It's how you handle that fear that separates the men from the boys."

Trace crossed his arms, needing the barrier as he told his father the truth about Brindle's lie. "I didn't handle it very well at the barn bash, Dad. Brindle lied because I accused her of something, and I did that because I was so damn scared I'd lost her, I couldn't see straight."

"That right?" His father rubbed his jaw. "She didn't let on that you handled it poorly. She said she got scared and didn't want you to feel trapped."

"She was protecting me," Trace said more to himself than to his father.

"That's the mark of a good woman. Learning how to handle fear with a modicum of grace is no easy task, and conquering it is even harder." He put a hand on Trace's shoulder and said, "When your pretty little filly sat down at that table tonight, she was one scared gal. But she looked us in the eyes and told us why she went on that godforsaken trip, and she apologized for any embarrassment she might have caused our family. I'd call that stepping up to the plate."

Trace filled with pride. In all the years he'd been with Brindle, his father hadn't said more than a handful of words about their relationship, and he'd always wondered what he really thought about it.

"You have always stepped up and handled things in ways that have made us proud. I have no doubt you're going to do the same thing with fatherhood."

Chapter Nine

BRINDLE HAD BEEN secretly admiring Trace from afar for so many years, it felt like coming home to be sitting on the hill at the edge of the athletic field by the community center, bundled up in her coat, with a to-go cup of decaffeinated coffee and a doughnut, watching him coach the youth football team. Her covert Trace-watching sessions weren't just limited to his sports practices. Before they'd ever kissed, she'd begun sneaking out to watch him and his brothers ride horses in the wee hours of the morning. She'd first caught wind of their predawn activities at a Friday-night jam session. Every few weeks the Jerichos opened their barn to the community. People of all ages played instruments together while friends and families danced. It was during one of those nights when Brindle had overheard her mother and Nancy Jericho talking about the differences between raising girls and boys. *Drama versus testosterone.*

Watching Trace train horses before the rest of Oak Falls even woke up? *That* she needed to see with her own two eyes. She'd woken Morgyn to go with her, and Sable had heard them sneaking out. Sable had given them hell, but even back then Brindle wouldn't let anyone stand in the way of what she wanted. Sable had gone with them, and she'd been joining in the fun ever since. Brindle would never forget the adrenaline that had rushed through her that very first time, as she lay on the hill overlooking the Jerichos' riding ring, or the tingling that had started in her chest when she'd seen Trace ride out of the barn on the back of a big black horse. She'd been mesmerized by the skill and strength he'd exuded. She'd held her breath when the horse bucked, laughing while Trace held his hat in one hand, the reins in the other, earning cheers from his brothers. Even back then he was as cocky and as confident as he was handsome. Morgyn had fallen asleep lying beside her, but Sable and Brindle had watched every second of the show. To Sable it had been two and a half hours of sneaky fun, but to Brindle it was the night she'd fallen in love with Trace Jericho.

Now she sipped her coffee, watching the kids huddle around Trace, his arms around the two closest boys. She was too far away to hear what they were saying, but she imagined he was giving them a pep talk. He put his hand in the middle of the group, and all the boys thrust their hands forward. They hollered something as their arms flew up, and then the boys ran toward the field.

Trace shouted something, and one of the boys circled back to him. Trace put his hands out, wrists touching, hands flexed back, and brought his hands close to his chest, as if he was teaching the boy to catch the football. The boy mimicked the motion, and Trace patted him on the head. He clapped a few times as the boy ran off to take his position. It was easy to imagine him teaching their child how to play ball, standing on the sidelines giving him pointers, and cheering him on. And she knew he'd find a way to be just as supportive if they had a girl who liked to dance, ride horses, or even play the guitar, like he did. He looked so happy, it made her wish he had more of this in his life.

"He looks good out there, doesn't he?"

Startled, Brindle looked up at Sin. He wore a baseball cap and sunglasses and carried an equipment bag over his shoulder.

"I've always thought so," she said. "He belongs on the field just as much as he belongs on a horse."

Sin crouched beside her and gazed out at the field. "He's good with the kids, patient and informative. He's helped me out five or six times and he never loses his cool. The kids respond well to him."

"He's helped that many times? He made it sound like it was just once or twice."

Sin said, "Yeah, well, you know Trace. He downplays the things he does for others. I really wish he'd take me up on my offer." Sin pushed to his feet. "He's just what we need."

"What *offer?*"

"To coach a team next year. I told him the position is his if he wants it."

"Really?" She looked at Trace talking with one of the boys and wondered why he hadn't mentioned it to her. "I thought it was just an off-the-cuff comment the other night."

"When it comes to coaching kids, I don't make comments I don't mean. It's too important to get the right person in the position. I know he's got a lot of responsibility at the ranch, but the offer stands, and if you can nudge him in that direction, I'd sure appreciate it."

I'm good at nudging.

Pushing. She was good at pushing.

But wasn't the elation on Trace's face worth a little push?

The old Brindle would have jumped on that bandwagon, but the new and improved version of herself needed to learn the art of nudging. She added that to her list of things to discuss next week during the meeting of the married minds with her sisters and mother.

"I'll see what I can do," she finally answered. "And, Sin? Thank you for seeing in Trace what most people overlook."

"What's that?"

"That he's so much more than just a good-looking cowboy."

LATER THAT DAY, Brindle went shopping with Lindsay and Trixie for a new outfit to wear on her date with Trace. She'd thought shopping would take an hour, maybe two, but three hours, four stores, and one power lunch later, she was standing in front of a three-way mirror holding her boobs and laughing hysterically.

"Seriously, you guys," she said. "*Look* at them! They're like grapefruits!"

"Melons," Trixie said. "*Big* ones. The kind people use for target practice."

Lindsay grabbed Trixie's arm, doubling over with laughter. "Little watermelons."

Brindle turned sideways in the tight black dress Lindsay had insisted she try on. She put one hand on her pooch of a belly and said, "I'm all belly and boobs. Trace is going to run the other way."

"No, babe. No way," Lindsay said. "I think you look beautiful. Besides, Trace is a boob man."

Brindle put a hand on her hip, raising her brows in amusement. "How do *you* know what he is?"

"He's with *you*, and according to Montgomery lore, you've got the best boobs in the family," Lindsay reminded her. It was a long-running joke between Brindle and her sisters about who had the best body parts. She'd sprouted C cups practically overnight the summer she'd turned twelve, and by fourteen she was a full D cup.

"Aren't all men into boobs?" Trixie said. "I swear, if we stared at guys' crotches the way they stare at our breasts, we'd be arrested."

"God, isn't that the truth?" Brindle agreed.

"Well, some of us don't have that problem." Lindsay glanced down at her perfect B cups. "But I'm glad I don't, actually. The last thing I want is to be hounded by guys. Anyway, you want to look special for this date, right? That dress is special. It will blow his mind."

"I don't know. I'm trying not to look like typical *me*, you know? We're starting over, and I don't want to look like I just want to entice him into bed."

They both gave her a deadpan look.

"Trust me, Brin," Lindsay said. "It doesn't matter what you wear; you're still going to look like that. You've got this natural seduction thing going on that most women would pay big bucks to master."

"Thanks!" Brindle smiled and shrugged. "What do you think, Trix?"

"I think that smile-shrug thing you do underscores what Linds just said." Trixie began leafing through a dress rack and said, "You could wear pajamas and my brother would still be gaga over you."

She knew that was true. "But I do want tonight to be special. We've never really gone on dates, you know? I'm not sure what to expect. He wouldn't give me any indication of where we were going. Do you guys know?"

Trixie turned away. "Did I tell you Nick's coming into town for the last jam session of the year? Yup, he's coming out."

"Good. I could use some man candy," Lindsay said. "Nick is the perfect mix of cowboy and biker, which is *so* not typical. Is his *you know what* as impressive as his biceps?"

Trixie laughed. "How would I know? He's an arrogant, pushy pain in my butt. I might like to check out his ass, but I'm *not* checking out his package."

Brindle rolled her eyes. "Okay, I get it. You both know what Trace has planned, and you won't tell me. Some friends you are."

"We're the best friends you could ever have *because* we aren't going to ruin your surprise." Trixie spun around, holding up a long-sleeved gray minidress with a boat neck, and said, "This is perfect! It's short and sexy, but it won't be tight, and if you pair it with those black thigh-high boots you love so much, you won't be too cold." She pushed Brindle toward the dressing room and thrust the hanger into her hands. "Go try it on."

She changed into the soft, cotton dress, and knew the second she slipped it over her head that it was perfect. It hung to the middle of her thighs in the front and was a little longer in the back. It was just snug enough to draw attention to her breasts without making them appear too prominent, and it hung loose around her belly, with a slight flare at the bottom, which enhanced her waist.

Before she could step out of the dressing room, Lindsay and Trixie barreled through the curtain.

"We found accessories," Lindsay said, putting three long necklaces over Brindle's head, while Trixie slipped a handful of bangles over Brindle's hand.

"And look." Trixie held up a pair of silver earrings with dangling gray and black jewels. "What do you think?"

"I think y'all are goddesses for spending so much time helping me find the perfect outfit." She admired herself in the mirror, imagining her thigh-high boots, and said, "This is perfect. It's understated, and the boots will make it just sexy enough. I'm not sleeping with him tonight, by the way."

"Uh-huh," Lindsay said.

"I don't want to hear about it if you do," Trixie reminded her.

"I'm seriously not going to. That's not what people do on first dates, right?"

Trixie looked from Brindle to Lindsay and said, "Don't look at me for answers. Jeb's scared off most of the guys around here. I'm like untouchable territory."

"Tinder users might disagree with you, Brin," Lindsay said as she gathered the discarded dresses.

"Tinder?" Brindle asked. "You use Tinder?"

"I never said that, and I have to go put these away." Lindsay hurried out of the dressing room.

"Do you think she does?" Brindle asked as she began undressing.

Trixie shrugged. "Maybe. I know she's not hoping for a ring on her finger."

"But neither was I, and I'd *never* use Tinder. That's a hookup app."

Trixie handed Brindle her shirt and said, "That's because your hookup is always ready and willing. Lindsay doesn't date anyone around here. She's mysterious about her personal life, isn't she?"

"Yeah. It's kind of weird," she said as she pulled on her jeans.

Trixie grabbed the rubber band Brindle used for the button on her jeans from the bench and handed it to her. "That's only because you've always put yours out there for everyone to see."

"That's the *old* me, and it's changing." Thinking of her discussion with Sin as she hooked the rubber band through her buttonhole, she said, "Do you guys have any trouble getting temporary help on the ranch? Like, if you needed someone to cover for a few hours two or three times a week, is that doable?"

"Trace and Shane handle the schedules for ranch hands," Trixie said. "I'm sure it can be done, but if it was that often, they'd need to find someone they trusted. Why? Are you worried that once the baby comes you might need Trace's help here and there?"

"I don't know what I was thinking," she said, because she didn't want to make the mistake of sharing her thoughts about Trace coaching with Trixie before she shared them with Trace.

Brindle pulled on her cowgirl boots, grabbed her coat, and said, "Come on. Let's go get Lindsay to spill her sexy Tinder secrets."

TRACE STOOD BEFORE Brindle's apartment door as nervous as he'd been the first time they'd had sex. He didn't know squat about first dates, and he didn't want to mess this one up. It was kind of hard to learn dating etiquette when he'd never formally dated anyone. He and Brindle had *met up*, *hooked up*, made plans with other couples, *skipped out* on other couples, and done just about every other form of dancing around the dating game there was. Which was why he found himself a few years shy of thirty, trying to figure out how to romance the woman he'd loved since he was a teenager.

Better late than never.

He hid the bouquets he'd brought behind his back and knocked on the door.

When Brindle answered, he nearly dropped the bouquets. She looked gorgeous in a little gray number with sexy thigh-high boots. "Holy smokes, darlin'. How am I supposed to behave with you looking like that?"

She looked down at her outfit and said, "I tried not to dress too sexy. Do you want me to change?"

A low laugh rumbled up his chest and he shook his head. "It wouldn't do any good. You could wear a burlap sack and you'd still be too hot to handle."

Her eyes darkened with the compliment. "You're looking pretty hot yourself, cowboy."

She grabbed the front of his dress shirt, pulling him in for a kiss. His hand slid down her back, coming to rest on the curve of her ass as their lips met. He couldn't resist deepening the kiss. She made a sweet, sexy noise, and that was all it took to make him hard as steel.

"This feels a lot like the old us," he said against her lips, holding her tight.

"I like the old us."

She tugged him down for another kiss, and he slanted his mouth over hers. His arm circled her back, crushing her to him.

She gasped, prying his arm from her side. "Something pricked me."

"*Damn.* Sorry, darlin'. Roses." He handed her the bouquets.

"I couldn't decide between a dozen red roses and chocolate roses, so I got you both. I know how much you love chocolate, and I figured red roses were a first-date tradition, right?"

She smelled the flowers, with a dreaminess in her eyes that made him want to bring her flowers every day.

"I don't know anything about first-date traditions," she said sweetly. "But this is about the most romantic thing you could have done. Thank you. Come in. Let's put the roses in water."

He followed her into the kitchen, and when she reached up to get a vase, he moved behind her, retrieving it for her. He set it on the counter and said, "You smell amazing."

"It's your favorite," she said as she filled the vase with water. "Juicy Couture."

"We should buy stock in it." He kissed her neck as she arranged the flowers.

"These are beautiful. You've never given me flowers before."

He turned her in his arms and said, "I've picked wildflowers for you before."

"Yes, and that was romantic, too. But being given flowers *before* sex feels totally different." She put her arms around his neck, brushing her body against his, and said, "Almost like foreplay."

"If you do that again, our first date is going to take place in your bedroom," he warned.

"I don't think so, cowboy. I'm a proper lady. I don't do that on the first date." She took his hand, leading him toward the door.

He snagged her keys and phone from the counter and pocketed them. As he helped her on with her coat, he said, "How about the second date? Because I could leave and come back in two minutes."

"Why, Mr. Jericho, you *are* a naughty boy."

He slipped his arm around her waist as they left the apartment and descended the steps. "Word around town is that Miss Montgomery has a thing for naughty cowboys, and you know how I love to be the teacher's pet."

"We'll have to straighten out that dirty rumor," she said. "I have a thing for only *one* particularly naughty cowboy, and he's already earned an A in romance."

"Mustang, you ain't seen nothing yet." He drew her closer as they crossed the parking lot and said, "I can't wait to earn extra credit."

TRACE DROVE PAST JJ's Pub. The parking lot was empty, and there were no lights on, but JJ's truck was parked out front. "Whoa. What's going on at JJ's? They're not supposed to be closed." He pulled into the lot and parked. "Do you mind if we run in just to make sure everything's okay?"

"Of course not. Let's go."

He came around the truck and helped her out. "Something must have happened."

They hurried to the front door, which was unlocked. Trace called out, "JJ?"

He pretended to try the light switch. "He must have an electrical issue. Come on, let's check the other light switches."

"You should lock the door," she said, holding on to his arm. "It's so dark in here."

"Good thinking." He locked the door, keeping her close as they headed for the office, which was also dark. "Let's check the back."

They went past the room with the mechanical bull, and he flipped the light switch in the bar, bringing her surprise to life. He watched with joy as Brindle's eyes swept over the lanterns he and his brothers had hung from the rafters and the canopy with cream-colored silk drapes they'd erected around a table in the middle of the dance floor. They'd decorated the canopy with red and pink roses and wound strings of tiny white lights around the frame. Three paper lanterns hung over the table, which was set with fancy place settings and silverware atop a red runner covering the center of the white tablecloth. Beside the table was a champagne stand, the bottle of sparkling cider peeking out the top.

"*Trace*," Brindle said breathlessly, gazing down at the trail of red rose petals leading from where they stood to the table. "You did all this for me? And you had JJ close the pub?"

He put his arms around her and said, "We've been in the spotlight of this town forever. Tonight I want you all to myself, basking in *my* spotlight."

Her eyes glistened with happiness. "I can't...You...Trace, there are no words big enough...I never wanted to be a princess, but you've just made me feel like one." A tear slipped down her cheek.

"You *are* my princess, Mustang. You're my princess, my wild girl, my *everything*." He touched his lips to hers in a tender kiss. "But I can't take all the credit. Lindsay helped me plan out the decorations, and my brothers helped me set up. I've always wanted to do things like this for you, and now that you've given me the okay, I want to be sure I'm doing enough."

"*Enough?* Trace, you literally blew me away. I will never, in my entire life, forget this feeling or how beautiful everything looks." She gazed up at him and said, "And I'll definitely never forget the way you're looking at me right this second."

"I've looked at you like this since you were a teenager, when I had no business looking at you at all. We're going to figure out how to do all the right things together so our baby, and everyone else in this town—in this *world*—knows we are unbreakable."

"I don't care what anyone else thinks. I only care that we're the best we can be together and that it's enough for our baby to feel safe and loved every day of its life."

"Aw, sweet darlin', we're going to be more than enough."

Chapter Ten

TRACE HAD THOUGHT of every little detail. They enjoyed a delicious steak dinner he'd brought in from the best restaurant in town and sipped sparkling cider, serenaded by all of Brindle's favorite songs playing on the jukebox. They held hands across the table and talked about everything from Trace's ranch work and coaching the morning game to Brindle's first week back at work and what she was planning for the drama club—a holiday play written by Natalie, who was being mentored by Grace. Brindle couldn't imagine a more perfect evening.

Except she could, because there was still an elephant in the room, and she wanted nothing more than to scatter mice, forcing them to deal with it so they could put it away once and for all. She'd gone someplace wonderful, and even though she knew it was a sore subject for both of them, it kind of hurt having to avoid talking about it. But she didn't want to ruin their evening by bringing it up, because that's what the old Brindle would do.

Navigating better communication was tricky, and she wasn't exactly sure how to handle this, but she knew it needed to come out.

Maybe just not right now.

Trace stood up and said, "I'll be right back, darlin'. It's time for your favorite course."

"*You* on a silver platter?" She reached for his hand, pulling him closer. "I never thought I wanted, or needed, to be wined and dined. I've always loved that we could hang out with friends, take advantage of spur-of-the-moment get-togethers and parties, and sneak away to be alone. I thought being treated like this would make me seem needy or materialistic. But I was wrong, Trace. I love spending time with only you, when we're not just making out, talking about work and our families. Thank you for doing this and opening my eyes to what I was missing."

He crouched beside her, gazing into her eyes with a sexy smile. "I've always wanted to take you out on dates and plan things for us that didn't include half the town. But you pretty much shut that down early on, and as I've said, I wanted you any way I could have you, Brindle. Thank *you* for letting me do it my way now."

"I think I ripped us both off. Everything feels different now that we've *finally* confessed our true feelings for each other. There's a sense of calm inside me that I've never felt before. I know we have a lot to work on, but I really believe we'll get there."

"I think we'll always have things to work on. It's kind of who we are." He kissed her, and then he said, "I'll be right back with dessert."

As he picked up their dinner plates, she said, "I can help you."

"I've got this." He winked, then carried the dishes away.

She watched him disappear through the kitchen doors, and her gaze fell to the rose petals scattered along the floor. She'd once said that Trace Jericho didn't need to romance a woman because he was six-plus feet of deliciously rugged seduction. She still believed that, but she couldn't deny the fullness in her chest that he'd put so much effort and thought into their special night.

He came out of the kitchen and set two bowls on the table. "Raspberry sorbet with whipped cream and chocolate sprinkles." He sat beside her and leaned in for a kiss. "My girl's favorite."

"It looks amazing. I practically lived on sorbet in Paris. I'm surprised I didn't gain twenty poun—" As the words left her lips, Trace's smile faded, and she realized what she'd said. "There I go again, shooting my mouth off without thinking. I'm sorry. I know my trip is a sore subject. It just came out."

His jaw tightened, and for a moment he stared down at the sorbet like it had become a villain. "It is a sore subject, but I guess we can't avoid it."

She sighed with relief. "Not if we want to move forward. I took a million pictures of things I wanted to show you. I also bought you the cutest shirt that said 'World's Best Daddy' in French, but I was so frazzled when I left Paris, I left my bag of gifts on the sidewalk when I got into the cab."

He lifted his chin, meeting her gaze. "I love knowing you bought that for me, that you think that way about me. Thank you." He rolled his shoulders back and said, "I'd like to see them and hear about your trip."

"Really?" she asked tentatively. "Because you kind of look like it's the last thing you want to do."

"That doesn't mean it's right for me to feel this way." He pulled her phone from his pocket and set it on the table. "Show me the pictures."

She scrolled through them, showing him the Eiffel Tower, the Louvre Museum, and other tourist attractions, but her heart wasn't in it. When she was there, she'd imagined he might be just as excited to see them as she'd been to take them, but now she realized how wrong she was.

When she came to a picture taken on a boat cruising the Seine with her, Andre, and Mathieu, Trace said, "*Stop.*" Anger flashed in his eyes. "Who are those guys?"

She pointed to the mahogany-haired man and said, "This is Mathieu. He's writes movies for television. He was only there for a few days, but he was nice." She pointed to the dark-haired man and said, "And this is Andre. He's a physician and he runs Operation SHINE, which brings medical clinics to newly developing nations. Andre was there longer than Mathieu. They showed me around Paris, and Andre and I talked a lot. He was pining for his ex, and I was pining for you."

"*Andre.* The guy you said was the father." He looked away.

"How do you know that?"

He met her gaze and said, "People talk."

"But I only told my family. Who…?"

"It doesn't matter." The muscles in his jaw jumped. "You left me here and then saw Paris, the most romantic city there is, with some other dude?"

"It wasn't like I planned it, or even enjoyed it," she said quickly.

He shifted his eyes away again, teeth grinding.

"Please don't do that. Don't look away," she pleaded.

The instinct to crawl into his lap and kiss the pain away was so strong, she fisted her hands to keep from moving, determined to change things for the better without using sex.

"Nothing happened with either of them. I have not even

kissed another guy since I was nineteen, despite the rumors that I *shouldn't* have used to fuel our fights. Andre *helped* me, Trace. He made me understand a lot of things, like that I needed to stop being afraid of the truth—that I *wanted* a commitment with you and that I love you with my whole being."

His eyes glowed with as much anger and hurt as love, and that stole her breath away.

"You took off without me, Brindle, and it doesn't matter if you were with friends or lovers. What matters is that being left behind sucked. And maybe that makes me a dick, but we said we'd be honest."

"It doesn't make you a dick any more than I'm one for going away for so long. We're really good at a lot of things, including fighting to cover up our feelings. But *look* where my trip got us. I'm sorry I needed to go, but we're finally at a point in our relationship where we can look at each other and say 'I love you' instead of hiding behind the pretense of loving only the sex we have or each other's bodies. We can finally tell each other what hurts and sit and talk instead of running away. That has to count for something."

"I know, but it still stings. I wanted to be the guy who saw those places with you. I want to be the guy you figure things out with, no matter how hard those things are."

"And I want you to," she said quickly. "Just like I want to be the girl who is with you when you figure things out. Not Heather, not anyone else. A lot of our old relationship *stings*, Trace. Before I left, you told me that girl you met on the ski trip you went on last winter was coming to see you on her way to Florida." A spear of jealousy sliced through her. "You want to talk about something that stung? I was in Paris trying to figure out how to fix our relationship, and I was miserable because I was thinking about you and *Skanky Suzie*."

"Damn it, Brindle." He pushed to his feet, his chest expanding. "I haven't had sex with another woman since we were teenagers! And I *never* cheated. We were broken up, and I was pissed and hurt, and *damn it*, I'd give anything to take those two times back."

The air left her lungs in a sound of disbelief. There was no faking the honesty in his eyes. "Two?"

"Yes, *two*. Don't you get it, Brindle?" he said angrily. "We both used jealousy to get back at each other, and the messed-up thing is that most of the time it was jealousy that caused the fights in the first place."

Tears burned her eyes, because all this time she'd thought he'd been with more women and because what he'd said was true. They'd behaved childishly for so long. Could they really learn how to have a mature relationship? "How can we possibly parent if we can't even have dinner without a fight?"

He sat beside her and took her hand in his, his dark eyes serious. "Do you love me?"

"More than anything," she said honestly.

"Do you want this commitment? The baby, us, no more running away and assuming the worst?"

"I do, Trace. I'm really trying to grow up and not make the same mistakes over again." Swallowing hard, she said, "Do you want this commitment?"

"Yes," he said firmly. "But I think we have to accept each other's shortcomings and not try to pretend they don't exist. Darlin', you're a gorgeous, smart woman. Guys are attracted to you like white on rice, and sometimes jealousy gets the best of me. I doubt any of that is going to change anytime soon, but I'll try not to overreact anymore."

"When women leer at you, I want to claw their eyeballs out, and even though I know it's not your fault, sometimes I flirt with other guys to get back at you for it." Admitting her immaturity was embarrassing, but she was determined to do everything within her power to make this right. "But I'm *not* going to repeat my old mistakes. There is nobody else I want to be with, and that's not just because you're handsome or good in bed. I love who you are, Trace, and I *love* who we are together despite our ridiculous fights. Yes, we have our faults, but we love each other, and if we both try, we'll get past that silliness. Don't you think we can get past it?"

"Yeah, but I still think it's part of who we are. We might always be jealous, both of us, but we need to find a better way to handle it. I'm not very good with words, so let me show you another way."

He turned the jukebox off and headed for the stage. She'd been so enthralled with the decorations and dinner, she hadn't even noticed his guitar leaning against a chair in the middle of the stage. Her pulse quickened as he sat down, set his piercing dark eyes on her, and began playing John Legend's "All of Me." As he sang about her smart mouth and not being able to pin her down, every word sank in. She'd never listened to the lyrics closely enough to realize how perfectly they matched her and Trace. When he sang about adoring her imperfections, her love for him drove even deeper. He called her his downfall, his rhythm, and his muse, and he was all of those things to her, too. He sang about giving all of himself to her, and when he hit the chorus, gazing at her with so much love in his eyes she could feel it wrapping around her, she was overcome. Her throat thickened, and tears burned.

Trace's soulful voice drew her out of her seat and to the

edge of the stage. This beautiful, patient man was all she'd ever wanted, and it pained her to think she'd nearly lost him over something as stupid as miscommunication. She was an English teacher, but when it came to Trace, the language she'd spent years studying and teaching others didn't come easily.

She was intent on fixing that. Starting right now.

AS TRACE STRUMMED the last note, a tear slipped down Brindle's cheek. Even though the shimmer in her eyes told him she was happy, that tear tugged at someplace deep inside him.

He set the guitar down, and as he descended the steps and came to her side, she put her arms around his neck and said, "You have all of me, and with your help and patience, you'll get the *best* of me."

He gathered her in his arms and kissed her, swaying to the beat of their hearts.

He pressed a kiss beside her ear and said, "I love you, Brindle, and every part of you *is* the best. We'll work on things, and no doubt we'll get better, but whether you're jealous, seductive, or bossy, I'll take it all, darlin', because I fell in love with all of you. Now, how about you show me some of those dance moves I love so much?"

He left her long enough to turn on the jukebox.

"Body Like a Backroad" came on, and he whistled, earning that sultry smile he adored. She took his hand and he spun her into his arms. *Man*, his girl could dance. They danced and kissed to songs of all speeds, dancing too slow to fast songs because neither one wanted to put space between them, then dancing all out to some of their favorites, like Hunter Hayes's "21." Trace felt an ethereal shift around them, like their very beings had changed and their lives were finally aligning on a path that would lead them in the right direction.

When "All About Tonight" came on and Blake Shelton sang about dancing with every woman in the room, Trace spun Brindle around, and she said, "Good thing I'm the only one here, or we might have gotten ourselves into an unwanted tiff."

He tugged her against him, loving the challenging look in her eyes, and said, "You are all I ever need, darlin'. Don't ever doubt that."

As they slow danced, he said, "For the record, I never saw Suzie while you were gone. She texted to try to see me, but I blew her off, and I never hooked up with her on the ski trip. The guys thought I did, and I never corrected them. That's on me, and I'm sorry about that. But you and I were arguing about something, and hell, Brindle, it doesn't matter why. What matters is that I was hurting, and I didn't handle the situation very well. When you told me about the trip you'd planned, I lost my footing. The idea of going six weeks without you?" He shook his head. "That was too much for me. I only told you I agreed to see her to get back at you for planning that trip. After you left, I spent the first two weeks working like a madman during the day and staring at the bottom of any bottle I could find at night."

"I was just as bad off, but I was eating instead of drinking," she said softly.

"Thank you for taking care of our baby." As he said it, the truth of his words hit him. That was exactly what she'd been doing by staying in Paris longer than she'd initially planned. She wasn't just figuring things out. She was protecting their baby as best she could until she had *them* figured out. She'd probably started changing the minute she realized she was pregnant. The same way he had when he'd found out.

Another song came on, jarring him from his thoughts. He realized Brindle was looking at him expectantly, waiting for him to say more. He twirled her around, and as they two-stepped, he said, "That was when Sin mentioned helping him with the football program. I figured it might keep me from going crazy wondering what you were doing halfway across the world without me. It was your voice in my head telling me that if I only get one shot at life, I should do the things that make me happy."

"I've said that to you a lot."

"Every damn time you pushed me to go away to school. I should thank you for that. All that pushing finally worked."

"Then that's *two* good things that came from a really hard time for both of us." She twirled again and said, "I saw you coaching today."

"You did? I didn't see you on the field."

"I was up by the parking lot."

"You sneaky girl." He dipped her over his arm, making her laugh. "Just like when I caught you and Morgyn watching us ride before dawn?" Before letting her up, he said, "Why do you spy on me, darlin'? Is it because it feels *naughty*?"

She rose, and they danced across the floor. "Maybe that's part of it. But did you ever think that maybe it's because even after twelve years I still find you the most intriguing man I've ever known, and secretly watching you lets me admire you without it being about sex or anything other than reveling in how lucky I am?"

"How do you do that, darlin'?"

She twirled, looking at him over her shoulder, and said, "Do what?"

"Make your sneakiness sound special."

"I'm just being honest."

The next song was faster, and she squealed. "Swing dance!"

He laughed and fell into step with her. Trace's parents had been holding Friday-night jam sessions for as long as he could remember. He'd learned to dance and play instruments practically since he could walk.

"It was fun to see how much the kids liked you today," Brindle said as they boogied. "And your smile while you were coaching? It was a crinkle-eyed smile."

He chuckled. "My skin doesn't *crinkle*."

"Yes, it does," she said. "And even from that distance, I could tell those crinkles were there." She moved flawlessly as she said, "Sin told me about your not-a-big-deal offer, and it sounded like a very big deal. I hope you're considering taking him up on it."

"There's a lot to consider, but working with the kids does make me happy, so yeah, I'm thinking about it."

"Oh, Trace, that's fantastic!" She launched herself into his arms. "You'll be the best coach ever!"

Her spun her around, and as he lowered her feet to the floor, he said, "Don't get carried away just yet. Like I said, there's a lot to consider."

"Well, consider this. If we have a boy, then one day you could coach *our* son."

His heart thudded harder. "Darlin', you sure have a way with words."

The song ended, and Brindle wound her arms around his waist, moving seductively. That was Brindle, going from playful to sinful in the space of a second.

"I've missed this so much, laughing, dancing"—he moved his hands down her back and grabbed her ass—"being each other's worlds."

"I missed it, too. While I was away, I kept wishing you were there. I don't ever want to be away from you again."

Trace wasn't sure how long they danced, but at some point they made it out to the truck and he drove her home. They kissed at all the stoplights, and when they reached her apartment, they stumbled up the steps, lips locked the entire way, which sparked memories of the day Brindle had moved there. Trace and her family had helped her move in. She and Trace had stolen private moments with extra trips to the truck, and with Trace "helping" Brindle move boxes in one room or another, which really meant they were hiding in a closet or a bathroom because they couldn't keep their hands off each other.

That was four years ago.

Not much had changed.

When they reached her floor, Trace backed her up against her door with a penetrating kiss. He was hard as stone, and she was squirming, rubbing her softness against him.

"How was your first date, Miss Montgomery?" he asked between kisses.

"Is it over?"

He looked into her wanting eyes and said, "Do you want it to be?"

She trapped her lower lip between her teeth, blinking up at him through her long, dark lashes, and shook her head. "But this is supposed to be us starting over," she said a little breathlessly. "If we're really starting over, then we probably shouldn't fool around on our first date."

Aw, hell. She was right, but the last thing he wanted to do was leave her tonight of all nights, when they'd been so close.

"Okay, darlin', but I'm going to make this up to you. To both of us. Now that you've finally given me the green light to treat you like you're truly mine, I'm *not* holding back." Her cheeks pinked up, and he said, "Mustang, you never blush. What's that heat rising in your cheeks?"

"I like hearing you say I'm yours."

"Could you repeat that?" His hand snaked around her waist, drawing her against him good and tight.

"I like being yours, and I like hearing you claim me."

"Darlin', that's all I've *ever* wanted to hear."

"Then tell me again so I can hear it in my dreams."

He gazed deeply into her eyes, falling even more in love with her as he said, "You're *mine*, wild one. You've always been mine."

"And in my heart, you've always been mine."

"Damn, woman, you sure do make it hard for me to leave."

He reclaimed her lips, crushing her to him with renewed passion. Her mouth was sweet and warm, and the longer they kissed, the harder it was for him to even think about walking away. But he'd committed to their new beginning and he didn't want to screw it up, so he forced himself to break their connection.

"I love you, Mustang," he said heatedly. "But if I don't go now, I'm not going to leave."

"I know," she said softly.

After many more kisses, he unlocked her apartment door, returned her phone, and keys, and gave her ass a light smack. "Get in there so I know you're safe."

She turned as she went inside and blew him a kiss. Then she

wiggled her fingers in a cute wave and closed the door behind her.

He stared at the door, itching to be on the other side of it. He took off his hat and raked a hand through his hair, thinking about how far they'd come. *I like being yours, too, darlin'.*

He put his hat on and reluctantly headed for the stairs, feeling a hell of a lot like when he'd walked out the night before she'd left for Paris. He stood on the first step, gripping the railing. He'd played by her rules that night, instead of telling her how much he loved her and how he really felt. Now the woman he loved, who was carrying his child, was inside that apartment and he was walking away?

"Fuck that," he ground out, and spun around—only to find her door opening and Brindle running toward him. Their mouths crashed together as he lifted her off her feet.

"Don't go," she pleaded. "I just want you to hold me tonight. We don't have to do anything."

"That sounds a lot like 'Come on, cowboy, we won't put it all the way in,' which got me into trouble once before." That was the line she'd challenged him with the first time they'd had sex, which had come after several hours of rolling around naked on blankets in the back of his truck, doing everything to each other except the final act. The fire of desire in her eyes, and that wicked challenge, had done him in, the same way hearing her say she liked being *his* had done tonight.

"Trouble *is* my middle name." She laced her fingers with his, leading him into her apartment. "Did I mention we're going to sleep naked?"

Chapter Eleven

BRINDLE AWOKE TUESDAY morning to the feel of Trace's warm, loving lips and big, eager hands traveling down her body. He caressed and cherished, making masculine, appreciative noises that caused her insides to simmer with desire. Ever since their date, which had ended with much more than sleep, their lovemaking had changed. They couldn't help but be wild with each other, but now Trace did things like framing her baby bump between his hands and talking to their baby between kisses, as he was now.

"Close your eyes, little one. Daddy needs to make Mama squirm." He tipped his handsome face up with a coy look in his eyes. "But Mama's going to keep her eyes *wide* open."

He kissed his way south, his dark eyes locked on her as he trailed kisses along her inner thigh, slowing only long enough to drag his tongue tauntingly close to the place she needed it most. Every touch of his lips caused a shiver of anticipation. By the time he finally lowered his mouth between her legs, bringing his hands in to play, she was a trembling, needy mess.

"*Trace,*" she pleaded, reaching for him. But he was intent on driving her crazy, and continued his relentless pursuit of her pleasure.

She squirmed and begged, her heels digging into the sheets. He pushed his fingers inside her, expertly sending her soaring. He loved her through the very last pulse of her orgasm, and when she collapsed to the mattress, panting for air, he moved over her. The love staring back at her made her feel melty inside.

"Good morning, beautiful," he said as their bodies joined together. "Ah, darlin', there's no better feeling than loving you with all I have."

They made love slow and sweet, kissing so deeply she got lost in the rhythm of his tongue sweeping over hers in time to his hips thrusting and gyrating, taking her up to the clouds again and again. Just when she thought she'd used every ounce of energy she had, his kisses became more intense and possessive, awakening carnal desires she hadn't known were lying in wait, and their bodies took over.

She was a fool to have held back for so long. Being with Trace was always exciting, but being openly loved by him? Being able to give that love back without insecurities weighing her down?

That was *magical.*

THAT MAGICAL HIGH pulled her through the school day. Well, that and the fun, sexy texts she and Trace had shared throughout the afternoon. She'd never realized how giving herself over so completely to him could change their lives, but she finally felt like she was really living. They'd spent Saturday night at her place, but Sunday and Monday nights they'd slept at his house. She liked knowing they were there for each other and talking things out. She was more committed and tied down than she ever wanted to be and loving every second of it. How crazy was that? The things she'd feared most were the things that had set her free.

She climbed from her car and looked up at Grace and Reed's Victorian home. She was meeting Grace, Morgyn, and their mother for their meeting of the married minds. She felt a strange sense of pride and nervousness, as if being committed and pregnant had thrust her into a new realm of existence. Into a new type of sisterhood. Would she pass muster? Could she learn to be as effective a communicator in her relationship as she was in her professional life?

She thought about her sisters, how easily Morgyn had fallen into her relationship with Graham and how seamlessly Grace and Reed had come together. They were definitely made for each other. As far as Brindle knew, they never even fought, and her parents practically finished each other's sentences. She'd seen them argue, but it was never mean-spirited, and it always ended with a kind word or a kiss.

When Brindle's fights with Trace didn't end with them storming off, there was always hot makeup sex. Was that just as good?

Better, she mused as she climbed the porch steps.

Brindle had been floored when she'd learned that Grace and Reed had carried on a secret love affair when they were younger. It seemed Brindle and Sable weren't the only sneaky sisters in the family. Knowing Grace's secret had brought her a notch toward *normal* in Brindle's mind. Grace was an overachiever, and Brindle had thought she'd *always* done the right thing. But her confession had also left Brindle wondering what she might find out about Amber and Pepper. Neither of them enjoyed parties, and Brindle had few memories of them dating when they were teenagers. Pepper was always busy with one science project or another, and Amber had always preferred books to boys. Brindle thought they were missing out when they'd stay home from creek parties or refused to sneak out to watch the guys ride horses before dawn. She *hoped* there were some secrets in their lives, because naughtiness was so fun, but she had a feeling it might take the right men to pry them out of their conservative shells.

She knocked once and then she pushed the door open. "Hello? Is this the place where girls come to learn how to communicate with men?"

"Honey, you've known how to communicate with men since you crawled into Poppi's lap when you were just a tiny thing," Lindsay's grandmother, Nina, whom everyone called Nana, said as she came through the living room. Nana and Poppi lived down the street from Reed and Grace. "You fluttered those long dark lashes, gazed at him with your big blue eyes, and wrapped that man around your little finger."

Brindle laughed and hugged the woman who had always treated her like a granddaughter. "Hi, Nana. I didn't know you were coming."

Nana looked stylish in a pair of dark slacks and a smart gray top. Her hair was short and layered, mostly white with hints of blond, giving her the appearance of a sweet grandmother. But the things that came out of Nana's mouth often rivaled Sable's unfiltered statements.

"Well, then, that makes two of us." Nana put her arm around Brindle, guiding her toward the kitchen. She lowered her voice and said, "Between you and me, when I heard Grace and Sophie talking about this meeting of the married minds, I thought I might be able to learn something." Sophie Roberts-Bad was Lindsay's older sister and Grace's best friend. She and her husband, Brett, had a little girl and they split their time between New York City and Meadowside.

"But, Nana, you've been married forever."

"Exactly." Her eyes glimmered with mischief. "You think I'd pass up a chance to hear all your sexy *communication* secrets?" She used air quotes around *communication*. "Honey, there might be snow on the roof, but there's fire down below."

"I want to be you when I grow up," Brindle said as they entered the kitchen.

Grace and Morgyn were sitting at the table, which was covered with plates of different types of cookies. Their mother stood at the counter transferring more cookies from a cooling rack to a plate.

"We all want to be Nana when we grow up," her mother said. "Hello, sweetheart. How are you?"

"It should be illegal to feel as good as I do." Brindle snagged a cookie and said, "But your grandbaby is hungry *all* the time."

"Well, we can't have that," her mother said with a wink.

"Hey, Brin." Morgyn patted the seat beside her. "Sit with us."

Brindle sat down and said, "What's with all the cookies?"

"You'll see. How are things at work?" Grace asked.

"Weirdly good," Brindle said. "Now that everyone knows the baby is Trace's, the staff is rallying around me, showering me with congratulatory hugs and well wishes. My students are so happy, you'd think they were graded on their enthusiasm."

"I'm glad. I bet you never thought about how your relationship with Trace affected everyone around you," Grace pointed out.

"Why would it affect my students?"

"Because kids hear and see everything," their mother said.

"I know. I'm careful about how I act around them."

"That's true," Grace said. "I've seen you with them, and you're a different person around your students than you are with adults. You talk to them on a level they can relate to. You guide them and show them that an adult can be professional and still be a normal person outside of work. But they have eyes and ears outside the classroom, Brin."

"I don't understand." Brindle looked at her mother. "I told you I haven't been with any other guys. I mean, I've flirted and had drinks with guys, but never…I've always been careful not to flirt with other guys around my students. Have I been a bad influence on them?"

"No, honey." Her mother put her hand on Brindle's and said, "But everyone in this town knows how much you and Trace love each other. They hear gossip, and they know when you're hurting. Your students *pull* for you, and pulling for you means rooting for you and Trace as a couple. They're invested, as is most everyone else around here."

Brindle looked at Morgyn, who was nodding in confirmation. "You think they were upset because they thought I was pregnant by someone else and that meant the end of the couple they were pulling for? That makes us sound like a soap opera."

"We were all pulling for you and Trace. If I weren't your sister, I'd have given you snide looks, too," Morgyn admitted.

"*Great*," Brindle said sarcastically.

Morgyn blew her a kiss.

"It's not because you're the town soap opera," Nana clarified. "Although there is the whole hashtag Team Trindle thing on Instagram."

Brindle's eyes widened. "What is *that*?" She picked up her phone and searched #TeamTrindle on Instagram. "Oh my God. There are more than three *thousand* posts about us?"

"You were gone a *long* time." Nana took Brindle's phone and turned it upside down on the table. "It started as a Facebook poll when you went to Paris. A will-they, won't-they thing. Then it moved to Pinterest on the Trindle boards, and now it's all over Insta. There are pictures of you two lovebirds all over the place. You've *really* got to get your nose out of Trace's sheets long enough to explore social media—but not this second."

"Holy cow," Brindle said under her breath. "Okay, seriously? Team Trindle? Nobody thought to tell me? I'm on social media. Why have *I* never noticed it?"

Grace said, "You have to know the hashtags to look for them."

"Graham said your Instagram followers grew by forty-five percent while you were overseas. Didn't you notice?" Morgyn asked.

"No, I didn't *notice*. I was a little busy figuring out my life." Brindle wondered if Trace knew about #TeamTrindle. She made a mental note to ask about it.

Nana sat up a little straighter and said, "Can we circle back to your students, please? You're not the Oak Falls soap opera, honey, but your love for Trace, and his love for you, gave everyone hope that true love really can last through anything."

"But we fought *all* the time," Brindle said. "I had to go to Paris to realize my love for him was everything I wanted and more. How could anyone else possibly know it was real?"

Their mother chuckled softly and said, "Because that's what

true love is, sweetheart."

"Not according to Grace and Reed or Morgyn and Graham. Or you and Dad, for that matter. Nobody fights like us."

"No two loves are alike," Nana said. "Poppi and I fought like cats and dogs when we were your age, but it was because we loved each other so much, we were afraid of losing one another. But look at us now. We've trained each other to communicate more effectively." She smirked and said, "I've trained him to agree with me."

"Well, let's get down to business, because if the whole town is rooting for us, they can get in line behind me. I want nothing more than to be able to talk to my man without either of us storming out, and I'm not easy, so hopefully you can fix me right up." Brindle bit into her cookie. "*Mm.* This is amazing. What is it, molasses?"

"It's my grandmother's recipe," Nana said as she set the plate of cookies in the middle of the table. "Do you want some hot chocolate before we get started?"

"Actually, I'd love some *milk*," Brindle said, surprising herself.

Her mother looked at her like she'd lost her mind. "Milk?"

"You hate milk," Grace reminded her. "You always said if we were meant to drink it, we'd be born as cows, which makes no sense since cows don't drink milk."

"I know, but I *really*—" Brindle gasped as realization dawned on her. Her hand fell to her belly and she said, "Oh my gosh! I think I'm having a *craving!*"

"Here we go!" Nana waggled her brows and got up to pour Brindle a cup of milk. "First it's cravings, and then it's an amped-up sex drive."

"This is *crazy!* I have to tell Trace!" Brindle grabbed her phone, suddenly realizing what Nana had said. "Wait. Amped-up sex drive?"

"They already hump like rabbits," Morgyn pointed out, and bit into a cookie.

"Morgyn." Their mother shook her head. "They're having a baby. I think you can say *make love* rather than *hump*."

Morgyn and Brindle looked at each other and burst into laughter.

Nana gave Brindle a cup of milk and sat down, while Brindle thumbed out a text. *I have my first craving! For milk! And apparently my sex drive is going to get even bigger. Think you can handle that?* She added a kissing emoji and hearts and sent it to him.

"Okay, let's do this. How can I communicate more effectively with my man?" Brindle's phone vibrated with a text from Trace. She read it, grinning like a fool—*Does this mean I should come to the school on your lunch break to make sure you're well taken care of? I'm game if you are!*

Morgyn snagged Brindle's phone and read Trace's text. "Seems to me you know how to communicate quite effectively with him."

"Give me that." Brindle took her phone.

Their mother put her hands flat on the table and said, "Okay, girls. We're here to help Brindle break some old habits. Let's focus on doing that." She waved to the cookies in the middle of the table. "I know how we tend to get off track when we're together, so I thought using cookies might help us focus."

"Or fatten us up," Grace said as she grabbed a cookie.

"Some pounds are worth it," Nana interjected.

Brindle put her hand on her belly and said, "Speaking of pounds, I'm using rubber bands to keep my jeans closed. Who wants to go maternity clothes shopping with me?"

"Me!" Morgyn and Grace said.

"You girls have fun with that," their mother said. "I've got Thanksgiving plans to make."

They made a date to go shopping the following weekend, and then Brindle said, "I can't believe Thanksgiving is only two weeks away. I need to talk to Trace and see where he wants to spend it. I don't really want to celebrate separately."

"You might consider dinner at one house and dessert at the other," her mother suggested. "Maybe next year we can do Thanksgiving as one big family with the Jerichos. It's something to think about."

"I was going to suggest we do that with Graham's family next year," Morgyn said.

"That sounds fun," Brindle agreed. "We can always do another holiday with Trace's family. We'll figure it out. There's so much to think about before the baby comes."

"Your life is changing so fast," her mother said. "Don't let the little things overwhelm you. Just take it as it comes, one thing at a time."

"No more Tuesday nights at JJ's," Grace said.

Brindle cringed. "What drugs are you on? Tuesdays are our dance nights. We're going tonight. Why would we give that up?"

"You may not want to leave your baby to go dancing," Grace said. "At least for a while."

"Oh, I thought you meant *now*." Brindle's mind sprinted into a future filled with cuddling their baby and snuggling as they watched television, and her heart warmed. But there was a longing just beneath all those warm feelings. She loved dancing with Trace, and she didn't want to give that up altogether.

"You know I'll babysit anytime," their mother said.

"Thanks, Mom, but Grace is right. I don't think I'll want to leave our baby to go dancing, at least not while it's little. We'll just have to get creative and have our own three-person dance party at home. Oh my gosh, can you imagine Trace dancing with our little baby boy or girl on his shoulder?" She sighed dreamily, imagining Trace holding their baby, and her insides turned to mush. "Oh, you guys, I haven't thought of that before. I have a feeling I'm going to be swooning over him even more once our baby is born."

"Seeing your man with your baby will do all sorts of wonderful things to you, honey," her mother said.

"We need to fix our fights for good," Brindle said, though she was really telling it to herself.

"You will, but remember, honey, no relationship is perfect," her mother reminded her. "You and Trace are going to have ups and downs. It's just the way life is. Let's talk about communication, because that's where it all starts." She looked at Brindle and said, "When you were little, if I wanted to hold your attention, I had to relate things to food or fun."

"I remember, Mom. I got the talk about bananas and doughnuts, when everyone else got the birds and the bees."

Nana threw her head back with a laugh. "That's brilliant! And visually accurate, too."

They all giggled.

"Some conversations are sticky and need to be carefully navigated." Her mother pointed to the molasses cookies. "Think of those as molasses discussions."

"Those are the discussions that make it hard for you to remember to root for Team Trindle," Nana said.

"Those are the ones Brindle normally runs away from, and

her next move is to make Trace jealous," Grace added. "You can't do that anymore, Brin. You're having a child together. You have to be able to talk to him about everything."

"When Graham and I hit sticky situations, I get quiet, and he gives me time to cool down," Morgyn said. "But, Brindle, you're not good at cooling down, so maybe you can tell Trace you need space instead of just walking off."

"That's a great suggestion," Grace said. "And try going into another room, or just walking a few feet away if you're out somewhere, so he knows you're not abandoning the discussion. Or even better, take him with you away from the group."

"Oh, that's good," Morgyn said. "Then you'd have his full attention."

"And the added benefit of a private makeup make-out session," Brindle said more to herself than to anyone else.

"Brindle…" Her mother gave her a half smile, half be-serious look.

Brindle sighed. "We're getting better at that. Not the makeup make-out part, but trying to cool down and talk things out. We've both been making the effort to do it."

"It's not easy, is it?" Nana asked.

"No, but it feels good afterward," Brindle said.

"She means makeup sex," Morgyn clarified.

"We all like makeup sex," their mother said.

"Ew!" Grace, Morgyn, and Brindle said in unison.

Grace held up her hand and said, "Mom, please…"

"That's not a visual I need," Morgyn added.

"Wait," Brindle said. "I just realized that we're talking about communication, but we're shutting our own mother down. That's not cool. Sorry, Mom. While I don't want to think about you and Dad like that, I like knowing that when I'm fiftysomething I'll still have makeup sex."

"It never has to end." Nana picked up a frosted sugar cookie and said, "That's where these come in. Because some conversations need a different type of help. When you want to do something different or go someplace and you have to lay the sweetness on thick to get your man's attention."

"Oh, that's never a problem." Brindle picked up a sugar cookie and dragged her finger through the frosting. She held up her sugarcoated fingertip and said, "All I have to do is crawl into his lap, whisper certain things in his ear, and…" She sucked the frosting off her finger. "Voilà! All is good."

Grace covered her face. "Oh my gosh."

"What? It works. Some types of conversations are easier than others." Brindle picked up a black-and-white cookie and said, "Is this representative of when we're right and they're wrong?"

Their mother shook her head. "It's more like when either party thinks their point is right, not just us. We're not *always* right."

"Yeah, I kind of hate that," Brindle said. "It's easier when I'm right."

"How do you handle it when you're wrong?" their mother asked.

"Usually I take off," Brindle said with no small amount of shame. "But sometimes, if I'm not *too* mad, there is another way to make my stubborn cowboy realize he's wrong, or forget I was wrong." She pulled her sweater off her shoulder, pushed the V-neck open wider, and gave them her best seductive glance, excited to share her expertise and not feel ashamed of it. She spoke in a sultry tone as she said, "First, I run my hand along his thigh, because a thigh stroke is just sexy enough to get his attention off the conversation and onto *me*. And then I usually go with something like, *How about we discuss it in the bedroom?* We usually have much better discussions after sex."

Her mother sighed and patted Brindle's hand. "Okay, honey, that's what we're trying to move past."

"*Wait*," Morgyn interjected. "I'm learning something. Give us a second."

"Yeah, me too," Grace said. "I think there's some value in going with a sexy coupling and discussing things afterward. Where did you learn these techniques?"

"I don't know. I was born with them, I guess," Brindle said.

Grace's brows knitted. "We have the same parents, and I didn't get those skills. I had to really reach outside my comfort zone to be the aggressor with Reed. And boy, he loves it."

"Reed has been gaga over you forever," Nana said. "Whatever is *in* your comfort zone has definitely been working, too."

"Yeah, but this is good stuff," Grace said. "The thigh stroke? I didn't even know there was such a thing. I want to know how my little sister was born with knowledge I wasn't."

Morgyn bit into a cookie and said, "Me too. Mom...?"

Their mother was humming, twirling her hair around her finger, and looking the other way.

"Did you *teach* Brindle?" Morgyn asked.

"What?" Their mother's cheeks turned crimson. "No, I didn't teach her that. But she must have paid more attention to me and your father during certain developmental years."

"You did the thigh stroke?" Grace gasped and waved her hand. "Don't answer that. Just tell me where *you* learned it."

"I don't know. It came naturally to me," their mother finally said.

"Some girls are more seductive, while others are sweet and

sexy," Nana said. "Take my Lindsay. That girl's got spunk, like Brindle, though she doesn't flirt much, which is a shame. But my Sophie is all sugar and sweetness, which works for her. She and Brett couldn't be happier."

"Well, I'm going to try Brindle's tactic next time." Grace crossed her arms, and Brindle could practically see the gears churning in her sister's mind. "This could be fun."

As much as Brindle loved knowing her sisters wanted to be more seductive, she knew what she'd described wasn't the right way to do it. "Wait, you guys. Those tactics are what got us into this communication pickle in the first place. Trace and I have been working on moving past *tactics* and pussyfooting around, or letting things stew between us. We're trying to face things head-on and talk openly about our feelings even when it hurts. It's really hard. Words hurt, which is funny, because that's what parents teach their kids from the time they're little. But it hurts less than stewing and doing backhanded things in retaliation. I kind of think emotional, verbal diarrhea is the way to go." She splayed her hands and said, "Like being naked. Show your cellulite and your freckles and all your sexy curves and learn how to navigate the hard ridges of masculine hips and thick thighs—"

"Slow down, hot pants, or I'm going to need a drink and a cigarette after this talk," Nana said.

Brindle shook her head to clear images of Trace's body from her mind and said, "Sorry. Sometimes my mind just goes to other things."

"*Big, hard* things, apparently," Grace said with a smirk.

"I can't help it! Look at my boyfriend!" Brindle said. "You guys, I just called Trace my boyfriend. I like that. But getting back to my point, I think talking honestly trumps using other tactics. Trace and I have gotten closer on so many levels since we decided to try to talk things out, and it's happened fast. We talk about everything now. He even asked about the play we're doing in drama club. It feels good to have a deeper relationship. I think I've always wanted it, but I was so afraid that we'd lose something in the transition."

"Love like yours can't be lost, honey. It can grow and change for the better, but only you and Trace can figure out what direction things move in," her mother said. "I don't think you needed this talk after all. It sounds like you and Trace are already figuring out what works for you."

"As good as that feels to hear," Brindle said, "I did need it. I wasn't sure I would fit into coupledom sisterhood like you guys do. But now I don't feel so far off the mark."

"Brindle, you always figure out how to handle things in a way that's right for you," Morgyn said. "You just do it on your own timetable."

Grace nodded in agreement. "And you'll always fit into whatever sisterhood we're in. You're Brindle Montgomery, and none of us is dumb enough to try to exclude you."

Brindle made a slapping motion in Grace's direction, and they all laughed.

"But you *are* going to be a mother," Nana reminded her. "Certain responsibilities come along with that, such as feeding your child. From what I know about you, you and ovens are not on very friendly terms."

"And you'll need to either learn to clean or hire a house-keeper," their mother added.

"*Ugh*, I know. On a more exciting note, did I tell you guys I have a sonogram next week? Trace is coming with me to see Dr. Bryant."

"That's one benefit of living in such a small town," Grace said. "In Manhattan you'd see a lab tech you've never met before."

"That's true," their mother said. "I'm sorry Dr. Bryant fled her old life because of a nasty divorce, but I'm glad she landed here. Our town needed a female obstetrician."

Morgyn sipped her hot chocolate and said, "Will you find out the sex of the baby?"

"We haven't decided yet, but we're leaning that way," Brindle answered.

"See how easily Brindle got our minds off of cooking and cleaning?" Grace said. "She really *is* good at distractions."

Caught! "Can we please table those topics for the next meeting of the married minds?" Brindle asked. "I'm not sure I can handle that much knowledge in one day."

"I'd say you did pretty well, considering we didn't even get to the *everything* cookies." Morgyn picked up a cookie that looked like a pie chart. "These have eight different types of cookie dough, they take forever to make, but they're *so* worth your while."

"They're for times when you need to pull out all the stops and just deal with it," her mother said.

"That's my new go-to cookie." Brindle picked up an everything cookie and bit into it. White chocolate, chocolate chip, oatmeal, cinnamon, and more sweetness than she could define spread over her tongue. She wanted to dive into a vat of them and eat her way out.

"And when you just want to tear your man apart." Grace picked up a gingerbread man and bit off the head.

"I'm Team Trindle all the way, so there will be no more biting off heads." Brindle couldn't resist embarrassing them all by saying, "But licking and sucking…"

As her sisters and mother covered their blushing faces, Nana put her arm around Brindle and said, "*Now*, you're in my sisterhood, too."

Chapter Twelve

THURSDAY AFTERNOON TRACE grabbed his toolbox from the back of his truck in the elementary school parking lot as Jeb and Shane climbed from their vehicles. Trace's gaze fell on Brindle's shiny red MINI Cooper. It was rare to see a MINI Cooper in Oak Falls among the masses of pickup trucks and SUVs, but it suited his girl perfectly, since she was one of a kind. She'd been mighty proud when she'd bought the used sports car. She'd driven straight to his place and they'd gone out for a drive—and they'd ended up pulled over on a dirt road, christening the front seat. She'd ridden him hard, and he'd loved every minute of it. But she couldn't exactly cart a baby around in that little car. He'd checked the safety rating on it when she'd bought it, and it was high, but putting a baby seat in the back would be a pain in the ass. At some point they'd have to think about upgrading to something more family friendly. Something sporty but big enough and safe enough for her and the baby.

Jeb sidled up to Trace and said, "You okay?"

"Yeah. I'm just wondering how Brindle would feel driving something a little bigger once the baby comes."

"Just don't get her a minivan," Shane said. "She's too hot

for a minivan."

Trace set a narrow-eyed look on Shane and said, "Stop checking out my girl. Let's go."

They headed into the school and made their way down the halls to the all-purpose room where Brindle was teaching drama club. In all the years Trace and Brindle had been together, he'd never seen her in the classroom. Their relationship hadn't been the type where he could show up and bring her lunch to catch an extra twenty minutes together, no matter how much he might have wanted to. She'd made an off-the-cuff comment a while back about Trace helping with sets. He'd given her the choice of continuing to hang out in the evenings, which usually ended horizontal, or using their time together to work on sets for the play. She'd chosen the former. But now that she was truly his, he wanted it all. He wanted to be the man who filled all the gaps in her life, whom she could count on to build sets, care for her when she was sick, and satiate her every sexual desire.

He heard Brindle's energetic, confident voice before they reached the entrance to the room, and he held out his hand, indicating for his brothers to hang back for a moment. He peered into the room, wanting to see her in action without causing a disruption. Brindle sat on the floor with about thirty elementary-age kids. She looked hot in the mauve sweater, dark jeans, and leather boots she'd worn out with him at JJ's many times. But sitting with her back pin straight with a reassuring expression as she patiently addressed each child's question, she was the epitome of a professional teacher. Brindle spoke in a careful, purposeful tone he had never heard before.

He had no idea how she could be a sensuous siren one minute and a caring and reserved role model the next, but seeing this side of her brought his mind to their baby. He'd been thinking a lot about parenthood and imagining Brindle as a mother, holding their sweet baby in her arms. She was his wild one, but he'd seen her with Sophie's baby, and he knew she'd be a nurturing mother. As he observed her reminding the children of the importance of keeping their grades up if they wanted to be in the play and her expectations of their supporting their friends even if they were competing for the same role, he realized that his wild girl didn't take her position over those young, moldable minds lightly. That gave him an even bigger sense of pride toward the woman who he knew would guide their child in all the right ways.

He imagined a stubborn boy who had Brindle's stormy eyes, or a little girl with Brindle's sassy mouth. He didn't care what they were like; he'd loved their baby from the second she'd told him he was the father. And the truth was, even if he weren't its father, he'd have stuck by them both and loved them just as much.

"Next week we'll hold auditions," Brindle said, bringing his mind back to the moment. "Remember to take a few minutes to read through the character list and descriptions after you finish your homework each night." Her eyes moved slowly around the circle, slowing on each of the children. "Think about which character you want to play. Natalie has included an audition sheet for each character. Those are the lines you'll need to memorize. It's important that you're prepared and you give the audition all that you have." She glanced at the studious-looking brunette teenager with dark-framed glasses sitting to her right and said, "Natalie, do you have anything to add?"

As Natalie spoke to the children, Shane whispered, "How does it feel to see your baby mama in action?"

"Really fucking good," Trace said softly.

Jeb leaned closer to Shane and said, "How many students at the high school do you think call Brindle a TILF?"

Trace glared at him. "*Enough* with the bullshit."

Jeb and Shane chuckled.

"Dude, all high school guys have a thing for teachers," Shane said. "Remember Miss McClintock?" Miss McClintock was a buxom blonde transplant from California who'd thought she'd wanted a more rural lifestyle. She'd stuck around Oak Falls for only two years, but it was enough time for her to become a teenage spank-bank legend.

"Okay, I'll see you all next week," Brindle said as she rose to her feet.

There was a flurry of commotion as kids gathered their papers and backpacks and put on their coats. Natalie helped the kids as Brindle talked with a few other children.

"Thank you, Miss M!" a lanky, towheaded boy called out.

Two curly-haired girls gave Brindle high fives. Kids called out thank-yous, and Brindle responded to waves, telling the kids to have a good week. A redheaded boy tugged on her sweater, frowning up at her as he said something Trace couldn't hear. Brindle crouched beside him, looking him in the eyes as she said something that made the little boy light up. Trace wished he could hear what she was saying. The little boy hugged her, then darted across the room and joined the other kids as Natalie guided them toward the parents standing by the side door to the parking lot, waiting to pick up their children.

"Hey, Mustang," Trace said as he and his brothers walked into the room.

Brindle turned with surprise in her eyes, and a smile spread across her beautiful face. "Hi. What are you guys doing here?"

Shane pointed at Trace. "Just following the boss."

With a quick glance to make sure the last child was out the door, Trace leaned in for a kiss. "We're here to help build sets for the show."

Her eyes bloomed wide. "*Oh*. Wow. That's so sweet." She wrinkled her nose, lifting her shoulders adorably. "The thing is, we won't be ready to start building them for another few weeks. We're usually into rehearsals by now, but we started the whole process a month late because of my trip, so we decided to move the play to after the New Year. But I *love* that you want to help. I can't believe you're really here. It's kind of weird seeing you in the all-purpose room."

"Go Team Trindle," Natalie said in a singsong voice as she came to Brindle's side. "Can I get a picture of you guys?"

Trace and his brothers chuckled. Brindle had come home from her meeting with her mother and sisters reeling about the social media frenzy. He'd admitted to hearing the rumors, but he'd never actually gone online to see what they were all about. He'd also admitted the reasons why he hadn't followed up on the rumors—he'd been in no frame of mind to deal with that kind of shit when she was gone. Brindle had called her sisters and given them hell about not clueing her in. He and Brindle had talked about the best way to handle it, and she'd tried to let it go and forget about the rumors. Maybe someone who didn't know her so well would have bought it. But Trace saw her struggle, and by evening, she'd decided to deal with the rumors the way she always had. She'd pushed her annoyance aside and buried the urge to address them down deep. It was a start, and they were making progress.

Brindle gave Natalie a don't-go-there look and said, "We're going to have a talk about that. I can't believe this whole hashtag thing was going on and you didn't tell me."

Natalie pushed her glasses up the bridge of her nose and said, "I'm sorry, but if it's any consolation, I was totally pulling for you guys. And what Trace did yesterday shut everyone down, so I just wanted to show that it was official with a picture of the two of you together. You know, to validate his post."

Aw hell…

"His *post*?"

Trace gritted his teeth at the fire in Brindle's eyes.

"You've been outed, bro," Jeb said.

"Trace doesn't even have any social media accounts." Brindle stalked over to the bleachers and dug her phone out of her purse.

"He does now," Shane said with a smirk, earning visual daggers from Brindle. "And his post has more than a thousand likes."

"It was *epic*," Natalie added. "I have to leave to meet some friends at the library, but I'll see you tomorrow in class, Miss M."

"Bye, Nat," Brindle said as she typed and swiped on her phone.

"I told you I was playing by my rules this time, darlin'," Trace said, watching her read his post. *It's official! Trace Jericho and Brindle Montgomery are exclusive! #TeamTrindleForever. Soon to be #TeamTrindleTrio.* The anger in her eyes softened, and he assumed she was looking at the picture. They'd taken the selfie the other night. Brindle was sitting on his lap in front of the fireplace in his house. She was wearing one of his T-shirts. Her hair was tousled and her cheeks were flushed from their lovemaking. Flames danced behind them, casting shadows over the blanket across her lap. Her head rested on his shoulder, her gaze soft and loving. One arm was draped around his neck as he pressed a kiss to her forehead. She looked beautiful and happy, and she was right where she'd always belonged, safely nestled in his arms. She'd been staying at his place, and they both loved falling asleep in each other's arms and waking up together so much, he wished they'd done it years ago.

He'd loved the picture so much, he'd made it the background on his phone.

As she lifted her eyes, love pushed the lingering frustration in them away. "You called your account TraceLovesBrindleForever."

He set down his toolbox, gathered her in his arms, and said, "You know I don't lie."

"But you *hate* social media."

"But I love you, darlin'. I know you're too proud to address rumors, but it was time to shut them down once and for all."

She peeked around him at Jeb. "And you used his post for your Instagram story. Does that mean you forgive me for lying?"

Trace's heart took a hit. He knew she was worried about that, but to hear her say it made him want to turn around and make sure his brother said the right thing. But he knew how Jeb felt. The question was, would he let her know the truth?

"We all make mistakes," Jeb said. "You guys might have gotten off to a rocky start, but I'll be lucky to find someone who loves me as much as you love this big lug. I might have to blow him away in the Turkey Trot race just to wipe that smug look off his face."

Trace felt Brindle relax a little in his arms.

"And I'll beat your ass over the finish line so you don't get an even bigger head," Shane said to Jeb. He looked at Brindle and hiked a thumb at Trace as he said, "This asshole told us he made a shitty comment when he found out you were pregnant. For what it's worth, I would have lied, too. And now that I know we're not needed here, I'm heading back to the ranch."

"Thanks for coming," Trace said as Jeb and Shane headed for the door.

Shane turned around, pointing at Trace, and said, "Don't think I'm picking up your chores so you can make out in the equipment closet. Get your ass back there in the next half hour or I'm going to come back and pull the fire alarm."

When they left, Brindle gazed up at him and said, "You took time off to help me build sets? I thought you couldn't take time off in the afternoon."

"Yeah, well, life changes. My priorities have shifted. I would have worked late to make up for the lost time." He pressed his lips to hers. "I told you we were living by my rules now. That means I get to do all the things I would have done over the years if circumstances were different." He kissed her again, deep and slow, and she melted against him. "Besides, knowing you'll be waiting for me at home changes everything." He kissed her jaw. "It's no longer a choice of helping with sets or spending my evening with you naked in my arms." He kissed her neck and then gave it one hard suck.

She made a needy sound and said, "It's not like I live there…"

"That's next on your list of priorities." He grabbed her ass, holding her against him so she could feel what she did to him. "So, about that equipment room…"

"Trace," she warned. "No."

He drew back, meeting her lust-filled eyes. "I don't think I've ever heard you tell me no before."

"I can't do that *here*," she whispered.

"How about behind the bleachers?" he teased, kissing her neck again.

"No," she said with a giggle.

He liked this proper side of her more than he probably should. It presented another type of challenge, even though he was only teasing right now. He didn't want to get her in trouble at work, but it was too much fun watching her blush to stop just yet.

"Parking lot? My truck?"

"You are relentless." She went up on her toes and kissed him. "It's just one of the many things I love about you. But Shane's waiting for you, and I have papers to grade before my hot cowboy gets home tonight." She dragged her finger down the open buttons on his Henley and said, "I promise to make it up to you."

"Just promise me you, darlin'. That's all I've ever wanted."

Chapter Thirteen

BRINDLE SHIVERED AGAINST the icy wind as she tied a blindfold around Trace's head Monday night.

"What's going on, Brin?"

"It's a surprise."

Brindle was excited to do something special for Trace. Their lives were becoming even more intertwined, and every day things felt a little more settled. Though she had her life and he had his, sleeping together every night really had changed everything. It had taken the pressure off. Neither of them felt as though they had to compete for the other's attention. Not that either one had ever had to, but that was the only way Brindle could make sense of the way things had changed. They'd gone from living in an immature world of insecurities to a mature, reality-based existence, which brought them even closer together. And surprisingly, they didn't long for more freedom or feel trapped. If anything, they wanted even *more* time together. They met Morgyn and Graham for dinner Friday night, since they were leaving to spend Thanksgiving with Graham's family. She'd gone out with Lindsay and Trixie to see Sable's band play Sunday afternoon while Trace met with Sin to discuss the coaching position for next year. He was helping Sin again next weekend, and she was excited to watch.

Their relationship had deepened in ways she'd never expected. Talking more had made them closer, and being closer made her want even more with him.

Once upon a time, her definition of *more* had been related to sexual things. But she learned that her new definition was much more in line with what Trace's had always been. She now understood that Trace's *more* had always included loving her until the end of time. It wouldn't matter if she was fat, skinny, pregnant, or sick. His love was the real deal, just like hers had always been, though she'd been too fearful to give in to it. Working together to better their relationship, and doing things as a couple, had driven that point home every day. They still had bristling moments of stubbornness, but they were becoming adept at counting to five—or ten—and then talking things out in a calmer fashion.

Trace reached behind his head and covered her hand with his as she finished tying the knot in the blindfold. "I like where this is headed, darlin'. But I'm not sure why we're standing in my parents' driveway."

"Oh, um, it was easier to meet you here since you worked late."

"What is with you and all the surprises lately?" She'd surprised him Saturday afternoon with his favorite lunch from the Stardust Café and they'd eaten while sitting on the fence watching the horses in the pasture.

"You always knew you wanted to do things for me, but I guess I never realized how much I wanted to do things for you." That was true. She found herself wanting to do more for him, and for them. But there was more going on in her head. Even though Trace had forgiven her for lying, she vowed to spend the rest of her life doing everything within her power to be the woman he deserved. And she was okay with that, because she should have been doing it all along. She'd mentioned that when she'd had breakfast at her parents' house yesterday and Sable had said, *Isn't that the very definition of living and learning? Stop beating yourself up. You love him, and he loves you. As long as you're learning from your mistakes, why fret over them?*

Maybe one day Brindle would feel that way, but it didn't hurt to go the extra mile.

She opened the passenger door to his truck and said, "Climb in, cowboy. I'm taking you for a ride."

As he climbed in, he said, "Now I'm really liking where this is headed."

"It won't be long now." She kissed his smiling lips, and his hand snaked around her.

"You're wrong, darlin'. It's getting longer by the second."

"I'm counting on it," she said seductively, earning a rough, enticing kiss.

She came away breathlessly, glad the truck was parked far enough from his parents' house that they couldn't be seen. As she pulled his seat belt across his broad chest, leaning in to buckle it in place, his hands were everywhere at once, groping and caressing. His hips rocked up against her chest, and she had visions of opening his jeans and taking his hard length in her mouth. Her body heated, and she reminded herself she wasn't out to seduce him.

She pushed upright and said, "You make it hard for me to concentrate."

"That's the plan," he said cockily.

"Let's just try to keep it in your pants for a little longer." She closed his door and went around to the driver's seat, grinning as he blindly felt his way across the seat to her shoulder.

His hand slid down her front and he fondled her breast.

"Trace." She pushed his hand away and he laughed. As she started the truck, she said, "We have to go for a little drive. Don't peek."

"I'm good with not seeing, but what's up with your new no-touching rule?"

"It's not a rule. I just can't drive if you're doing that."

She drove around the block to throw him off, and then she drove back to his parents' house and down the long driveway toward the barns. She followed the narrow driveway through the pasture to the west side of their property and backed the truck through the open barn doorways.

"Smells like horses," he said.

She'd forgotten he'd pick up on the scents. "Everything in Oak Falls smells like horses. I have to do something. Promise you won't peek?"

He made an X over his heart.

"Okay, sit tight." Brindle's heart was beating so fast as she climbed from the truck, she was afraid she'd forget something.

She'd been planning this surprise for days, but the weather gods had been dead set on ruining it for them. They were calling for snow tonight, and she'd had to move the surprise indoors. Thanks to Shane, who had kept Trace away from the barn, Morgyn, who spent two hours over FaceTime teaching Brindle how to turn a broken umbrella into a starry sky, and Trixie, who had helped her set up, she knew it would be as close to perfect as it could get. She'd even gotten up the guts to tell Trace's mother what she'd planned so they weren't interrupted. That conversation had been more embarrassing than she'd anticipated. She had a feeling when she'd said the truck was an important part of the plan, his mother had known *why*. But heck, his mother had been young once. Surely she'd made out in the back of a truck at some point. Hadn't all country girls?

When she'd told Amber about her plans, her demure sister had informed her that *no*, all country girls *hadn't* made out in the back of a truck. To which Brindle had replied, *It's time for me to play matchmaker for you.*

Brindle spread out the pillows and blankets she and Trixie had hidden in the barn, hoping they were enough to keep them warm, and then she laid out the rest of the surprise. She opened the rear barn doors, and a gust of wind assaulted her.

Shivering, she rounded her shoulders and headed for the passenger door. She pulled it open and took Trace's hand. "Ready?"

"Always," he said in a husky voice.

She led him to the bed of the truck and realized she'd set everything in the middle and he might crawl right over it. How could she plan plays for thirty kids and mess up a simple surprise for the man she loved?

"You need to climb into the truck without taking off your blindfold. And put your hand on the right side, so you stay close to it."

"Brin, I hear your teeth chattering. What's going on?"

"Don't worry about me," she said. Suddenly realizing her man was *blindfolded*, she decided to taunt him a little. She slid her hand down his stomach and cupped his package. "You should probably climb in before I take advantage of you."

He didn't move, except for the smirk that formed on his lips. He covered her hand with his, keeping it right where he wanted it. *Oh boy*, right where she wanted it, too.

"*Up*, cowboy," she said, trying to regain control of her runaway hormones.

"Oh, I'm *up*."

She laughed, and he moved her hand higher, squeezing it around his erection. Her temperature spiked as he lowered his mouth in search of hers. She went up on her toes, greedily meeting him. She came away light-headed, just as she'd been the first time they'd made love in the bed of his truck all those years ago.

"I'm at your mercy, darlin'. Any other commands for me?"

"I have a long, dirty list that starts with you on your knees and ends with me riding you like a bronco." Her cheeks burned, and she quickly added, "But if we do that, you'll never see your surprise."

"I don't *ever* need to see again."

He reclaimed her mouth with savage intensity. *Yes!* Oh, how she wanted to forgo the surprise and satisfy their every fantasy—in the bed of the truck, against the wall of the barn, bent over the front seat. But even stronger was her desire to show him how much he meant to her—beyond sex and passion and all the naughty things she loved about him.

She forced herself to break their connection, and after several deep breaths she said, "I need you"—*naked*—"in the bed of the truck."

"Your wish is my command."

He climbed into the truck, and the sight of his ass in those snug jeans made her even needier.

"I feel you staring at my ass, darlin'."

God, I'm such a perv. I'll probably still be checking out his ass, and grabbing his package, when he's sixty.

TRACE HEARD BRINDLE climbing into the truck behind him. He spun around, quickly moving to the end of the bed, and held out his arms. "Let me help you, darlin'."

"I can climb into the truck," she said with enough sass for Trace to conjure the image of a scowl behind his blindfold.

"I know you *can*." He jumped from the truck, following her voice as she griped at him for getting out of the truck. He lifted her by the ribs and set her in the truck.

"Trace! I'm perfectly capable of climbing into a truck," she said as he climbed in. "If this is your type of *rule*, then we are going to have a problem. You can't treat me like I'm—"

"Like what? My pregnant girlfriend?" he said firmly. She was quiet for so long he imagined his sweet, stubborn girl trying to figure out a retort that made sense.

But there wasn't one.

He reached blindly for her and heard her scooting back. He laughed. "Really? You're mad? Count-to-five mad, or just irritated because you have an independent streak a mile wide and you're afraid I'll crush it?"

"That second thing," she said stubbornly, but he heard her smile.

He sat back on his heels and said, "This is the real me, darlin'. I'm going to be protective of you and of our baby. I won't ever try to take away your independence. You want to go out with your girlfriends? Go. You want to climb into my truck after the baby is born? I'm all for it. Hell, Mustang, I've never held you down. Lord knows if I back you into a corner you'll come out swinging. But I'm your man, darlin', your *protector*, and I'll be damned if I'll ever let you put yourself or our child in danger."

She groaned, and then there was a beat of silence, and he prepared himself for an argument. But the most remarkable thing happened. She *laughed*, and he heard her scooting closer. She put her hands on his thighs, and damn...the electric shock she caused should be illegal.

"I'm sorry. You're right. But this is going to take some getting used to." She touched her lips to his, and then she said, "How many stages of grief are there? I might have some mourning to do..."

She removed his blindfold, and her beautiful face came into focus. Even though in his heart she'd always been his, it hit him anew each time they were together, bringing feelings of happiness and completeness like he'd never known possible. "Forget mourning, babe. Celebrate that we just made it through a conversation you hated and we didn't fight."

"Tonight *is* a celebration."

She motioned to the blankets beneath them, the pillows piled around the back of the cab, and in the middle of it all was a plate of cookies, a quart of milk, two chili dogs, and fries. A metal web of white lights shimmered above them. The barn doors were open. Rain lights twinkled and danced in the breeze against the weathered wood. The gray night sky reflected in the creek a short distance from the barn.

He pulled her onto his lap, his heart full to near bursting. "You re-created the first time we ever made love."

"Well, more like the first time we ever *went at it*," she said playfully. "But yeah. I wanted to do it at Jericho Ridge, where we were that night, but they're calling for snow. So I created our own starry sky." She pointed to the metal web of lights.

"Morgyn showed me how. I ruined four umbrellas trying to get it right. Since we're starting over, I thought it might be nice to go back to the beginning. You know, to symbolize how far we've come."

"I love that idea, darlin'. I love it so damn much I'm kind of all choked up. I had no idea you remembered so much about that night. Right down to the chili dogs."

"I'll never forget the night I gave you my V-card, or the way you held me afterward, stroking my back and kissing my temple. Or how we went skinny-dipping in the creek. I remember lying in the truck with my head on your chest when we wished on the same star."

"Know what I wished for?" He'd wished she'd be his forever.

"Don't tell me. It's bad luck. That was the first time I asked you to close your eyes when we talked, remember?"

"Every word of it. But that was the only time you've ever asked me to close my eyes and talk *before* having sex." He remembered her innocent eyes closing and the nervous energy that had billowed off her, despite her confident seductress attitude, as she'd said, *This will be my first time, so go easy.* He'd known his brazen girl had a vulnerable side, but hearing it that night had changed him. He'd no longer wanted to conquer her as much as he'd wanted to protect her. He'd been so afraid of hurting her, he'd gone slow, loving her carefully until she'd said, *Now go hard.* He'd nearly lost it at those words coming out of her sexy mouth.

"Did you close your eyes then?" she asked.

"No," he said honestly.

Her eyes widened. "So you've been lying to me from the *start?*"

"No, darlin'. I've been watching out for you since the start," he clarified. "But there is one thing I don't remember about that night. Did we have cookies and milk?"

She wrinkled her perky nose and said, "I didn't have cravings back then."

"Oh, yes, you did." He brushed his scruff along her cheek and said, "If my memory serves me correctly, you had a taste for cowboy flesh." He bit her earlobe. "I'm glad that hasn't changed…"

"It's only gotten stronger, which is what I wanted to talk to you about." Her expression turned serious. "We have the sonogram tomorrow."

"I'm looking forward to it." He was nervous as hell to see their baby, but he was also excited. She climbed from his lap, and he draped a blanket over her belly and legs.

"Thanks." She smoothed the blanket nervously. "I'm not sure how to say this without it sounding weird, but I need you to hear it. We were both thrust into this situation—"

"Are you having second thoughts?" Worry prickled up his spine.

She shook her head. "No, I promise. But it's important that you hear what I have to say. You have to remember that I didn't know I was pregnant when I made my travel plans. I had an inkling the week I left, but I hadn't confirmed it."

"You told me this already. Did something happen in Paris that I need to know about?"

"Not with another guy or anything, if that's what you're thinking."

"I'm not thinking that. I don't know what to think."

"Because I'm confusing you." She was shivering. "Okay, here it is. Tomorrow we're going to see our baby, and I'm so excited I can barely see straight. But I don't want you to think that's why I agreed to a commitment. During that first week in Paris, *before* I took the pregnancy test, I realized how much I loved you. How much I've *always* loved you. The pregnancy complicated things, but I need you to know that with or without a baby, *this* is what I want. *You* are who I want."

He gathered her in his arms. "I know, darlin'. I feel it in your touch, and I see it in your eyes when you look at me. Everything has changed for us, and it's going to change even more. Hopefully starting with this."

He dug the key he'd had made for her out of his pocket and dangled the key ring with the mustang charm in front of her. "I love falling asleep with you in my arms, and your sleepy kisses when I get out of bed to go to work at the crack of dawn. I like seeing your belongings mixed with mine, smelling your body wash in the shower, and seeing your face when I walk in the door every night. Move in with me, darlin'. Let's start building a home together."

He placed the key in her palm, and as her fingers curled around it, she beamed like she'd been waiting her whole life for this very moment. "Trace, this is *big*. We've only been sleeping at your place for a little while. You know I can be a pain. You might get sick of having me around all the time. And I suck at cooking and cleaning. Are you sure?"

"I've never been more sure of anything in my life." He pressed his lips to hers and said, "Team Trindle forever, darlin'."

TRACE HALF EXPECTED Brindle to misguidedly see moving in as a strike against her independence and argue with him about it. But she was as elated as he was, and she couldn't keep it under wraps. As they ate their chili dogs, she made comments between each bite. *You're really sure? You want me there every day? Every night? Oh my gosh, Trace! We're moving in together!*

Trace was riding high as they fed each other French fries between kisses. When the first snowflakes drifted down from the sky, shimmering against the lights on the doors, Brindle popped to her knees and said, "It's snowing! Come on."

She knee-walked to the edge of the truck and then turned her smoky blue eyes on him and said, "Help me down?"

How could something so small feel so huge?

He hopped off the tailgate, and when he reached for her, she put her arms around his neck and her legs around his waist. She pressed her lips to his, and when he set her feet on the ground, she twirled out of the barn, tipped her head back, and opened her mouth, catching snowflakes on her tongue.

"Do it with me!" she urged.

He laughed, and he couldn't take his eyes off her. She looked so beautiful and happy, he wanted to memorize this moment to relive it over and over again.

She tilted her head up and studied his face. "Why are you looking at me like that?"

"Because I just figured out what you're made of."

"What? Just now? Equal parts of sugary goodness and stubborn pain in your ass, at your service."

"I'd have gone with the perfect combination of wild filly, sexy TILF, and *mine.*"

They kissed as snowflakes melted against their cheeks and

steam rose from their mouths.

"TILF is Teacher I'd Like to Fuck. I think you mean TIDF," Brindle said as he set her on her feet.

"What's the D for?"

"Teacher I *Do* Fuck."

"Always the English teacher," he said with a wink. "I'm sticking with TILF. Teacher *I Love* to Fuck. Come on, let's take our baby for its first walk down by the creek."

He took her hand and they strolled down to the water. Snow gathered on rocks and caught on Brindle's long eyelashes as they followed the creek along his parents' property, stealing kisses between conversations. Trace wrote *T + B* in the snow with the toe of his boot, and then Brindle walked the shape of a heart around it. When they stopped to watch the creek trickle by, Trace secretly admired Brindle as he remembered something JJ had asked him when he was twenty years old or so. His brother had asked if he thought he was missing out by not pursuing other women. JJ wasn't exactly a playboy, and Trace had wondered what was behind the question. But his answer had come easily. He'd said he had the prize mustang and he knew he wasn't missing a thing. JJ had gotten a funny look in his eyes and said, *Good to know you're not an asshole after all.*

He might not be an asshole, but even now he wished he could erase the two other women he'd slept with. Because he'd been right all those years ago. There wasn't a woman alive who could hold a candle to Brindle Montgomery, and he would be honored to say she was the only woman he'd ever slept with. But he'd been young and dumb, and he chalked it up to a learning experience.

By the time they made their way back to the barn, Brindle's nose and cheeks were bright pink.

He gathered her in his arms and said, "Darlin', I don't know much about romance, but I think you nailed it. I loved every second of my surprise. But you're freezing. How about we wrap this up in front of a roaring fire back home?" He pressed his lips to hers, and then he said, "*Our* home."

Chapter Fourteen

"WHAT'S TAKING SO long?" Brindle said to Trace Tuesday afternoon in her obstetrician's waiting room.

"We've been here five minutes. Relax."

"I am relaxed." She grabbed a magazine, then put it back on the table. They hadn't done a sonogram at the clinic in Paris. But since she'd been home, she'd read all about what they could see on the ultrasound at this stage of her pregnancy, and it was terrifying. All of the baby's fetal organs would be formed, even though immature. The doctor would use this scan to evaluate the anatomy of the baby. She'd look for spinal cord abnormalities, brain defects, heart defects, and more abnormalities than Brindle could handle thinking about. They could also tell the sex of the baby, which was the one thing she was excited about. "I lied. I'm not relaxed."

"Really? I never would have noticed." He reached for her hand, giving it a reassuring squeeze. "I told you not to read all that stuff online. It's going to be fine."

"I had to read about it. I'm a teacher. I like to be informed. Besides, you read the pregnancy books. That's the same thing."

"Well, they didn't freak me out, so they must have been different."

"This is crazy. I shouldn't be so nervous." If stressing out about the results weren't enough, she'd drank so much water for the scan, she had to pee like a racehorse. What if she peed on the table? She kept that worry to herself. "What if she sees something bad?" She felt queasy. "Oh God, Trace, what if—"

He moved from his seat and knelt before her, placing his hands on her waist, his dark eyes holding her attention just as they had last night when they'd made love in front of the fire.

"Take a deep breath," he said calmly. "Everything is going to be fine, and on the off chance they find something worrisome, we'll deal with it together. There's nothing we can't handle." He pressed his lips to hers. "We've got this, and I've got *you*, Brindle. Always."

"Okay, right. We do. But what if we don't?" Her fears grew with every passing second. "What if they see something that can't be fixed? I want this baby even if it has issues. I love it already. What if they find one of those things where they have to do surgery while the baby is in the womb? What if they mess up? What if—"

"Brindle," the nurse called out.

Brindle flew to her feet, knocking Trace's jaw with her chest and sending his head flying back. "Oh no! I'm sorry!"

She reached for him as he rose to his feet, rubbing his jaw. "It's fine. Relax."

"I'm so sorry. I'm just nervous." Everyone in the waiting room was looking at her like she'd lost her mind, which she kind of had.

"There's nothing wrong with being nervous." Trace's gaze swept over the gawkers as he said, "Someday I'll deserve to be socked in the jaw. You're just one step ahead, darlin'." He put an arm protectively around her. "Let's go get a look at our little cowpoke."

A few minutes later, Brindle lay on the examination table with her pants pushed below her belly and her sweater pulled up to her sternum as Dr. Bryant, a pretty thirtysomething with blondish-brown hair, put gel on Brindle's stomach. Trace sat in a chair beside the table, holding Brindle's hand.

"Are you excited to see your baby?" Dr. Bryant asked as she moved a wand over Brindle's stomach, applying just enough pressure to make Brindle feel like she was going to pee right there on the table.

"Yes," Brindle and Trace said at once. He held her hand so tight, she knew he was nervous, too, which made her even more nervous. *Nothing* rattled him. She looked over and he was staring intently at the monitor, the muscles in his neck corded tight.

"Good," Dr. Bryant said, focusing on the monitor as the grayish-black blobs took shape and their baby's profile became clear. A fast *whoosh*ing sound filled the room.

"Holy…" Trace rose to his feet, astonishment written in his wide, emotion-filled eyes and in the strength of his grip on Brindle's hand. "Is that him? Her? Our baby? What's that noise? Is something wrong?"

"No, Trace," Dr. Bryant said. "That is the sound of your baby's strong, healthy heartbeat." She pointed to the monitor, where the baby's arms were moving, it's hands sweeping near its mouth, its knees pulling up toward its chest. The image went out of focus, and she moved the wand, and it became clear again.

"Look, Brindle. Two hands, two legs." Tears glistened in Trace's eyes as he leaned down and kissed her. "That's our baby, darlin'. We did this. Look at it. It's perfect." His head whipped toward the doctor. "Is it perfect? Is everything okay? Can you tell? You should be able to tell, right?"

Dr. Bryant nodded and pointed to the screen as she spoke. "Everything looks good so far. This is your baby's heart. See it beating? And the spine looks good. This black area is amniotic fluid, which looks sufficient." She manipulated the machine. "I'm just taking a few measurements and pictures."

The baby moved in and out of focus.

"That's our baby, Brindle." Trace brushed her hair away from her face and kissed her forehead, her cheek, and her hand, murmuring about their baby and how incredible it was. Every word was filled with love. "It has your perky nose."

Brindle laugh-cried. "Is it a boy or girl?" She looked up at Trace and said, "You still want to know, right?"

"Yes, definitely," Trace agreed.

"Okay, let's see if the baby will cooperate." Dr. Bryant moved the wand, applying more pressure, and the baby shifted.

"I can't tell what we're looking at," Brindle said.

"I know. Hold on," Dr. Bryant said. "With any luck your little one will open its legs and give us a peek." She pointed to the monitor and said, "This is a leg, this is a leg, and this is your baby's bottom."

"Whoa! That baby's got a huge package," Trace exclaimed. "Just like his daddy."

"Actually, that's the umbilical cord," Dr. Bryant said kindly. "Everyone makes that mistake."

Brindle giggled, and she swore Trace blushed.

"Okay, we have visuals," Dr. Bryant said. "Congratulations. You're having a baby girl."

"Holy smokes, a *girl*." Trace kissed Brindle hard. "A girl, darlin'. We're having a girl."

As happy tears rolled down her cheeks, Brindle said, "We're going to need to read more parenting books."

AS THEY LEFT the doctor's office, Brindle chatted excitedly about telling their families, but Trace was only half listening. He couldn't stop looking at the sonogram picture Dr. Bryant had given them. Their baby had already been real in his mind, but seeing it on the monitor like that? Watching it move, seeing and hearing its heart beating, had brought *real* to a whole *new* level.

"I don't think we should tell anyone yet," Brindle said. "We should do something fun, like reveal the gender at the Turkey Trot. They'll all be there, your family and mine. What do you think? Trace? *Trace*, are you even listening to me?"

Brindle touched his arm, gazing up at him with those big blue eyes, which he now imagined on their little girl. Love swamped him like a tidal wave, and he stopped in the middle of the parking lot.

"What's wrong?" she asked.

"We're having a baby girl," he said absently, his mind trampling well past babyhood and toddler years to the images of teenage Brindle challenging him to kiss her. His protective urges surged, every muscle in his body flexing as tunnel vision took over. He snagged Brindle's hand, half running toward the truck.

"What's wrong? Where are we going?"

"To see Jeb," Trace ground out as he helped her into the passenger seat.

"About making a crib?"

"*That*, and to make sure he knows how to make a chastity belt."

Chapter Fifteen

TRACE AND BRINDLE didn't ask Jeb about the chastity belt after all. They decided to keep their baby's gender a secret and reveal it at the Turkey Trot. The week flew by with talks of baby names and parenting styles. Trace wanted to choose a name that their daughter wouldn't have to "live up to," which had confused Brindle at first. Then she realized what he was really saying was that he wanted their little girl to have a traditional name, like Mary or Margaret, so boys wouldn't hear it and think it was sexy. How could he not know that names had nothing to do with sexiness? Brindle knew Marys and Margarets who were hot enough to catch fire. They were also at odds with parenting styles. Brindle felt it was important that children be taught about everything, even touchy topics like sex and drinking, and that they be given enough rope to make mistakes so they could feel the sting and learn from them. But Trace appeared to have an overprotective-daddy streak she hadn't seen coming. *No boy-girl parties until she's sixteen. No thongs or sexy underwear—ever—and she's not dating until she's eighteen. We're getting one of those tracking apps on her phone. Actually, forget the phone; they only lead to trouble.*

It was Saturday morning, and Brindle was setting out snacks

for after the game. She looked across the football field at Trace standing on the sidelines and warmed all over. She'd bought him a black baseball cap with the No Limitz logo on the front. He looked rugged in a different way from when he wore his cowboy hat, bringing her right back to their high school days. That overprotective-daddy streak was sexy as hell, because who didn't want their man to protect their child? But she knew he was in for a hot shot of rebellion if he didn't ease up before their daughter was a teenager.

Luckily, she had plenty of time to talk some sense into him.

"Look at our baby sister going all domestic on us," Sable said as she and Amber approached. Amber's trusty companion Reno lifted his nose for some love.

"Hi, you guys. Thanks for coming out to support the team." Brindle reached down to pet Reno.

"Support the team, scope out the hot, single dads. Same-same." Sable crossed her arms over her quilted leather jacket, her jeans-clad hip jutting out as she smirked from beneath her black cowgirl hat. "I guess those meetings with the married minds are working."

They'd had another meeting the other evening. Morgyn was in Maryland visiting Graham's parents, so Grace had brought Sophie in her place. Sophie had Brenna, her baby girl, with her, and they'd spent more time admiring her and talking about midnight feedings, schedules—or lack thereof—and sneaking sexy times in while the baby napped, than they did about cooking and cleaning. That was just fine with Brindle. She hadn't thought about the lack of sleep, schedules, or privacy that would come along with motherhood. She'd not only scheduled *another* meeting of the married minds, which she realized she desperately needed, but she'd gone right home and discussed their upcoming potential *lack ofs* with Trace. Apparently he'd already been debriefed by his father, because he had it all figured out. *Don't worry, darlin'. The great thing about working on the ranch is that when you're on maternity leave, I can come home when the baby naps and take my Mustang for a ride, which'll free us up to sleep at night. Two birds, one stone,* he'd said with a wink.

They'd started moving her things into Trace's house, and she found herself wanting to do more for him, so learning to cook was high on her list of priorities. The cleaning? Not so much.

"I'm trying, but I'm still better in the bedroom than I am in the kitchen," Brindle said. "I do want to learn to cook, though."

"If that's what having a baby does to you, then count me out," Sable said.

"Count me in!" Amber flipped her brown hair over her shoulder and reached into the snack bag, helping Brindle set out juice boxes. "I can't wait to do things like this. I want to be the snack mom, the carpool mom, and make family dinners, sew Halloween costumes…" There were potential complications associated with epilepsy and pregnancy, and Amber was aware of them. She'd talked on and off about adoption and surrogacy.

"You'll be an incredible mother," Brindle said. "You've got the patience of a saint."

Sable's gaze swept over the bags of sliced apples and carrot sticks, pretzels, Goldfish crackers, and Pirate's Booty, and she said, "Think you went a little overboard with the snacks?"

"I looked up snack ideas online and there was a huge list," Brindle said as she set more bags of Pirate's Booty on the table. "I don't know what the kids like or what their parents are used to bringing for snacks. I asked about food allergies, and we're clear there. I want to support Trace's coaching in every way I can. Besides, it's the last game of the season, and I didn't want to let any of the kids down. This way they have choices."

Sable grabbed a juice box from the bag of snacks and looked at it. "These things are tiny." She set it on the table and said, "So...Are you ready to tell us if you're going to have a cowboy or a dancing girl?"

"Sorry, sis, but my lips are sealed. You'll find out the same time everyone else does, at the Turkey Trot." Not only had her and Trace's families been begging for answers, but her students and the other teachers were, too. She and Trace had come up with the perfect gender reveal, and Brindle's lips were sealed.

"You know you and Trace have more hashtags now, right?" Amber informed her. "There's Team Trindle Filly for a girl and Team Trindle Colt for a boy. The whole town is making bets."

"I know," Brindle said, spotting Jeb and Chet heading their way from the parking lot. Jeb was watching Trace like a hawk. "Some of my students made T-shirts. I can't believe our pregnancy is that interesting to the whole town."

"Why wouldn't it be?" Amber said. "The two least likely people to ever settle down are having a baby and moving in together. You two are what urban legends are made of. People will still be talking about Team Trindle when we're old and gray."

"Are you guys in on those wagers?" Brindle asked her sisters as Jeb and Chet joined them.

"Is she really asking Amber which team she bats for?" Jeb teased.

Amber rolled her eyes. "I'm Team Filly." She glared at Jeb and said, "And *no* comments from the peanut gallery."

"Hey, it's all good," Jeb said.

Amber added, "I can't wait to see Trace with a baby girl in his arms."

"Down, girl," Brindle teased. "That's my man you want to ogle."

"I'm Team Colt," Sable said, eyeing Chet. "Every generation needs hard-bodied men who are good with their hands."

Chet and Jeb chuckled.

Brindle set her hand on her hip. "Okay, hold up. It feels weird to hear you say that about my potential future son—your nephew."

"I meant to train horses and work with power tools," Sable said. "Geez, get your mind out of the gutter. What are you, Chet?" she asked with a seductive lilt to her voice. "Team Colt or Team Filly?"

"That's a trick question if I've ever heard one," Jeb said, nudging Chet with his elbow.

Chet held Sable's stare as he said, "Personally, I'm into *women*, not horses. But as far as Trace and Brindle's baby goes, I'm Team Colt. I'm not sure Oak Falls can handle a Montgomery-Jericho filly."

Sable lifted her chin at the surly firefighter with a look that would have most men stepping back. Chet stood taller, meeting her challenging stare with one of his own.

"You got a problem with strong women, Hudson?" Sable asked.

"Nope. Strong suits me just fine. But strong and *reckless*? That's a dangerous combination."

"Shouldn't a badass fireman like you be prepared for anything? Reckless can be fun." Sable flashed an arrogant smile, her eyes raking down his body. "Unless your hose isn't capable of dealing with the flames?"

Chet stepped closer to Sable, the muscles in his jaw strung tight. "There's nothing I can't handle."

"Holy smokes," Amber whispered to Brindle. "I thought you and Trace were hot."

As Sable and Chet had a stare down that could melt steel, Brindle finished setting up the snacks, and Amber headed over to the sidelines. Jeb stood with his feet planted hip distance apart, arms crossed, chin dipped low, and his eyes locked on Trace, oblivious to the Chet and Sable drama unfolding just a few feet away.

"He's really good with the kids, isn't he?" Brindle said. She was proud of Trace for finally taking steps toward doing the things he loved beyond ranching. Trace hadn't told his family that he was thinking of coaching next year. He said he wanted to be sure before getting anyone riled up over changing schedules and hiring more help for the ranch, but at least he was exploring it as a possibility.

Jeb nodded, jaw tight. "If you have a boy, he could coach him one day."

"Mm-hm," she agreed, though she was dying to say, *We're having a girl!* Keeping their secret was torture. She'd almost blurted it out with Trixie yesterday when she stopped by the ranch to see Trace. She'd have to duct tape her mouth shut if she wasn't careful.

"He never should have given up those scholarships," Jeb said. "He had a promising career in football."

"I know. If I were a better person, I'd have broken up with him for good back then, so he'd have gone away to school. But I was selfish. I loved him too much."

"That wouldn't have done it anyway." Jeb turned toward her with a serious expression. "He'd never have left even if he believed you were really done with him. My brother doesn't give up, and his love for you was too deep even back then. I knew it before he'd even graduated from high school. If he were JJ or Shane, I'd have thought differently. But Trace has always loved hard and forever. Ask him someday about Riviera."

"His old dog?" She knew he'd had a basset hound named Riviera when he was young.

"Yeah. She got real sick, and my parents should have put her down. She was incontinent, could only eat if the food was pureed, and she'd whine so loud half the night she kept the whole family awake." Jeb stared just past Brindle, as if he were reliving the memory. "Trace wouldn't let them put her down. He couldn't bear to say goodbye to her, so he made her diapers, pureed her food, and slept in the barn with her for a month, until she passed away in her sleep. He couldn't have been older than eight or nine."

"Aw, he must have been heartbroken."

"He was, and after she died he scared the piss out of our parents. They thought he ran away in the middle of the night because he was so grief stricken. Our old man found him sleeping in the barn. The fool did that every night for a week until my father finally forbade him." Jeb sighed heavily and said, "That love and loyalty goes for the people in his life—you, our family, friends—and for the work he does. Ranching is in his blood, Brindle, like my father and Shane, and to a point, Trixie. Although she's got other dreams to fulfill. But Trace would be miserable if he didn't work the ranch. What I hadn't realized until these past few weeks when he started working with the kids was that he needs *this* in his life, too."

"Right?" was all Brindle could manage. "I'm so glad you see that!"

He nodded. "He was a miserable son of a bitch while you were gone. When you two used to fight, working with the animals would get that ornery shit out of his system. But that wasn't enough when you were gone. When I first heard he was helping Sin, I wondered if he'd be able to shake missing you enough to be patient with the kids. But it's like being around them filled at least some of the gap you'd left behind."

"I'm sorry I left for so long, but we both needed to grow up."

"It's been painful watching you two play games for so long. But I'm glad you're both figuring it out." Jed slid his hands into his coat pockets and said, "He's going to make a great father, and I hope he'll keep this up, too."

As he headed for the sidelines, Brindle said, "I hope you'll tell him that."

Jeb turned with an amused grin. "You think anyone can tell Trace anything that'll make a difference?" He shook his head and said, "You are two stubborn peas in a pod. This has to be *his* idea, but you probably already figured that out."

Figured it out? As cheers rang out and the players barreled into Trace, hooting and hollering because they won the game, she wondered how she could have been such a fool. They really were two stubborn peas in a pod. She thought she'd been planting seeds about coaching, but she'd really shoved them down so deep they risked suffocation. She'd also thought escaping Oak Falls had given her the clarity she needed to find the answers she was looking for, but it turned out those answers were only a starting point.

As the kids ran over to collect their snacks, Trace's eyes locked on hers, and he grinned with his team's victory. A familiar zing of heat skated through her veins, reminding her that their true answers could only be found through the power of #TeamTrindle.

Chapter Sixteen

TRACE COULD COUNT on many things in his small hometown, like gossip running thicker than sludge in a creek, a community that rallied together in hard times and came out in droves in celebration of events like the Turkey Trot, and unpredictable weather that could thwart one's plans at a moment's notice. Luckily it wasn't snow they faced Thanksgiving morning, but an unusually warm, sunny day. Perfect weather for the 5K race, but not so perfect for the plans they had for their gender reveal. But his quick-thinking girlfriend had found a solution, and a little paint had done the trick.

Trace's brothers and friends stood with the crowd of runners beneath the enormous banner hanging over Main Street announcing the race and marking the start and finish lines. Usually, there were fall-colored balloons dancing above the banner, but this year the balloons were pink and blue with #TEAMTRINDLECOLT and #TEAMTRINDLEFILLY printed on them. Main Street Sweets, the local bakery, had set up tables along the sidewalk and were selling pink and blue lemonade, blueberry and strawberry pies, and pink and blue frosted cookies. Spectators and racers wore pink or blue shirts with the Trindle hashtags and matching wristbands. Hell, even Trace's father sported a pink wristband, while his mother wore a blue one. While he and Brindle had planned to do their gender reveal at the end of the race, they'd had nothing to do with the balloons, bracelets, food, or T-shirts. They were both shocked to find themselves at the center of so much excitement.

"Let's go, Trace!" Beckett hollered, waving him over.

Trace held up his finger. "Almost done, darlin'?" Brindle was pinning his number on the back of his shirt.

"Yup." She looked adorable in the new maternity jeans and top she'd bought with Grace and Morgyn. She'd gone shopping just in time. Rubber bands no longer did the trick. "You're all set to win."

"Can you at least tell us how you're going to do the reveal?" Trixie asked. She was sporting a bright pink and black flannel shirt tied at the waist and a matching pink wristband.

"Nope," Trace said, pulling Brindle into his arms. In the past, she'd walked the race to set a good example for her students, but this year she wanted to cheer Trace on, and he fucking loved that.

"You suck," Trixie said. "I'll remember this when I have a secret you want to know."

Trace narrowed his eyes. "You have secrets?"

Trixie, Lindsay, and Brindle laughed. He didn't like the idea of Trixie having secrets, but he had bigger things on his mind than what secrets his sister was keeping. Mainly, winning this race and finally revealing the gender of their baby so his family would get off his back. His mother had tried to sweet-talk it out of him, while his brothers had tried to bully it out of him. His father had tried buddying up, sharing stories about when each of his children were born, trying to coax it out, father to father. While Trace loved having that new commonality with his father, he'd stayed strong and kept their secret. But it was Trixie's efforts that had amused him the most. She'd tried a little of everything. She'd brought him cookies, called him names, and even offered to dish long-held secrets about Brindle. The thing was, he knew more about Brindle than Trixie—or anyone else—ever would. He didn't cave.

But he'd be glad when the time came for their big announcement, because he hated secrets almost as much as he'd hated being away from Brindle.

"I still can't get over how much everyone is pulling for us," Trace said to Brindle.

"I know. It's crazy, isn't it? I plan on taste testing the cookies while I'm cheering you on." Brindle had been ravenous lately—in the kitchen and in the bedroom.

"Did you have a hand in all this pink and blue, Lindsay?" Trace asked.

"Who, *me*?" Lindsay's feigned innocence gave her away.

"Linds, as fabulous as this is, why didn't you tell me?" Brindle asked.

"Did *you* clue me in on the gender of your baby? See what happens when you mess with the party princess?" Lindsay said smugly. "But I can't take full credit. I found an order form for the balloons on Nana's kitchen counter. She and her partner in crime, Hellie, had already ordered them. That was my inspiration for the bracelets and T-shirts. Once those were ordered, word spread fast. We had hundreds of orders before they were even made."

"I can't believe you guys didn't hear about it sooner," Trixie said.

Lindsay waved her hand and said, "That would be because of my threats. I told everyone who ordered one that if they let the cat out of the bag to Trace and Brindle, I'd not only never plan an event for them, but that I'd sabotage whatever events they held."

"*Man*, you're vicious," Trace said.

"Attention, racers," boomed from the speakers by the podium where the mayor was announcing the race. "Please take your places. The race will begin in exactly five minutes."

"Gotta jet, darlin'." Trace kissed Brindle and said, "Wish me luck."

He noticed everyone around them lifting their phones, taking pictures of the two of them kissing. He didn't know how he felt about pictures of him and Brindle all over social media, but heck, she was his, and any way he looked at it, people knowing about it was a damn good thing.

"You don't need luck," Brindle said. "You're already the winner in my book."

"God, you two are so cheesy right now," Trixie said.

"We're ready to cheer you on!" Lindsay reached into a bag beside her feet and whipped out pink and blue pom-poms. She handed them to Brindle and Trixie.

Trace shook his head and headed into the street to join the other racers.

"About damn time," Jeb said, sporting a blue #TeamTrindleColt shirt and wristband. "You all stretched out?"

Trace's stretching had come in horizontal form earlier that morning with his beautiful girlfriend. "I'm good."

"Not good enough to win, because that's going to be me this year," Beckett said.

Shane scoffed. "If you can see through the smoke I leave behind." He was the only one of the Jericho brothers wearing a pink #TeamTrindleFilly shirt.

"You think I'm having a girl?" Trace asked.

"You're not manly enough to produce a son," Shane said. Then he high-fived some dude wearing pink behind him.

"Jackass," Trace uttered. "It takes a bigger man to raise a daughter than a son."

"One-minute warning," the mayor announced, and the runners got into position.

"Does that mean he's having a girl?" Chet asked, starting a debate among the others.

When the horn sounded, Trace took off fast, determined to win. Chet and Reed kept pace with him and peppered him with questions, which made him want to push himself to run faster, just to escape their inquisition.

"So? It's a girl?" Reed asked.

"He's just throwing us off," Chet said. "Right?"

Reed said, "Dirty trick, dude."

Shane and JJ caught up to them, and within seconds, Beckett and Jeb started asking questions like, "Has Brindle bought baby clothes? Are they pink or blue?" and "What names are you thinking of?"

"You need to have a kid every year," Chet said as they neared the end of the first mile marker. Spectators lined the streets, cheering them on. "The turnout hasn't ever been this good."

There were only a handful of guys ahead of them when they turned at the halfway mark and headed down a parallel street.

"Think you and Brindle can stop by my shop this week to look at designs for your crib?" Jeb asked.

"Yeah. Sounds good. Thanks for doing that."

"No sweat, bro. Want to tell me what color to paint it?" Jeb asked with a sly grin.

"White." Trace sprinted off, leaving Jeb's disgruntled sounds in his wake. As he ran, he thought about how his brothers and friends had always been there for him, and he hoped his daughter would find the same long-lasting friendships. He thought about who else had kids or was pregnant, and though Sophie and Brett came to mind, one child in their circle of friends wasn't nearly enough.

At the second mile marker, he blew past the guys who were ahead of him, and one by one, Shane, Reed, and Beckett caught up, giving him shit about holding his secret, but Trace kept his eyes trained on the road, determined to win.

"Reed, you and Grace planning on having kids?" Trace asked when the finish line came into view.

"At some point."

"Care to wager?" Trace taunted.

"On the gender of your child?"

"On yours. If I beat you, you guys have a baby right away."

Reed laughed. "And when I win? You'll let me in on the secret?"

"Sure." He wasn't going to lose to Reed.

"You're on," Reed said, and sprinted toward the finish line.

There was a collective murmur of curses as Trace took off after him. He was neck and neck with Reed when Brindle's cheers carried into his ears. She was shaking pink and blue pompoms, yelling, "Come on, cowboy!"

Seeing her cheering for him should have made his legs move faster, but only his heart took off in the right direction as he ran to the sidelines, vaguely aware of people taking pictures and videos, hollering at him to finish the race as he said, "Come on, darlin'. Time for us to shine."

He took her hand, walking fast toward the finish line, kissing and laughing.

"I love you, Mustang," he said as they crossed the finish line surrounded by other runners. Then, with his starry-eyed girl beside him, he whipped his shirt over his head, revealing the bright pink paint on his chest and abs that read IT'S A GIRL! and #TEAMTRINDLEFILLY on his back. Cheers and congratulations rang out in front of them, while laughter sounded behind them.

"What are they laughing at?" He looked over his shoulder.

"I might have also painted 'Property of Brindle Montgomery' on your back." She unexpectedly whipped off her shirt, revealing a pink tank top with #TEAMTRINDLEFILLY written across her belly in black marker. More cheers rang out as she turned around, showing Trace where she'd written PROPERTY OF TRACE JERICHO on the back.

He kissed her as the crowd converged on them in a mass of cheers and embraces.

A long while later, after it seemed like the whole town had congratulated them, Trace's brothers and friends gave him shit for their losses in the baby-gender wagers.

"I'm out seventy-five bucks, man. Not cool," Sin said.

"You owe me a hundred bucks," JJ said.

Trace shook his head. "It's not my fault you were dumb enough to bet."

"Dude, I can't believe you didn't win the race," Reed said. "You were right there with me, and then you were gone."

A few feet away, Brindle was eating pink cookies with their mothers and showing off their sonogram picture, while stealing glances at Trace. She turned her back to him, flashing the writing on her shirt, and she looked over her shoulder with a seductive glimmer in her eyes. She'd claimed him in front of the whole town. It might have seemed like a small, unnecessary gesture to some, but Trace knew how important independence was to Brindle. He might not have won the race, but he was definitely the biggest winner of all.

THEY FACETIMED AXSEL, Morgyn, and Pepper from the race so they could see the balloons and T-shirts and feel the excitement of their big day. Sable had already clued them in on the bets. Morgyn and Axsel had bet they were having a girl, but Pepper had wagered for a boy. Pepper had purely scientific reasons behind her choice, something that had to do with male sperm swimming faster than female and Brindle's overeager eggs. Regardless of the bets, everyone seemed genuinely excited for them. Although Brindle's mother had taken a little *too much* pleasure in the idea of Brindle trying to raise a daughter who could turn out as rebellious and stubborn as she was. Of course, with Brindle's luck she'd have a girly-girl who was all about frills and lace, and she'd have no idea how to relate to her.

Perhaps in addition to meetings of the married minds, she needed to start penciling in some time with Amber to learn how the other half lives.

Now they were back at home, getting ready to have Thanksgiving dinner with Trace's family and dessert with her family. Brindle had offered to make the pies. Not that she had any baking experience beyond slicing premade cookie dough, half of which ended up in her stomach and not the oven, but she wanted to contribute. And now she had something to prove since most of her sisters had suggested their mother make pies *just in case* something went wrong. As if she couldn't handle baking pies? She'd show them!

"Hey, darlin', you got the pies in the oven yet?" Trace called down the second-story bridge that ran between the guest room and the master bedroom, overlooking the kitchen and living room.

"Yes," she called up to him. Her mother had shared her great-grandmother's famous bourbon pumpkin pie with pecan streusel recipe. Brindle made two pies, and they'd looked amazing when she'd put them in the oven.

She wiped her hands and looked up at Trace leaning over the bridge, watching her.

"Can you come up here for a sec? I want to show you something."

"Sure."

She remembered when he'd bought the cabin. He'd gotten it for a steal because it had been empty for quite a few years and had needed a lot of work. Brindle would never forget the pride in his eyes when he'd shown her the house. She'd seen the same look in his eyes when she'd agreed to move in with him. They'd already moved in most of her belongings, though they were still figuring out what to do with some of her furniture. Her lease wasn't up for a few months, so they had time to figure that out.

Trace met her at the top of the stairs wearing only a pair of jeans. He smelled fresh from his shower and looked handsome with his wet hair brushed away from his face.

"What's up?" Her eyes trailed down his body.

He pulled her against him and said, "Eyes up here, darlin', unless you want to end up naked."

She bit her lower lip, her insides already thrumming with desire. Nana hadn't been kidding about pregnancy hormones. She was hornier than a dog in heat.

He kissed her lower lip free and said, "I might have to keep you pregnant all the time."

She playfully swatted him, and he chuckled.

"Come with me." He reached for her hand, leading her into the guest room. The heavy wooden dresser and headboard gave the room a masculine feel.

Each of the bedrooms was built at one end of the A-frame and had four triangular windows that connected with wooden frames, forming one big triangle. The top triangle, and the two bottom triangles twisted open, while the middle, upside-down triangular window was stationary. The master bedroom overlooked the creek in the backyard, while the guest room had a beautiful view of the front yard.

The bedrooms were large, with slanted walls. "I'm thinking about putting in a knee wall with storage behind it. That way the crib can sit against a straight wall."

"A nursery," she said softly. They'd been so busy, she hadn't even begun thinking about the nursery. She loved that he had.

"Our little girl needs one. I thought we could put a rocking chair by the window, and maybe a dresser and changing table over there." He pointed across the room. "What do you think?"

"I think that sounds perfect, and I'm sorry I didn't think of it first."

He drew her into his arms and said, "You've been busy with drama club auditions, grading papers, our gender reveal, meeting with your mom and sisters, planning surprises for me..."

"Still. I should have thought of it." The auditions had gone well but had taken two full afternoons.

"We're a team. You brought me dinner at the ranch last night when I worked late. That's what it's all about, teamwork."

He kissed her. "Jeb asked what color we wanted the crib. I told him white, but that was just because we hadn't revealed our little cowpoke as a girl yet. If you want it pink, we can do that."

"Pink?" She wasn't a big fan of pink furniture, but this was Trace's baby, too, and she didn't want to rip him off if he had visions of pink in his head. "What do you want?"

He waggled his brows and kissed her again. "What I want." *Kiss, kiss.* "Has nothing to do with paint colors."

"But you brought it up," she said as she leaned her head to the side, giving him better access for those enticing kisses.

"It seemed like a good idea at the time." He kissed her softly and said, "But now you're in my arms, and my mind went someplace even more intriguing."

Oh, how she loved that!

"White?" He slicked his tongue around the shell of her ear. "Yellow?" He kissed her cheek. "Green?" He gazed deeply into her eyes and said, "*You. Naked.*"

"I like that idea best of all."

"Me too."

He lowered his lips to hers, kissing her hungrily. As they always had, they quickly lost themselves in each other, tearing at their clothes, as if it had been weeks rather than hours since they'd last made love.

"I'll never get enough of you," he said, kissing and groping her nakedness.

Every touch of his lips sent sparks searing beneath her skin. She pushed at his briefs, and he stripped them off. A wolfish grin spread across his handsome face as he hooked his fingers in the side of her panties, pulling them off as he kissed a path straight down her belly.

He rubbed his hands over her baby bump and then he

kissed it and said, "It's that time again, sweetness. Buckle up for a wild ride while Daddy satisfies Mama's every whim."

"I love *whim time*," Brindle said as they stumbled to the bed.

They lay on their sides, kissing and groping, teasing each other into panting, pleading frenzies. He rolled onto his back and locked his hands around her waist, lifting and guiding her so she was straddling his face. He covered her sex with his mouth, and electricity shot through her. She grabbed the headboard with one hand and his hair with the other as he masterfully drove her out of her mind. She tugged on his hair, earning a lustful growl. He clutched her ass so tight his nails dug into her flesh, and the roughness sent her spiraling into oblivion. Her hips bucked, her sex pulsed, and his name flew from her lungs loud and uninhibited. Just when she began coming down from the clouds, he did it again, hard and purposeful, and she shattered against his mouth. He stayed with her through the last aftershock. Then he kissed her inner thighs soft as a feather as he teased her oversensitive nerves with his fingers, keeping her at the brink of madness.

It took her a second to catch up as he slithered out from between her legs, grabbing her hips from behind.

"Let go of the headboard, darlin'," he commanded with a touch of Southern charm that did her in.

Her limbs trembled as she pushed back, needing more, but Trace took his time, rubbing his shaft against her sex until the length was slick with her arousal. One hand moved up her body, cupping her breast as he kissed her spine. His chest and leg hair tickled her skin, and the pressure of his arousal sliding between her legs made her swell with desire.

"Trace, please. I need *more*."

She moved his hand from her breast to between her legs, nearly shooting off the bed when he zeroed in on the spot he knew so well. Lights exploded behind her closed lids, and she arched back. She felt the broad head of his erection pressing against her entrance, and she thrust her hips back, forcing him into her in one fast motion.

"Aw, *fuck*, darlin'." He fisted his hand in her hair, pulling just hard enough to send shocks of lightning to her core.

"Yes! Take me hard, Trace. Don't hold back."

He pounded into her, groping and tugging on her hair as she coaxed, challenged, and praised his every effort. He was a sexual god, an orgasm *king*, and he was all *hers*.

THEY LAY TOGETHER afterward, floating in a lust-filled haze.

"Sarah Louise," Trace said as he ran his fingers over her belly.

"*Brindle*, asshole," she teased.

He kissed her lips and said, "The baby, Brin. My grandmother's name was Louise. I never really knew her, but I've heard stories about how amazing she was. I was thinking that it might be nice to honor her by using her name."

"Aw, that's really sweet, but Sarah is a little plain, don't you think?"

"It's feminine and strong."

She looked at him, and he kissed the tip of her nose. "I can get on board with your grandma's name as a middle name, but I'm not sold on Sarah. What if we just jumble those letters a little? Sahara?"

"Nope. Guys will make jokes about her being dry as a desert."

"Only if they want to deal with my fist hitting their mouths."

"That's my girl." He kissed her again. "Rachel?"

"That's pretty. Emily? We could call her Emma."

"I like that. Emma Lou."

She gave him a deadpan stare. "No. You're not calling our daughter Emma Lou. That makes her sound too country."

"Do you know where we live? We're about as country as it gets."

He placed his hand on her belly, and she felt a flutter beneath it. Her eyes flew wide open. "Did you feel that?"

"Feel what?"

"The baby! I think it moved." She pressed her hands to her belly. "Maybe it'll move again." They stared at her belly, and a few minutes later she felt the fluttering again. "There! Did you feel that?"

"No. Are you sure it's not just all those cookies you ate?"

"I don't know. I've never been pregnant before, but all the books talk about a fluttering, and this is *definitely* a flutter."

He pressed a kiss to her baby bump and said, "Emma Lou, can you move for Daddy?"

She smiled at his tenderness. "She's not moving. She doesn't like it."

"Or maybe she's just stubborn like her mama and she doesn't want to *admit* to liking it." He kissed her belly, and then he kissed her lips and placed his hand over her belly. "Let's see if we can get her to move. How about Jessica?"

"That's pretty, too. But kind of overused. What about Shiloh? Vivica? Monica?" she suggested, catching wind of a faint beeping noise, but she was more interested in the names Trace was tossing out.

"Kelly? Clara? Maribelle? Lucy?"

"Shh. Do you hear that?" She sat up, listening more intently. "What is that noise?"

He pulled her down to the mattress. "The sound of my body begging for more."

"Trace, I'm serious." She pushed up again, and the long, faint beeping noise finally registered. "Oh my gosh. The pies!"

She pulled on her tank top and underwear and Trace reached for his briefs. "I hope I didn't ruin them!" She rushed out of the bedroom and saw smoke coming from the oven. "Shit!"

She ran down the stairs and grabbed the oven mitts. Trace was right behind her.

He snagged the mitts from her and opened the oven. Smoke poured out. "Get the window before the smoke alarm goes off."

She opened the windows as he pulled the burned pies from the oven. "I had one job for Thanksgiving. *One!* All I wanted was to do this right, and what do I do? I—"

"You loved your boyfriend," Trace said, pulling her in close.

"That's not an excuse, Trace. What am I going to do, say *Sorry, everyone. I was horny, but I had fun, so…?*" Her pulse raced as the importance of the pies magnified in her mind.

Trace chuckled, and she glowered at him.

"Sorry, but they're just pies, darlin'. We'll go buy some at the store."

She stared at the smoke swirling in the breeze and said, "The bakery is closed. It's a holiday, remember?"

"I'm sure they have frozen pies at the dollar store, and

they're always open."

"Don't you see? They're not *just* pies. They're symbolic of who I am in everyone else's eyes. I'm the reckless one, the rebellious girl who's better at sex than being domestic. I wanted to prove them wrong. I don't want to be Sara Lee, serving frozen pies. I want to be Martha Fucking Stewart and bring perfect home-baked pies for Thanksgiving!"

Trace's eyes narrowed. He strode over to the refrigerator and pulled out the carton of milk. "Grab the boxes of chocolate pudding from the pantry, and the graham crackers."

"Why?" She grabbed both from the pantry.

"My girl wants to bring homemade pies, and I'm going to make it happen." He washed his hands and said, "We've got this, darlin'. Now get over here and wash your hands, or we're going to be late."

As she washed her hands, she said, "What are we doing with instant pudding? And why do you even have it?"

"We're making chocolate pudding pies. I bought it for a special occasion that would end with us naked." He waggled his brows.

"*Oh.* I really like your surprises."

They threw out the burned pies, and while Brindle washed the pie pans, Trace left the room, returning with his hammer.

"What's *that* for?"

"We have to make the crust." He grabbed two Ziploc quart bags and put the packages of graham crackers in them. Then he wrapped them in a clean towel and beat them with the hammer.

She laughed. "You could just break them with your hands like normal people do."

"I don't know what type of people you hang out with, but that doesn't sound nearly as effective. What makes the crust stick together?"

"I don't know. I've never made graham cracker crust. I'll google it." She grabbed her phone from the counter and began searching. "We need sugar and butter."

"On it!"

They made two beautiful chocolate pudding pies. Afterward, they used their fingers to eat the extra chocolate from the bowl, feeding it to each other, and ended up with chocolate pudding everywhere.

Brindle giggled as Trace licked chocolate from her chest. "We're breaking my family's tradition of eating my great-grandmother's pies."

"We're starting our own tradition." He kissed her belly and said, "Right, Regina Louise? From now on, we have pudding pies on Thanksgiving."

"You are *not* calling our daughter that." She looked at their pies and said, "I'm never going to be one of those moms who all the kids love to visit because she makes the best treats. I'll never be Martha Fucking Stewart."

He rose to his full height and lifted her onto the counter. "You'll be the cool mom who kids want to spend time with because you make them laugh and you listen when they talk." He pressed his lips to hers and said, "You're one-of-a-kind, big-hearted, seductively sinful Brindle Fucking Montgomery, and you're better at sex than baking, which your boyfriend happens to adore." He dragged his finger through the bowl, and then he painted her lower lip with the chocolate and kissed it off. "If you want to learn to bake, I'm in. But make no mistake, darlin'. I think you're perfect just as you are, and our daughter will, too."

Chapter Seventeen

THANKSGIVING HAD ALWAYS been a celebration of family, but this year, with Trace by her side, their baby in her belly, and the new start to their relationship, the word *family* had taken on a whole new meaning. When they'd gone around the table sharing what they were thankful for, it wasn't just the unconditional support of both of their families and the support of their community Brindle was thankful for. She was thankful for the time she'd spent in Paris learning about herself and about counting to five, or ten, or even sometimes twenty, because whatever it took to make things better for her and Trace was worth it.

Family wasn't the only thing with a new definition. What Brindle and Trace had together finally had a meaningful label. They had a loving *relationship* and Brindle knew it would get even better with time.

A week after their first wonderful Thanksgiving as a couple with their families, Brindle gazed out their kitchen window at Trace traipsing across the front yard carrying an enormous bundle of Christmas lights as JJ and Jeb set up ladders to help him string them. Her heart was full. Her family had applauded her effort to make their traditional pies and teased her about burning them, and his family had thought the pudding pies were scrumptious. Nancy Jericho offered to give Brindle their family recipes, too, and to help her learn anything else she wanted to about being a wife. Although Nancy had winked and said from what she'd heard, Brindle was sharing all sorts of lovely relationship secrets with others in the meetings of the married minds. She'd even mentioned joining in on the next one.

"Let's go, pretty mama," Trixie teased as she came to Brindle's side in the living room. She and Lindsay had come to help her decorate the Christmas tree, and later, Brindle and Trace were cooking everyone dinner. "You can't stare at my brother *all* day."

"Wanna bet?" Brindle said, picking up another ornament.

"She's all domesticated now, like a tamed stray cat," Lindsay said as she arranged holiday candles and greenery along the mantel, and they all burst into hysterics.

"That'll be the day." Trixie glanced outside to where the guys were now wrestling in the front yard. "Some things will never change."

And some things can, Brindle thought happily.

They went back to decorating, and a little while later, the front door opened and Sable and Amber came in, their cowgirl boots clicking across the hardwood floors.

"Is this where the party is?" Sable held up a tray of cookies from the Pastry Palace. "We brought food, and Grace, Reed, and Chet were right behind us."

"Who said there was a *party*?" Brindle asked, mentally going through her refrigerator, trying to figure out how to cook for more people.

"I don't remember. Nana, maybe, when she came into the

bookstore yesterday." Amber shrugged off her coat and laid it on the back of the couch.

Nana? Brindle looked at Lindsay, wondering what her grandmother, who loved to celebrate every little thing, was up to now.

"Don't look at me. All I did was tell her we were decorating your house," Lindsay said. "She might have immediately gotten on the phone with Hellie, though…"

"Oh no." Brindle laughed. "Our house is way too little for one of Nana's celebrations."

"That's not true. Mom has always said that when a house becomes a home, it's even better when it's full of people who love you. And look how *pretty* your *home* is. You have pictures of you and Trace on the mantel, too!" Amber hugged Brindle. "I'm just so happy for you."

More than anything, Brindle hoped that one day Amber would meet her soul mate, someone who would love her for all she was and never let her down. "Thanks, Amb. It feels amazing to come home to Trace every day. I wish we'd come to our senses a long time ago."

Sable snort-laughed. "For what it's worth, we had a lot of fun in your pre-domestic life."

Jeb, Chet, and Trace barreled through the front door in a fit of laughter and slaps on the back. Chet's eyes met Sable's, and though his expression turned serious, Brindle felt the heat between them from across the room. Amber and Lindsay were whispering, eyeing JJ and Shane as they came through the door.

Brindle rubbed her hands together and said, "Don't worry, sis. I have a feeling our good times have only just begun."

FRIENDS AND FAMILY arrived throughout the afternoon, filling their house to the brim with unexpected, and very welcome, guests. Trace had always loved his privacy, but watching Brindle in the role of hostess was as adorable as it was sexy, and he loved being the host because it was with her by his side. In between making sure there was enough food for everyone and mingling, they stole kisses and silently touched base with furtive glances.

Brindle had been so busy enjoying herself, she hadn't even noticed when he and the guys had snuck upstairs to prepare the surprise he'd hidden for two days.

"I think we're ready," Chet said as they came down the stairs. "But promise me you'll turn off all the tree lights before you go to bed at night."

"Of course, man," Trace said. "Think I'd put Brindle or our baby in danger?"

"Always the fireman," Shane teased.

"I know. Sorry." Chet had lost both his parents in a fire, and his brother, Boyd, had suffered severe burns.

Trace put his hand on Chet's shoulder and said, "Don't be. One day I might need the reminder. When I get old and senile, it'll be your voice keeping me safe. Come on. Let's light this party up."

There was standing room only in the living area, so Trace stood on the steps and raised his voice among the din of their friends. "Who's ready to see the lights?"

Cheers rang out as everyone scrambled for their coats and headed out the front door, into the snowy night. Trace put his warmest winter coat around Brindle, keeping her in the house for a moment after everyone else rushed out. He gazed into her eyes, seeing a settledness that had developed recently. It looked good on her.

He put his hand on her belly and said, "How're my girls holding up?"

"According to our moms, we've started a new post-Thanksgiving, pre-Christmas tradition, and it feels pretty great. I never imagined having all of this, and now I can't imagine a life without it."

"Me too, darlin'." He lowered his lips to hers.

"Cripes, you two," Sable said as she came through the door. "Can't you keep it in your pants for a little while longer? We're freezing out there."

"Jealous?" Trace asked, earning one of Sable's trademarked glares as they followed her out.

His parents stood arm in arm beside some of their friends. Brindle's father had one arm around Amber, the other around her mother. He wished Pepper and Axsel could have been there, but from the way Trixie, Lindsay, Grace, and Reed were huddled around Grace's phone, he had a feeling they were FaceTiming at least one of them.

"Go on, babe," Trace said to Brindle. "Find a place where you can see."

"Let's go, lover boy. I'm getting grayer over here," Nana called out from beneath her fake-fur hat. She and Hellie had set up this whole night, spreading the word among their closest friends and family that it was time to *christen* another Jericho home.

Trace couldn't be happier.

"I've got this," Jeb said as he joined Trace on the porch.

"Go in the yard with Brindle so you can experience the first look together, and don't worry; Shane is videoing it for you."

"Thanks, man."

"Hey," Jeb said as Trace stepped off the porch. "You look good as a family man."

How could one sentence get Trace choked up?

He went to Brindle's side, and when he gave Jeb a nod, Jeb plugged in the lights, breathing even more life into their home. White lights decorated the frame and windows, and through the second-floor window, a white Christmas tree with pink lights and a vibrant pink star lit up the nursery.

There was a collective gasp, followed by everyone talking at once. But it was the happy tears in Brindle's eyes that Trace was looking at as she threw her arms around his neck, thanking him in between kisses.

"It's so gorgeous." *Kiss, kiss.* "When did you do this? I didn't see you carry in a tree!"

"I can't give away all my secrets."

"This is the most spectacular surprise ever!"

He gazed into her beautiful eyes and said, "This is only the beginning, Mustang. I've got a lifetime of surprises in store for you."

Chapter Eighteen

TRACE CLOSED THE equipment shed and headed for his truck. He lifted his hat and swept his arm across his forehead as Jeb pulled up. Trace righted his hat as his brother stepped from his truck, sawdust clinging to his jeans and shirt.

"Hey, Trace. You look whipped."

Trace dug his keys from his pocket. "Just frustrated. I've been working on the tractor all afternoon, but I can't seem to find the cause of the noise it's making."

"Going to call Sable?"

"Probably." Sable was the best mechanic around. She knew her way around cars, trucks, and machinery.

"Bet you hate that," Jeb teased.

"It is what it is. I got better things to do than spend any more time on it, like go home and see my girl."

"I won't hold you up," Jeb said. "I just wanted to catch you alone for a minute and figured this was the only time I could do that."

"What's up?"

Jeb walked with Trace toward his truck and said, "I know you're thinking about taking that coaching job."

"Actually, I am taking it. I'm meeting with Sin tomorrow

afternoon." It was mid-December, and Brindle was all moved in. Over the last couple of weeks her belly had popped out to the cutest baby bump. She was more beautiful than ever, and the more pregnant she looked, the more he felt like a father-to-be. They were both changing, and their relationship was evolving in directions he hadn't expected. They'd skipped going to JJ's the last two Tuesday nights in lieu of spending that time focusing on each other without the noise and the crowds. His desire to coach had strengthened. He was excited about the prospect of being more involved with the kids, helping them learn the value of sportsmanship, friendships, and helping them build confidence.

"Good. I'm glad, man. You're great with the kids. Listen, I know we've never really talked about why you didn't go away to school, but my gut tells me that part of the reason was because I didn't step in to take over when Dad's arthritis got bad."

"No, it wasn't," he lied, because he didn't want Jeb to feel the weight of that guilt. "You had your own shit going on. Dad could have hired someone else. I just didn't want to be that far away from everyone, from Brindle." He opened his truck door and said, "Besides, I'm a cowboy at heart, not a football player. Now I've got my girl, a life I love, and a coaching job on the horizon. Life is good, bro. Don't give it another thought."

Jeb sighed and rubbed his jaw, as if he was weighing Trace's response.

"Look, Jeb. To be honest, even if you'd stepped up to run the ranch, I still would have stayed home. I've never wanted to leave Oak Falls or had dreams of doing something different than exactly what I'm doing now. I made the right decision. Don't overthink it."

"A'right. For what it's worth, if I had anything to do with

that decision, thank you for having my back. I'm going to head in to tell Dad I'll step in while you coach, to pick up the slack. My shop's doing great, and I've got the extra time."

"That means a lot to me, and I know it'll mean the world to Dad, but Shane, Trixie, and I had a meeting with him this morning. We decided to hire a few extra hands on a permanent basis. I'm going to have a baby and, hopefully one day, a wife, to look after, and Trixie doesn't want to work the ranch forever. It's time."

As Trace climbed into his truck, Jeb said, "About the *wife* thing. You've been in love with Brindle forever. When are you going to put a ring on her finger?"

"I've been thinking about that. But you know Brindle. She can't be rushed. I'll know when she's ready."

"Uh-huh, sure, okay," Jeb said with a chuckle. "You riding with us this weekend?"

"Who do you think set it up?" He started the truck and said, "Four thirty Sunday morning. Bring coffee, and be ready to be blown away."

Jeb pushed Trace's door closed and said, "In your dreams."

"Dude, my dreams are all becoming realities. Maybe you should be taking notes."

"AT LEAST I'LL see you at Christmas," Brindle said into the speakerphone to Morgyn as she graded papers on the couch. She couldn't believe Christmas was less than two weeks away. "Unless you've become such an adrenaline junkie that you've decided to go skydiving or something over the holiday?"

"Hardly." Morgyn and Graham were on a ski trip with Graham's cousin Ty and his wife, Aiyla. "But I definitely have to teach you to ski. You'd love it. We're planning a cross-country ski trip in February with Ty and Aiyla. I wish you could come."

Brindle rubbed her belly. "You'd have to roll me down hills. Did I tell you my belly popped out more? I look like I'm carrying a basketball."

"Aw, Brin. I can't wait to see you. I bet you look cute."

"Trace seems to think so." She set her papers aside and picked up the phone, taking the call off speaker. "You should see him. He's always running his hands over my belly, kissing it, talking to the baby. She really likes when he plays his guitar."

"She'll probably like dancing as much as you do. I'm glad about Trace. Isn't it weird how we both fell in love at the same time?"

"I fell in love with him ages ago." Brindle took a bite out of a carrot stick. She'd switched to healthier snacks after reading about how hard it was to lose the weight gained during pregnancy.

"You know what I mean. Do you think you'll go back to work after you have the baby?"

"That's the plan, but Mom says I might change my mind after I hold our baby for the first time." She'd stopped by her parents' house earlier to go through her mother's recipes, and they'd had a long chat about motherhood, relationships, and life changes. Brindle had come home armed with a number of easy recipes and a heart full of love. "Did you know that Dad cried when each of us were born?"

"No, but I believe it. He's a softie. I bet Graham will cry when we have a baby."

"Really? Trace will probably sweep me and the baby off the birthing table and into his arms and totally freak out the doctor." She smiled at the thought. "Want to know a secret?"

"Is it one you want me to keep? Because you know I suck at secrets."

Brindle leaned back against the cushions, excited to tell Morgyn what she'd been thinking about. "Yes, you do need to keep it. Maybe I shouldn't tell you, because it's a big one."

Morgyn groaned. "Now I *have* to know."

"Remember how you said you asked Graham to marry you because you wanted the world to know how much you loved him?"

"Yes, why? Oh my gosh, Brindle! Are you going to ask Trace to marry you?"

"*Shh!* Graham will hear you!"

"He's outside with Ty, and Aiyla's in the bathroom." Morgyn lowered her voice and said, "Are you really going to do it?"

"I'm thinking about it."

Morgyn squealed. "I can't believe it! I want to be there. When are you doing it? I'm so excited! Does Mom know?"

"No! Nobody knows, and you promised to keep it to yourself."

Morgyn groaned again. "*Brin-dle!* You shouldn't have told me. Can I just tell Graham?"

"No! You can't tell anyone. I mean it, Morgyn." She heard Trace's truck pull up out front and said, "He's home. I gotta go."

"Are you doing it *now*?"

"No," Brindle said. "Remember, you cannot say a word."

"I'll try…"

"Morgyn!" she warned as Trace came through the door. "I'll

see you at Christmas. Love you!"

Trace sauntered over as she ended the call and he sat down beside her. "How're my girls?" He kissed her, and then he kissed her belly. She would never tire of the love he showered on them.

"Awesome. I'm almost done grading papers, and there's a chicken roasting in the oven." She and Trace had been learning to cook together, trying different recipes, often burning them because they got too lost in each other. But she was so happy and excited about the baby, their relationship—*their lives*—that she wanted to do something extra special for him tonight. Her mother told her she was *nesting*, but Brindle had read about nesting, and usually it came along with an urge to clean, and she definitely didn't have that. But she had an overwhelming desire to do things for Trace, like cooking, getting the nursery ready, and spending time alone with him. He'd painted the nursery pale yellow last weekend, and they were deciding on themes. Trace wanted horses, and Brindle leaned toward something different every day. Luckily, they still had three months to decide.

Trace moved a stack of papers to the coffee table. He put his arm around her and rubbed her belly. "Hear that, Lilly Sue? Mama's making dinner. She gets more amazing every day."

"Lilly Sue?" She arched a brow. "That's a pretty cute name, but I thought her middle name was going to be Louise, after your grandmother?"

"Lilly Lou? Hm…"

She rolled her eyes. "I came up with another list of ideas today." She grabbed her notebook from the floor and flipped to the list. "I alphabetized them. Aria, Brooklyn, Emily *again*, because it's stuck with me since Thanksgiving. Georgia. We could call her Gia."

Trace picked up his guitar from behind the couch and strummed as he sang, "Aria, Brooklyn, Emily *again*—"

The baby moved, and Brindle gasped. "Oh, she likes that. Sing it again."

He repeated the line, adding in some of his own names as he strummed the guitar. "Anna, Aria, Bethany, Brooklyn, Emily—"

The baby kicked so hard Brindle said, "Whoa! That's it. I think she likes Emily. You have to feel this." Trace hadn't felt the baby move yet, but her movement was stronger than ever before.

He set his guitar down and put both hands on her belly.

"Emily," she coaxed, both of them staring at her belly, waiting for their little girl to do her trick. "Come on, baby girl. *Please* kick again."

Trace leaned closer to her belly and sang, "Anna, Aria, Bethany—"

The baby kicked, and Trace gasped. "Holy shit. Did you feel that?" He splayed his fingers, covering almost her entire belly as he pressed more firmly. "That was amazing. You feel that all the time?"

"No, only sometimes, but more in the last week or so. I think she likes your voice."

The baby moved again, and Trace laughed. Then he grabbed Brindle's face between his hands and kissed her hard. "She's amazing. *You're* incredible."

"I think you mean *we're* incredible, all three of us," she said between excited kisses.

They sat on the couch trying to coax their little girl into moving until the oven timer went off. And after eating dinner, which wasn't quite as delicious as when her mother roasted a chicken but was good enough for Trace to praise her endlessly,

Trace made a fire. Warmed by the dancing flames, they discussed trading in Brindle's car for a bigger, four-door vehicle. She knew she'd have to do that before the baby was born, and she was glad Trace was looking into sportier cars and not minivans. They went back to discussing names, and both of them became giddy every time the baby moved hard enough for Trace to feel it.

Brindle knew how much he loved her and the baby. But over the course of the next few hours, as he sang to her belly and they laughed about Whoville names like Cindy Lou Who and Dr. Mary Lou LaRue, she felt him falling deeper in love with her. With *them*. And when they turned on a movie and cuddled on the couch, his strong arms wrapped around her, she was overcome with a sense of complete happiness.

Trace pressed a kiss to her cheek and whispered, "I love you, darlin'."

Everything she wanted, and everything she needed, was right there in that room. As she told him she loved him, she knew those three little words weren't nearly enough to convey what was in her heart.

Chapter Nineteen

"ARE YOU STILL meeting your brothers at four thirty?" Brindle asked Trace late Saturday night as he filled a glass with ice water.

Her stomach had been in knots for two days. She planned on going to watch him ride, but she hadn't told Trace. Even though he'd found out she'd been secretly watching him before she went to Paris, it felt all kinds of wrong to tell him what she was planning. She and her sisters never told *anyone* before they went on their secret adventures. It was a tradition. They rarely even told each other ahead of time. Dragging unsuspecting siblings out of bed was half the fun. Otherwise she might as well just go sit on the fence with Trace's brothers and watch him ride, and what was the fun in that? When he wasn't aware she was watching from the hill, he was even more macho because he and his brothers were wicked competitive. He laughed harder, rode rougher, and got himself all worked up, so the next time he saw Brindle, he did *everything* more aggressively.

And she loved that.

"That's the plan." He kissed her and said, "I'll try not to wake you when I leave."

Another pang of guilt sliced through her. He was so good to

her. He never kept secrets, and here she was wanting to hold on to hers. She followed him into the living room and said, "I have to tell you something, and telling you goes against everything I believe in, but not telling you feels wrong, so…"

"Go for it, darlin'." He sat on the couch, and she sat on the coffee table in front of him.

"I'm sneaking out tonight. Not *sneaking* actually, because I'm telling you about it. I'm going to watch you ride tonight, but I don't want you to—"

"No, you're not." He set the glass of water on the coffee table.

"Excuse me?" she said with disbelief.

"You're six months pregnant and it's freezing out there. You're not going to sit on a hill before dawn and watch me ride. You can watch me during the day."

She pushed to her feet and said, "Are you *forbidding* me?"

"Nope. I'm being your boyfriend, protecting you from getting sick or falling on the way up the hill. Last time you and Morgyn did that shit, she fell down the hill, remember?"

Brindle paced. She didn't want to fight, but she was not going to sit back and let him forbid her from doing a damn thing. "Hold on. Since when do you tell me what I can and cannot do?"

He pushed to his feet, towering over her as he said, "Since you're pregnant with my baby and I don't want anything to happen to either of you."

"*Your* baby? Where the hell is this coming from, Trace?" Her voice escalated, but she was too mad to slow down. "Don't pull this crap on me. What happened to talking things out and discussing them?"

"We are," he said sternly, his jaw tight.

"This is *not* a discussion. This is a dictatorship. What happened to you? You're being completely ridiculous."

"I'm being ridiculous?" he hollered. "You're the one who wants to go traipsing around like you have no responsibilities."

"Oh, really?" She crossed her arms, glaring at him. "You think I act like I don't have any responsibilities? Who's the one carrying the baby? Who's the one who doesn't drink, has to get enough sleep, and goes to the doctor every four weeks? Oh yeah, *me!*"

"Well, this is a hard limit for me. You want to watch me ride? Come with me during the day. I'll set up a heater in the barn and make sure you're safe. No hill climbing."

"Listen to you, telling me what *you'll* do. Did you have to ask for *my* permission to ride?"

He scoffed. "Why would I?"

"*Exactly*," she fumed. "Why should *I?*"

"Because it's dangerous, Brindle, and reckless, and—"

"Stop," she hollered, too angry and hurt to listen to any more. They'd come so far. How could they spiral backward so fast? "Sitting on a frigging hill is about as dangerous as sitting in my yard. *You're* the one in danger, riding your wildest horses before daylight. *That's* reckless!" She was breathing so hard her entire body heaved with every word.

"I'm a *man*. I can take care of myself," he said so fucking calmly it pissed her off even more.

"Because you have a penis? Well, let me tell you something. That penis of yours? It makes you say stupid shit sometimes, and this is one of those times. I'm *not* doing this with you," she seethed, and headed for the stairs. She stopped at the bottom step without looking at him and said, "And I'm *not* storming off. I just can't do this with you right now. I...*can't*. I'm going to bed before I say something I can't take back!"

"You do what you gotta do," he ground out as she stomped upstairs.

She paced the bedroom, seeing red. Where was all this coming from? She tore off her clothes and put on one of his T-shirts she slept in, swiping at the unrelenting tears streaming down her cheeks. She brushed her teeth too hard, nicking her gum, and her anger turned to hurt. She didn't understand any of this. Was it *her*? Was *she* being ridiculous? Or was he being a controlling ass?

She had plans for tonight. *Big* plans that included *great* things between them.

She should want to cancel those plans.

But she didn't.

She wanted to figure this out and keep moving forward, but she was too hurt by his demands to think clearly enough to figure out how to do that.

She opened her jewelry box, carefully lifting out the velvet shelf inside, revealing the black box she'd hidden there. She took it out and sat on the edge of the bed, breathing deeply to try to regain control of her emotions. She opened the box. Inside was the sturdy, masculine ring she'd had made for him. She ran her fingers along the textured silver edges and the brushed gold in between. The ring was unpolished and rugged. It was *perfect*. It looked weathered, with uneven edges, some parts darker than others, so Trace would never have to worry about it getting banged up at work. Her heart squeezed as she read the inscription, the date of their first kiss, followed by COWBOY and MUSTANG with a heart etched between them.

She set the box in the bedside drawer and climbed beneath the covers with the ring in her fist. She lay listening to him pacing downstairs, telling herself this would blow over. She tried to convince herself to tell him he was right and let it go.

But she didn't want to let it go, because who the fuck did he think he was?

She had no idea how long she lay stewing in the dark. At some point she must have fallen asleep, because she woke to the sound of Trace getting ready for bed. She pretended she was sleeping as he climbed into bed behind her and wrapped his arm around her.

He whispered, "I'm sorry, darlin'."

Tears burned, but she didn't move, didn't apologize. She was too busy solidifying her plans.

BRINDLE AWOKE HOURS later as Trace slipped from the bed. She kept her eyes closed, anger and hurt still eating away at her. The hurt probably outweighed the anger, but the line was so fine, it was hard for her to commit one way or the other.

She listened as he padded downstairs in his socked feet, as he did every morning, though not usually this early. The familiar sounds of Trace making coffee, putting on his boots, and the faint jingling of his keys drove the hurt deeper. She hated that they'd fought. Her mother told her that going to bed angry was allowing a villain into their bedroom, but she'd been too freaking mad to think of that last night. She heard the front door open and close, then the faint *click* of the lock. She closed her eyes, imagining Trace striding toward his truck, his broad shoulders rounded against the cold. She heard his truck door close. That was where she lost track of the sounds, but she looked out the window and saw his headlights sweep over the dark backyard. He was turning the truck around and leaving.

She counted to ten and realized her hand was still fisted around the ring. When she hit ten, she threw the blankets off and popped out of bed. She pulled on jeans and shoved the ring in her pocket. Then she put on a tank top and a sweater, pulled on socks, pocketed her phone, and hurried downstairs. She grabbed her coat, hat, and scarf, shoved her feet into her boots, snagged her keys from the hook by the door, and ran out to her car.

The cold air stung her cheeks as she climbed in and revved the engine. She didn't wait for the car to warm up as she peeled out of the driveway and drove straight to Sable's.

Sable lived in an apartment above the auto shop she owned. Brindle hurried up the stairs. She fumbled with her keys, let herself in, and tripped over a pair of boots by the door.

"Damn it." She turned on the lights, shocked to find Aubrey sleeping on Sable's couch. The coffee table was littered with bags of Cheetos, Skittles, and Stewart's orange soda bottles.

Aubrey groaned and pulled the covers over her head. "It can't be morning."

"It's not. What are you doing here?"

"I was going over changes to the script with Grace."

"I don't mean in Oak Falls." Brindle pulled the blankets from Aubrey's head, earning another whining groan. Aubrey's hair was tangled, her makeup smeared. "I mean, at *Sable's*."

"I slept at Grace's last night, but the walls are thin." Aubrey pushed up to a sitting position.

"Oh. Good for Gracie, getting some action."

"Right? I was going to stay with Amber. Sable, Amber, and I went out to JJ's, but Amber left early because Sable and I were apparently scoping out guys for too long. By the way, you can keep your cowboys. Not my type…"

"Whatever. You should wash your makeup off at night. You look like a raccoon."

"What are you, my mother?" She picked up her phone and looked at it. "Good God, woman, it's four fifteen!"

"No shit. Get up. We're going out." Brindle headed for Sable's room. "She's alone in there, right?"

"Yes."

Brindle burst into Sable's room and turned on the light.

"What the fu—" Sable bolted upright.

Brindle grabbed her jeans from a chair and tossed them to her. "Get up. I need you to go to the hill with me."

"Seriously?" Sable swung her long legs over the side of the bed. "You live with the guy. Do you really have to go watch him ride at this hour?"

"Don't start with me unless you want to join Trace on my shit list. Can you believe he told me I *couldn't* go watch him ride? He tried to *forbid* me. If I didn't love him so much, I'd have clocked him for that."

Sable laughed as she pulled a sweatshirt over the little tank top she'd slept in. "Dude's got balls."

"Big ones," Brindle said. "If he thinks he's going to ruin my fun just because I'm pregnant, he's about to learn how wrong he is. Nobody tells me what to do."

Sable shoved her feet into her boots and said, "I thought you guys were doing better, talking shit out?"

"We were. We *are*. I think he's on the rag or something. Guys get like that, right? All weird and hormonal once a month?"

"In my experience," Aubrey said as she appeared in the

doorway, "guys are like that most of the time."

Brindle rushed them out the door, and they drove over to the hill. As they trudged up the grass, Sable and Aubrey flanked Brindle, clutching her arms.

"Why are you holding on to me?" Brindle asked.

"Because you could fall," Sable pointed out.

"You sound like Trace, which is *not* a good thing right now," Brindle said as they ascended the hill. "We were communicating *so* well. I don't understand his complete turnaround. I know he loves me, but he usually loves *all* of me, including my spontaneous, fun-seeking ways. And he definitely knows better than to forbid me from anything." Brindle looked at Aubrey and said, "What am I missing? Is it me? Am I being foolish?"

Aubrey released Brindle's arm and held her hands up in surrender. "Don't look at me. I have no intention of ever doing something crazy like moving in with my fuck buddy. I'm of the belief that men and women should live separately and come together to fulfill each other's needs. Then…" She waved. "*Bye-bye.*"

"Yeah, well, good luck with that. I thought that's where we were, too, but now I know better. I thought I was happy when we were just having fun together, without a commitment, but now I know I wasn't. Trace changed all of that for me, and despite this asinine fight, I never want to be without him." She stopped walking halfway up the hill, breathing hard. She rubbed her belly, hating the question nagging at the back of her mind, which she was futilely trying to ignore.

"What?" Sable asked.

"Do you think I'm making a mistake? I love Trace, but what if he thinks he can run my life and this is just the tip of the iceberg? I know some women like to be told what to do, but I'm not one of them. I always thought he knew that about me. What if I'm wrong?" She swallowed hard, hating herself for even verbalizing that fear. "What kind of a man would forbid his partner from doing anything at all other than, you know, cheating or something insane?"

Brindle waited for her sister's snappy retort about how all men were a pain in the ass, or how she agreed with Aubrey about men and women living separate lives, but Sable was quiet for so long, she wondered if she was even paying attention.

"Sable?"

Sable rolled her eyes. "God, Brindle. Who does that? A man who truly loves you, that's who. If he didn't care, he wouldn't be so concerned."

"Who *are* you?" She stalked up the hill, leaving Sable and Aubrey to catch up.

Sable grabbed her arm and said, "Trace changed the way I think about guys."

"What?" Brindle wondered if Sable was still loopy from whatever she drank earlier in the night. "Why?"

"Because he *does* love all of you, and he's never asked you to change who you are beyond calming your ass down enough to communicate better. That's *love*, Brindle."

Brindle stopped walking again. "So, do you think he just overreacted because he was scared I really would get hurt, or cold, or something?"

"Probably," Sable said. "You are pregnant, and that pretty much changes everything."

Brindle groaned. "I need to talk to him. We need to fix this, because my heart hurts so much right now, it's like the stupid fight tore it in half."

They climbed the rest of the way in silence, Brindle's anger easing with her decision to face their fight head-on and try to fix it. She'd known there'd be setbacks in their starting over. That was all this was, right? They could get through this.

They could get through anything.

"What's that?" Aubrey asked, pulling Brindle from her thoughts.

Brindle followed her gaze to a pile of something she couldn't make out at the top of the hill. They hurried toward it, and there on the crest of the hill was a pile of blankets, a massive thermos with hot chocolate, something written in black marker on the side, several mugs, a basket with two apples, a box of granola bars, a bag of M&M's, a box of cookies, and several packages of air-activated hand and toe warmers, like hunters used. Leaning against a pair of gloves was a piece of paper with *Love you, Mustang* written in Trace's handwriting, signed, *Your cowboy.*

Brindle melted on the spot, literally dropping to her knees on the blanket. Her gaze fell to the ring below, where Trace was riding a horse as it leapt over a jump. She watched him as he took jumps like a pro, handling the horse with the same strength and grace as he usually handled her.

I'm such an idiot.

He wouldn't let one of his horses walk into dangerous territory. Why would he let her? The hill *was* dangerous, and it *was* freaking freezing out.

"Damn, Brin," Sable said as she and Aubrey knelt on the blanket and began grabbing snacks. "Maybe you should fight more often."

"The man knows how to apologize," Aubrey added.

"This isn't an apology. He whispered an apology when he

got into bed, and I was stupid enough to pretend I was sleeping. This is Trace taking care of his wild, crazy girl. You guys, this fight is just a bump in the road. Like a rite of passage, something we needed to go through to remember how we *don't* want to react."

"Morgyn would call it a sign from the universe," Sable said.

Trace's horse slowed to a trot. Trace looked directly up the hill, and like metal to magnet, she rose to her feet, feeling his love heating up the space between them. She waved and blew him a kiss. He lifted his hat, charming her once again. He put the hat on and rode into the barn.

"Now I understand why Trace made you see guys differently," Aubrey said. "He's definitely one of a kind."

"And he's mine, so keep your grubby hands off him. I've got plans to follow through with. I'm doing it," Brindle said. "I'm apologizing and proposing."

"*Proposing?*" Sable and Aubrey said in unison.

"Yes!" Brindle paced, her eyes trained on the ground so she wouldn't trip or fall. "He loves me as much as I love him. He knows what he can and can't do, and yes, he tried to forbid me, but we all make mistakes. He's always been there for me, and I've been there for him. We're soul mates. He's loyal, and loving, and—"

"Brindle," Sable said, but Brindle was on a roll and she couldn't stop.

"I have loved him since I was thirteen years old, and I will love him until the end of time. And yes, we'll fight," she admitted as she paced, her plan so solid now, she saw their future clearly, their daughter, more children, fights and making up, lazy evenings in front of the fire and Saturday afternoons cheering him on as he coached. "But we'll always make up, because our love is stronger than our stubbornness."

"Hey, Brindle," Aubrey said.

"Don't even try to stop me, Aubrey. I'm going to march down there, apologize, then I'm going to propose the fuck out of that man. And I'm going to marry him, because I am his and he is mine, and I want the entire world to know it."

"Brindle!" Aubrey and Sable hollered.

"What? Don't you see I'm having a moment?" She spun around and followed their pointing fingers to colorful lights spelling MARRY ME, BRINDLE across the roof of the barn. The air left her lungs in a rush of shock and disbelief.

"Did you mean all those things?"

She turned at the sound of Trace's deep voice and found him standing beside a black horse.

TEARS SPRANG FROM Brindle's eyes as she ran into Trace's arms and said, "Yes! I meant every single one of them. I love you, and I don't know why we fought, but I know we'll figure it out."

"I had to make sure you got here. I thought, with the baby, at the last minute you might decide you were too tired and stay home. I couldn't let that happen, darlin'. I wanted to see you on this hill one last time before our baby was born and predawn rides were a thing of the past." He cradled her face in his hands, gazing into her beautiful blue eyes as he confessed, "The only way to do that was to make sure you were so riled up, you wouldn't miss coming up here for the world."

"You started a fight on *purpose*? What if I hadn't argued?

What if I'd just said okay?"

He laughed. "Mustang, everyone knows what happens if you back a Montgomery into a corner. I was just lucky you didn't deck me. I was also petrified you'd be done with me for talking to you like that. You know I love your wild, crazy heart, and I always will."

He dropped to one knee, holding up the halo engagement ring he'd bought for her, with a teardrop-shaped chocolate diamond surrounded by round pavé diamonds, with a diamond-encrusted rose-gold band. Rivers of tears cascaded down her cheeks. Her hands trembled as she tried to wipe the tears away.

Trace was vaguely aware of his brothers approaching and of Sable videoing them as he put one hand on Brindle's belly and leaned in close to say, "Listen up, sweet baby girl. Daddy's about to make things official."

There was a collective *aw* from the girls and murmurs from the guys.

Trace reached for Brindle's hand as he said, "Darlin', I have loved you since you first set those stormy eyes on me, and my love for you has grown stronger every single day. You're stubborn as a mule, smarter than I could ever hope to be, and as forgiving as the open sky. Our relationship will never be like anyone else's, but that's because there's only one of you, and I would be the proudest man alive if you would be mine forever. I will love you through every argument, every ruined pie, every sleepless night and spur-of-the-moment outing. Will you marry me, Mustang? Let me be your cowboy, and we'll ride our wild, crazy love forever?"

"*Yes!*" she said through tears as he slipped the ring on her finger. "You just ruined my surprise in the best way possible, and I can't even pretend to be mad."

"Only Brindle…" Sable said under her breath as Brindle reached into her pocket and dropped to one knee in front of Trace, holding up a masculine-looking ring.

Holy shit. "What are you doing?"

"What I had planned to do," Brindle said sassily. "Nothing could have stopped me from being here tonight, because I *want* to be your wife. I want to raise our rebellious children, who will probably sneak out and drive us crazy, and I want the world to know that I am yours and you are mine. I know the question doesn't matter as much now since you've already asked me, but will you marry me, Trace? Will you let me try to be the woman you deserve for the rest of our lives?"

He was so choked up, it took all his focus to force his voice to work as he pushed to his feet, bringing her up with him, and said, "That question matters more than anything ever has. Yes, darlin'. I'll marry the hell out of you."

Everyone cheered and clapped as he drew Brindle into his arms and they sealed their promises with a series of long, steamy kisses. When their lips finally parted, he went in for more.

"Dude, let the woman breathe long enough to put your ring on," JJ teased.

Trace glared at him.

"Over here, cowboy," Brindle said, drawing his eyes to hers. "Read the inscription first." As he read it, she said, "You may not recognize the date. It's the—"

"First time we kissed," he said, his heart beating so hard he was sure she could feel it pulsing in the air between them. "How could I ever forget the date that changed my world?"

"Oh my God, these two *almost* make me believe in true love," Aubrey said, and everyone laughed.

As Trace put the ring on, he said, "I never figured myself for a ring guy, but I'm never taking this off."

He kissed her again, good and hard. Shane pried them apart and said, "Bro, some of us don't want to watch you two make out."

Trace and Brindle were passed from one congratulatory embrace to the next.

When Brindle finally landed back in his arms, smiling like she'd never been happier, Jeb said, "I can't believe you relied on a fight to get her here."

"I told you I know my girl. Besides, if she hadn't shown up, Sable was going to drag her out here."

Brindle gasped and looked at Sable. "You *knew*?"

"Yes, and Amber is going to kill me for not telling her. I tried to get her to stay out with us tonight, but your boyfriend—"

"*Fiancé*," Brindle corrected with a wiggle of her ringed finger and an air of pride that made Trace's heart sing.

"Fiancé," Sable said supportively, "swore me to silence, *even* to our sisters."

"Don't feel bad. The asshole didn't clue us in, either," Shane said. "And I don't want to be around when Trixie finds out. She's going to be pissed."

Brindle eyed Jeb and said, "Well...*one* of your brothers knew."

Trace shot a look at Jeb. "Seriously?"

"Who do you think made your ring?" Jeb said. "The other day when we were talking, I thought it was *you* who was going to be blown away tonight."

Trace locked his eyes on his beautiful fiancée and said, "I've been blown away every day since I first set eyes on my pretty little Mustang."

"And I'm going to blow you away every single day for the rest of our lives," Brindle said. Then she went up on her toes, and as he lowered his mouth to hers, his brothers told them to get a room, which was exactly what he planned to do.

Epilogue

THE TWINKLING LIGHTS strung throughout the Jerichos' barn had nothing on the sparkle in Trace's eyes. It was New Year's Eve, and the Jerichos were holding their annual celebration. Snow fell like secrets outside the open barn doors, and nearly all of Oak Falls was enjoying the winter wonderland and jam session. Brindle stood with Amber, half listening as she ogled Trace. He was talking with his father, Shane, and Axsel by the Christmas tree, which was decorated with gold and silver tinsel. Even from across the dance floor, Brindle's husband's eyes shimmered with love.

My husband.

Gosh, I love that.

She sighed, playing her new name over in her mind. *Mrs. Trace Jericho, Mr. and Mrs. Trace Jericho, Trace and Brindle Jericho.*

Trace turned, catching her watching him, and blew her a kiss. She swore she felt it land, warm and tangible, on her cheek. She touched her rose-gold wedding band, thinking about how perfectly the circle symbolized their relationship. This barn was where their new beginning had *really* started, and now it was also where their future would begin.

Several people played instruments on the stage, where less than an hour ago, Brindle and Trace had exchanged vows. They hadn't sent out invitations or planned anything other than writing their vows. They told family and friends they were engaged and would make it official at the last jam session of the year. The community, who had rallied in support of their baby, carried their good news far and wide. Nearly the whole town and people from other areas who had followed their hashtags on social media showed up to see Team Trindle get married.

"I wish Aubrey could have come," Brindle said to Amber, who looked stunning in a green dress that really made her eyes pop. Amber had been upset about missing their proposals, but luckily Sable had caught it all on video.

"She wanted to be here, but she never misses the LWW New Year's Eve gala." Amber whispered, "I mean her New Year's Eve hookup. I think she's hoping Knox will be there."

"Good for her," Brindle said.

"I've never seen so many pink shirts," Jillian, Graham's younger sister, said, as she and Morgyn joined them. Jillian looked gorgeous in a festive gold dress she'd probably designed, with a pink #TeamTrindleTrio pin, which Lindsay had put out on a table by the entrance. Morgyn looked equally stunning in one of her own colorful creations.

"Isn't it awesome?" Amber said, reaching down to pet Reno, who wore a pink pin on his collar.

"Lindsay told me they've sold hundreds of shirts since Brindle and Trace got engaged," Morgyn added.

"This is what happens when you ask a party planner not to plan anything," Brindle said. Lindsay told her she couldn't resist offering pins and hanging a banner across the stage that read CONGRATULATIONS #TeamTrindleTrio. "I practically had to threaten violence to get her not to order food and napkins and the whole nine yards."

"She said she felt lucky that you allowed her to have a horse-drawn carriage waiting to drive you and Trace to the bed-and-breakfast tonight," Amber said. "But honestly, you only get married once. I think you should have let her plan the whole nine yards."

"Why? This has been perfect," Brindle said. "The community has been there since Trace and I first got together. We didn't want to be in the spotlight. We just wanted to get married in a way that everyone could enjoy it. I'm still not sure what the allure of our relationship is to everyone, but it feels good knowing that our little girl will be welcomed into so many hearts."

"I think the way you handled the wedding is fabulous," Jillian said. "I mean, who gets married at a jam session? And I have to say, Morgyn found you the *perfect* wedding dress,"

"Isn't it magnificent? I *love* it." Brindle twirled in her cream-colored gown with a pink sash. It had sheer sleeves and a plunging neckline, which drew eyes away from her burgeoning belly. The simple silk dress fell to just above her knees, with a floor-length lace overskirt. "Morgyn is a miracle worker, as you know, since you carry some of her things in your shop. This was actually two dresses that she made into one."

"Jax was bummed that he didn't get to design a dress for either of us," Morgyn said. Graham's brother Jax was a wedding gown designer. He, Jillian, and Nick had come for the wedding. "I told him not to worry, because by the looks of Nick and Trixie, he might have another chance."

Morgyn motioned across the room toward Nick, who was talking with Jax and Jeb. Nick's bulbous biceps were seriously straining his dress shirt. His eyes were locked on Trixie, who was talking with Lindsay a few feet away.

"Wow. He's not very discreet, is he?" Brindle said. Then she looked at her husband again. Trace was watching her with an intense expression. She mouthed, *I love you.* His lips curved up into a sinful smile and he mouthed, *I love you more.* He tilted his head in the direction of the stairs that led up to the hayloft and winked. She laughed softly. Her naughty boy was always in the mood to play.

"Uh-oh, we're losing her again. She's been Traceified." Jillian touched Brindle's arm, bringing her attention back to the girls.

Brindle blinked repeatedly to try to clear her head. "I'm sorry. I can't help it. I swear something happens when you say *I do.* I just want to be with him every second. What did I miss?"

"From the look on Trace's face, I'd say *nothing*," Amber said happily.

Jillian leaned in close and lowered her voice as she said, "Amber was telling me about the meetings of the female minds. I want to join in. When's the next one?"

"The third Saturday of the month. Can you come down for it?" Brindle asked.

When word had gotten around about the meetings of women sharing relationship secrets, more women started showing up. Though some were married, some were not, so they changed the name of the group to be inclusive of everyone. There were thirty women at the last meeting. Nana and Amber had taken it upon themselves to create a directory of members and a schedule of the now *monthly* meetings. Amber's lessons in all things feminine were as popular as Brindle's seduction tips and their mother's communication suggestions. Whoever said it took a village to raise a child had it wrong. It took a village to become healthy, well-rounded individuals and significant others.

"Oh, I'll be here." Jillian's eyes surfed the faces of the crowd. "I never knew Oak Falls had so many hot cowboys."

"According to Trixie, you have plenty of hot guys in Pleasant Hill," Brindle said, looking at Trixie, who was now being glowered at by her brothers. They must have seen her ogling Nick.

"Yeah, well, dating is easier without Mr. Biceps over there hulking around." Jillian pointed over her shoulder to Nick.

"Stick with us. We'll hook you up," Morgyn said. "Amber, too. She needs a man in her life."

"I'm good," Amber said. "I have so much going on with my bookstore. I have no time for a man. I'm setting up a bunch of signings for the year."

"Oh, honey." Jillian put her arm around Amber's shoulder and said, "We need to talk about priorities." She guided Amber away.

Brindle spotted Trace and Graham heading their way. Love and desire swam in Trace's dark eyes as he closed the distance between them. "Look at them, Morgyn. Are we lucky or what?"

"We're lucky, but you know luck has nothing to do with it, right?" Morgyn said. "Our stars aligned, and we were fated to fall in love when we did."

Brindle didn't know about fate, but whatever had brought them together at the exact moment in time when they were both ready to make the changes they needed to in order to truly let each other in was bigger than both of them. It was an unstoppable force that had propelled their love to new heights and permeated every aspect of their lives.

Trace put his arm around Brindle and kissed her temple.

"Hello, my beautiful wife."

"I still can't believe your beautiful wife didn't let Lindsay throw her a quick bridal shower," Morgyn said as Graham took her hand.

Brindle gazed up at her man and said, "I can't imagine what anyone could give me that would be better than what I already have."

"WOULD YOU MIND if I stole Mustang away for a dance?" Trace asked.

"Only if you tell me why you call her that," Morgyn said.

"Sorry, babe, not a chance." Trace led Brindle to the dance floor and drew her into his arms. "How's my girl?" He kissed the tender skin beside her ear and said, "Mm. I missed you."

"I missed you, too." She ran her finger down the center of his open dress shirt and said, "But now that Morgyn brought it up, I'm curious. Why *do* you call me Mustang?"

"Do you really want to know?"

"I want to know everything about you and about us, so yes."

"Okay, darlin', but it's probably not the reason you or anyone else thinks. I would imagine people think it's because you're wild." As they swayed to the music, their bodies pressed tightly together. "But there's a lot more to it than that. Mustangs aren't *wild* horses. They're descended from once-domesticated horses, so they're *feral*, free-roaming horses, and they think they're happiest without any hindrances on their independence."

"That sounds like me," she said sweetly.

"You have no idea how true that is. You see, mustangs are

the hardest horse to befriend because they're stubborn, and they're super smart. They have to be, to survive in the wild. In the mustang world, we're predators, and predators are negative forces. They don't understand why we would try to reach out and bring them into a quieter space. They have to learn to trust, which can take a really long time and a vast amount of tact and patience. They can't be forced into submission. In order to gain their trust, you have to know when to back off and when to hold a little tighter. Once they realize you're trying to *communicate*, not *overtake*, they eventually learn to see you differently. There's still a long road ahead where we stand on the cusp between rejection and acceptance. But once a mustang *chooses* to trust you, when they *choose* to let you in, they're the most devoted horse of them all. However, even that comes at a price. You see, my beautiful wife"—he gazed into her loving eyes— "Mustangs are always *partners*, not just simple rides. They expect more out of their people than other horses do. But when they let you in, when you've earned their devotion, it will never be broken, unless you turn on them. They're the most loyal horses you'll ever find. They'd give you their dying breath."

"That's the most beautiful thing I've ever heard," she said dreamily, and just as quickly, her eyes darkened. "I probably shouldn't tell you why I call you cowboy, because it's not nearly as romantic."

He chuckled, holding her tighter. "Does it have something to do with the way I ride you?"

"Possibly…" She trailed her hand down his arm and took his fingers in hers. "Come with me and I'll show you." She led him off the dance floor with a seductive glimmer in her eyes, glancing around the room as she headed for the barn doors.

"You need a coat," Trace said.

She shushed him with a finger to his lips as she stepped out into the snow, and there by the entrance was their horse-drawn carriage, decorated with holly and silver and gold tinsel. A banner hung across the back proclaiming them JUST MARRIED.

"Get in," she said excitedly, quickly untying the horses from a post. As she climbed in, he put his hands on her butt, giving her a boost. She scooted over to the driver's seat and said, "Hurry, before our families or friends notice we're escaping!"

He climbed in, and before he even sat down, she flicked the reins and the horses trotted away. Her unabashed, contagious laughter and smile lit up the night sky as he sank down beside her.

"I can't wait to ring in the New Year as husband and wife!" she said loudly as they raced along the snow-covered ground toward the barn on the back of his parents' property, where they used to sneak up to the hayloft when they were younger.

With his arm around her, he said, "Only you, Brindle Jericho, would have the guts to sneak out of your own wedding."

Her eyes shimmered in the moonlight, and snow wetted her cheeks as she said, "Not true, cowboy. I've got the perfect partner for a lifetime of shenanigans. Do you think I'm crazy?"

"I think you're feral and fantastic!"

"Hell yes, you're crazy! Stop! You stole our carriage!" Her mother's voice came from behind them, and they both spun around. Brindle's parents sat in the carriage, hair tousled, clothes disheveled, and their cheeks flushed. Her mother's lipstick was smeared over their mouths.

"Aw, heck. Just keep driving," her father said as he pulled his wife back down to the bench and out of sight, their laughter silenced by their kisses.

Trace and Brindle burst into laughter, and Brindle said, "I don't want to know what's going on back there, but we've got dibs on the hayloft!"

Ready for your next Bradens & Montgomerys love story?

Fall in love with Graham Braden's brilliant and sexy business partner, Knox Bentley, and the Montgomerys' favorite female billionaire, LWW founder, Aubrey Stewart, in their hilarious and sensual love story, *Making You Mine*.

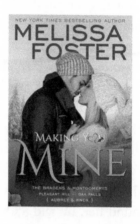

Knox Bentley never liked like the pomp and circumstance that came with being wealthy. He'd distanced himself from his pretentious family and their fortune as a young adult and found his own path to success. But even with the world at his fingertips, he realizes something is missing, and after a long stay overseas, he finally knows exactly what it is. His no-strings-attached hookups with Aubrey Stewart, an exquisite and stubbornly independent blonde, are no longer enough for him. They connect on every level, but Aubrey is a fierce business-woman with a new movie channel on the horizon and no time for much else. She is the deal he can't close, the precious jewel even his billions can't buy. Now that he's back in the States, he's determined to show her that what they have goes beyond the bedroom and finally make her *his*.

Have you read the hilarious Seaside Summers series?

Start this series *FREE in digital format with
SEASIDE DREAMS

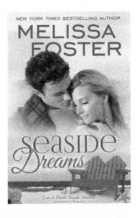

Seaside Dreams features a group of fun, sexy, and emotional friends who gather each summer at their Cape Cod cottages. They're funny, flawed, and so sexy, you'll be begging to enter their circle of friends!

Bella Abbascia has returned to Seaside Cottages in Wellfleet, Massachusetts, as she does every summer. Only this year, Bella has more on her mind than sunbathing and skinny-dipping with her girlfriends. She's quit her job, put her house on the market, and sworn off relationships while she builds a new life in her favorite place on earth. That is, until good-time Bella's prank takes a bad turn and a sinfully sexy police officer appears on the scene.

Single father and police officer Caden Grant left Boston with his fourteen-year-old son, Evan, after his partner was killed in the line of duty. He hopes to find a safer life in the small resort town of Wellfleet, and when he meets Bella during a night patrol shift, he realizes he's found the one thing he'd never allowed himself to hope for—or even realized he was missing.

After fourteen years of focusing solely on his son, Caden cannot resist the intense attraction he feels toward beautiful Bella, and Bella's powerless to fight the heat of their budding romance. But starting over proves more difficult than either of them imagined, and when Evan gets mixed up with the wrong kids, Caden's loyalty is put to the test. Will he give up everything to protect his son—even Bella?

*Free in digital format at the time of this publication. Price subject to change without notice.

Have you met the Bradens at Weston?

Treat and Max's story is the one that started the Love in Bloom sensation. Discover the magic of the fiercely loyal and wickedly naughty Bradens at Weston and see why millions of readers have fallen in love with these sexy billionaires!

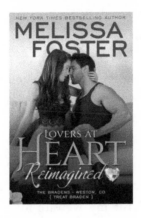

Treat Braden wasn't looking for love when Max Armstrong walked into his Nassau resort, but he saw right through the efficient and capable facade she wore like a shield to the sweet, sensual woman beneath. One magnificent evening together sparked an intense connection, and for the first time in his life Treat wanted more than a casual affair. But something caused Max to turn away, and now, after weeks of unanswered phone calls and longing for the one woman he cannot have, Treat is going back to his family's ranch to try to finally move on.

A chance encounter brings Treat and Max together again, and it turns into a night of intense passion and honesty. When Max reveals her secret, painful past, Treat vows to do everything within his power to win Max's heart forever—including helping her finally face her demons head-on.

New to the Love in Bloom series?

I hope you have enjoyed getting to know the Bradens and Montgomerys. If this is your first Love in Bloom book, you have many more love stories featuring loyal, sassy, and sexy heroes and heroines waiting for you. The Bradens & Montgomerys (Pleasant Hill – Oak Falls) is just one of the series in the Love in Bloom big-family romance collection. Each Love in Bloom book is written to be enjoyed as a stand-alone novel or as part of the larger series. Characters from each series make appearances in future books, so you never miss an engagement, wedding, or birth. Visit my website for more information on Love in Bloom titles.

www.MelissaFoster.com

Download **free** first-in-series ebooks and see current sales here: www.MelissaFoster.com/LIBFree

Visit the Love in Bloom Reader Goodies page for free ebooks, downloadable checklists, family trees, and more! www.MelissaFoster.com/RG

More Books By Melissa Foster

LOVE IN BLOOM SERIES

SNOW SISTERS
Sisters in Love
Sisters in Bloom
Sisters in White

THE BRADENS at Weston
Lovers at Heart, Reimagined
Destined for Love
Friendship on Fire
Sea of Love
Bursting with Love
Hearts at Play

THE BRADENS at Trusty
Taken by Love
Fated for Love
Romancing My Love
Flirting with Love
Dreaming of Love
Crashing into Love

THE BRADENS at Peaceful Harbor
Healed by Love
Surrender My Love
River of Love
Crushing on Love
Whisper of Love
Thrill of Love

THE BRADENS & MONTGOMERYS at Pleasant Hill – Oak Falls
Embracing Her Heart
Anything For Love

Trails of Love
Wild, Crazy Hearts
Making You Mine

THE BRADEN NOVELLAS
Promise My Love
Our New Love
Daring Her Love
Story of Love
Love at Last

THE REMINGTONS
Game of Love
Stroke of Love
Flames of Love
Slope of Love
Read, Write, Love
Touched by Love

SEASIDE SUMMERS
Seaside Dreams
Seaside Hearts
Seaside Sunsets
Seaside Secrets
Seaside Nights
Seaside Embrace
Seaside Lovers
Seaside Whispers

BAYSIDE SUMMERS
Bayside Desires
Bayside Passions
Bayside Heat
Bayside Escape
Bayside Romance

THE RYDERS

Seized by Love
Claimed by Love
Chased by Love
Rescued by Love
Swept Into Love

TRU BLUE & THE WHISKEYS

Tru Blue
Truly, Madly, Whiskey
Driving Whiskey Wild
Wicked Whiskey Love
Mad About Moon
Taming My Whiskey

SUGAR LAKE

The Real Thing
Only for You
Love Like Ours
Finding My Girl

HARMONY POINTE

Call Her Mine

WILD BOYS AFTER DARK (Billionaires After Dark)

Logan
Heath
Jackson
Cooper

BAD BOYS AFTER DARK (Billionaires After Dark)

Mick
Dylan
Carson
Brett

HARBORSIDE NIGHTS SERIES
Includes characters from the Love in Bloom series
Catching Cassidy
Discovering Delilah
Tempting Tristan

More Books by Melissa
Chasing Amanda (mystery/suspense)
Come Back to Me (mystery/suspense)
Have No Shame (historical fiction/romance)
Love, Lies & Mystery (3-book bundle)
Megan's Way (literary fiction)
Traces of Kara (psychological thriller)
Where Petals Fall (suspense)

Acknowledgments

I hope you enjoyed Trace and Brindle's story and are looking forward to reading about the rest of their siblings and friends. You can start with the first book in the series, EMBRACING HER HEART, Grace and Reed's love story.

If you haven't yet joined my fan club on Facebook, please do. We have a great time chatting about our hunky heroes and sassy heroines. You never know when you'll inspire a story or a character and end up in one of my books, as several fan club members have already discovered.
www.Facebook.com/groups/MelissaFosterFans

Remember to like and follow my Facebook fan page to stay abreast of what's going on in our fictional boyfriends' worlds.
www.Facebook.com/MelissaFosterAuthor

Sign up for my newsletter to keep up to date with new releases and special promotions and events and to receive an exclusive short story featuring Jack Remington and Savannah Braden.
www.MelissaFoster.com/Newsletter

And don't forget to download your free reader goodies! For free family trees, publication schedules, series checklists, and more, please visit the special Reader Goodies page that I've set up for you!
www.MelissaFoster.com/Reader-Goodies

As always, loads of gratitude to my amazing team of editors and proofreaders: Kristen Weber, Penina Lopez, Elaini Caruso, Juliette Hill, Marlene Engel, Lynn Mullan, and Justinn Harrison. And, of course, I am forever grateful to my husband, Les, and the rest of my family, who allow me to talk about my fictional worlds as if we live in them.

Meet Melissa

www.MelissaFoster.com

Melissa Foster is a *New York Times* and *USA Today* bestselling and award-winning author. Her books have been recommended by *USA Today's* book blog, *Hagerstown* magazine, *The Patriot*, and several other print venues. Melissa has painted and donated several murals to the Hospital for Sick Children in Washington, DC.

Visit Melissa on her website or chat with her on social media. Melissa enjoys discussing her books with book clubs and reader groups and welcomes an invitation to your event. Melissa's books are available through most online retailers in paperback, digital, and audio formats.

CPSIA information can be obtained
at www.ICGtesting.com
Printed in the USA
BVHW030131070619
550370BV00011B/118/P